The Blue

"How do I know they are still ⟨alive⟩ ⟨You⟩
wouldn't let me speak to them. You may have killed
them already."

"Don't judge us by your own standards, Herr
Doctor," replied Ward. "If you answer my questions
they will be released unharmed. You now only have
nine minutes so don't waste time."

"What is it you want to know?"

"First of all," said Ward, fishing Messenger's three
pieces of yellowed celluloid from his jacket pocket,
"what are these?"

Six looked at all three quizzically and looked up
again. "I've no idea. I've never seen them before in my
life. It's true, I promise you."

"Take another look," ordered Ward. "You may have
seen it in a different form."

"I promise you, I really don't know. Some kind of
message perhaps, in code. But I swear I don't know
what it is."

The old man's forehead was beginning to show beads
of sweat forming; Ward was inclined to believe him, but
he pressed on. "These were found on the body of a
British officer who was killed in August 1940. Does that
jog your memory?"

"Mein Gott," exclaimed Six. "Die Blauliste."

NIGEL WEST

The Blue List

A NOVEL

Mandarin

A Mandarin Paperback

THE BLUE LIST

First published in Great Britain 1989
by Martin Secker & Warburg Limited
This edition published 1990
Reprinted 1990
by Mandarin Paperbacks
Michelin House, 81 Fulham Road, London sw3 6rb

Mandarin is an imprint of the Octopus Publishing Group

Copyright © 1989 by Westintel Research Limited

A CIP catalogue record for this book
is available from the British Library
ISBN 0 7493 0291 7

Printed in Great Britain by
Cox and Wyman Limited, Reading, Berks.

Berlin, 1940

The green internal telephone jangled noisily. The Chief of the Department, Standartenführer Dr Six, spoke briefly to the man who answered it: "Knoechlein, I have just been informed that See-Löwe has been postponed until further notice. You know what has to be done, so please carry out your instructions and tell the others."

Obersturmbannführer Knoechlein replaced the handset in the cradle and leaned back in his chair. From his desk on the fourth floor of the Prinz Albrechtstrasse building he overlooked some playing fields and, in the distance, the Anhalter Station. He gazed slowly around the room and feasted his eyes on the card-index files covering every part of the wall.

In the two short months since July he and the rest

of the Amt II team had worked tirelessly preparing details for the invasion of England scheduled for 24 September. When the Wehrmacht spearheaded the attack they would be accompanied by crack SS *Einsatzgruppen* who would ensure that resistance within the newly occupied areas would be stamped out and that the military government was established successfully.

All through the hot summer the members of the Enemy Information Department had been compiling documentation to assist the invading forces. Experts had been drawn from throughout the *Reichssicherheits-hauptamt*, the Reich Security Agency, to assist in the processing of all the names that were to be included in the *Sonderfahndungsliste*, the Special Search List that identified all those prominent persons who were to be arrested by the Gestapo. So far, some 2,700 names, together with home addresses and other pieces of information, had been drawn up. In spite of the short time that they had been allowed, Knoechlein felt that the result was a triumph of efficiency. Within the Arrest List's 350 pages were a number that had been ruled blank for any last-minute entries, together with a summary of 171 commercial firms that would require special attention and nearly 400 addresses of trade union offices, political organizations and religious groups that were to be singled out. In order to aid the men

of the *Einsatzgruppen* in the field, a town-by-town
cross-index had been constructed so few of those
wanted would escape the net.

Under the supervision of SS officers like Richter
and Mahnke, every potentially subversive group,
from the Freemasons to the Boy Scouts, from the
Communists to the Church of England, had been
examined and their leaders given a mention. The
research involved had been unrivalled, and now the
work was not, after all, going to be put to use – or
not, at least, during 1940.

Knoechlein lifted himself out of his chair and
walked the length of the passage outside his office,
stopping briefly to give Helmut Jonas the news.
Jonas' role had been to index all the "liberal" movements that had been allowed to flourish under the
British parliamentary system, and his analysis had
certainly been thorough.

At the end of the corridor was the office of perhaps one of the most difficult men in the section to
work with. He had been among the first to join the
Sicherheitsdienst, the Nazi Party Intelligence Service
(his operational number, as he frequently reminded
everyone, was IC/0006) and had been appointed to
Major General Jost's special Grossbritannien section
in August 1939. Since that time he had worked preparing a more general guide for the invading forces
to the strange country they intended to dominate.

Walter zu Christian and Walter Schellenberg would, he knew, be bitterly disappointed to learn of See-Löwe's postponement. Their up-to-date study of the British Isles was a superb example of intelligence, invaluable to any officer coping with a strange and hostile population.

Zu Christian and the Colonel had originally penned a 600-page study for the High Command on conditions in England that became the basis for *Informationsheft Grossbritannien*, a reference work that was slimmed down to a 100-page volume packed with essential pieces of intelligence.

From a brief survey of the geography and climate of the islands, the book went on, with the aid of maps, to give a detailed examination of the roads, railway and canal systems. The handbook covered every aspect of life in England and even included an authoritative chapter on *Der Nachrichtendienst*, the British Secret Service.

Knoechlein knocked on the door before him and heard an invitation murmured from within. The bespectacled, quiet-spoken SS Major zu Christian was seated behind his desk.

"Standartenführer Dr Six has just told me that Operation See-Löwe has been postponed more or less indefinitely, Herr Major. We are to put everything into winter-storage."

Zu Christian nodded. "This is the third time there

has been a delay. It may be for only a few weeks." It seemed a question more than a statement.

Knoechlein shook his head. "I think we shall have to wait until the spring. Apparently the Directive from the Führer was quite specific. It's off this year . . . It's probably due to the weather."

Both men knew that the weather was not the only reason; they had become too involved in the See-Löwe planning sessions not to recognize the lack of co-operation between the various services and High Commands, and had seen the unreasonable demands each made upon the other. The OKW, flushed with their capture of France, saw the invasion of Britain only in terms of an exaggerated river-crossing, an operation they were well experienced in. The OKM were always pessimistic about keeping the supply lanes across to the Kent coast free of interference, and the Luftwaffe were increasingly anxious about an Air Force that, during the battle for France at least, had been proved to be obsolescent and completely lacking in numbers.

These troubles, combined with the current policy of massing the invasion barges and tugs into concentrations that were easy targets for the enemy, were more than enough to delay the attack into the next year. But nevertheless both men were disappointed. They had visited England shortly before the outbreak of war, and knew the coastal defences to be non-existent. Perhaps more important than physical barriers, they strongly believed that the population didn't really have the will to resist the organizational skills of the Reich. Many people in London, especially those holding positions of responsibility, would welcome a new order that would rid them of the Jewish speculators and bankers who had profited so well out of the depression years.

Reluctantly, zu Christian accepted the message that he was given. The 20,000 copies of *Informationsheft Grossbritannien* would stay in the storage room next door to Schellenberg's office and the card-indexed files accumulated would be sent off for use by some other *Amter* within the RSHA until they could be resurrected.

He realized the implications of postponement only too well. Tremendous resources had been devoted to keeping the *Informationsheft*'s material right up to date. A delay would mean further work, checking and re-checking each entry, ensuring that every item was accurate. The secret document represented the culmination of years of patient research, from public sources as well as old-fashioned espionage. The details had been amassed over a long period by the Reich's agents abroad in an operation that had been given a high priority. The resulting product, collated from literally thousands of individual reports, was nothing if not comprehensive.

Zu Christian was justly proud of the achievement. He had dedicated himself to the project with impressive zeal, and had made a useful contribution to ensuring its reliability, especially in the section dealing with the topography and economic assets of the county of Sussex. After all, had he not been educated at Eastbourne College? In spite of his superior's apparent pessimism, he hoped the news was nothing more serious than just another hiccup. He had no knowledge of the decisions taken by the Führer or his strategists, but he was determined that his efforts should not have been wasted. He would continue to revise and update the *Informationsheft* until it was needed, even if that did mean a delay until spring the following year.

Knoechlein, however, did not share his subordinate's confidence about See-Löwe's future. This was not a delay, but a general postponement. In his perception, the whole enterprise was in jeopardy. He was a man of action who believed in seizing opportunities. It was a mistake to follow the ever-cautious advice of the old-timers who comprised the Wehrmacht's High Command. Indeed, he mused, if it had not been for the imaginative undercover missions executed by the SD, the Wehrmacht would never have been able to sweep through Poland so efficiently. He knew that SD agents had been behind the series of provocative frontier incidents the previous summer that had provided the pretext for the *Blitzkrieg* attack eastwards, to Warsaw.

Knoechlein had not been indoctrinated into the exact details of what had occurred on the Polish border in the days immediately before the offensive had begun, but he recognized fully the role of clandestine operations in modern warfare. He knew too the importance of that most potent of unseen weapons, referred to by General Franco as his "Fifth Column". He had seen their influence earlier in the year as governments toppled in anticipation of a Nazi occupation.

Knoechlein made his way back to his office and collected his high-swept black peaked cap from the hook behind the door. He looked for a moment at the skull emblem under the eagle and swastika insignia and considered that the chances were that he would not have the opportunity to wear the cap in England – at least, not this year.

He still had one more task to complete before winding down the department, and that involved a visit to the Foreign Ministry. He spoke briefly on the internal telephone and then walked slowly down to the entrance hall where a Mercedes was waiting to whisk him straight over to the office in the Wilhelmstrasse of State Secretary Bohle, the man who had been appointed as the Head of State for the German-occupied areas of Britain.

With little delay Knoechlein was ushered into the office of the State Secretary, a man who had been born in England, in Bradford, and who had been a member of the Party since 1933. His English was faultless, except perhaps for just a trace of a South African accent that occasionally crept into his speech, originating from the three years he had spent in Durban shortly before the Great War. Despite the magnificent surroundings of the room, the trappings of power within the Ministry, Bohle treated the young black-uniformed man before him with courtesy. It was always useful to have friends at Prinz Albrechtstrasse.

"I suppose you're here because of the Directive," said the State Secretary.

"Yes," replied the Obersturmbannführer, "Operation See-Löwe is to be postponed so the special file must be returned to the Sicherheitsdienst, as agreed."

Ernst Bohle picked up the plain brown folder before him and passed it over to the younger man, who placed it carefully into the briefcase he was carrying. Knoechlein snapped to attention and saluted, "Heil Hitler," and with that dismissed himself.

The "special file" that he now had in his possession

contained, apart from general documentation for See-Löwe, one of the most crucially important items of all . . . the *Blauliste*, a list of prominent Britishers who were willing to support a German military Government in England. Whether through blackmail or from genuine ideological interest, the names on the list had already been approached by the SD and had expressed their potential allegiance to the Nazi cause. Some had openly shown their politics by joining various societies and movements; others had either been "caught with their trousers down" by the ever-vigilant SD agents in London before the war, or had been sympathizers with positions that could be put at risk if their true beliefs should be revealed.

Because the action of this latter group, this Fifth Column, was fundamental to the success of See-Löwe, the identity of each name on the list was protected by a unique code, the Blue Code, hence the *Blauliste*. The list itself was unintelligible, and only four copies were ever made.

Ernst Bohle's copy and the Amt II copy were destroyed by fire when Colonel Schellenberg's office in Prinz Albrechtstrasse was bombed. The third copy went with Gestapo Müller to the Russians in 1945. The fourth had been sent to England on 24 August 1940, in preparation for the invasion.

South Armagh, 1977

As the bleak morning sun burnt the remaining mist patches off the fields, eight weary pairs of eyes kept watch on the farmhouse. The soldiers, their faces blackened, had crawled into their concealed hides long before dawn, following a request from the Royal Ulster Constabulary in Middletown to respond to an emergency call. But this was bandit country, less than a mile from Glaslough in the Republic by unapproved roads. Bitter experience had taught the Royal Green Jackets to dig in, keep the suspect premises under observation, and wait for daylight before moving across the exposed terrain. Sometimes they would set up a clandestine observation post for up to a week before getting the order to close in. Too many milk churns packed with nails and stolen industrial gelignite had been left for unwary British patrols in conduits under local roads. These home-made mines had taken an appalling toll of armoured Land-Rovers, detonated either by the weight of the vehicle passing above, or remotely by a hidden Provisional. They had learned to keep away from road signs and other tall features which were used by "the oppo" as visual aids for them to set off their radio-controlled charges at exactly the right moment from a safe distance.

Sophisticated counter-measures had been devised to prevent such incidents, but most of the men waiting patiently for the order to start their search were on their third tour of duty in the Province, and they were sceptical of the electronic gadgetry designed to explode hidden charges, preferably while they were still being handled by the Provo technicians. Even the impressive number of "own goals" scored by the kit would not persuade any of the older sweats concentrating on the farm buildings in the distance to break cover and risk presenting an easy target for a sniper equipped with an image-intensifying nightscope.

Shortly after seven the dawn chorus was joined by the familiar thud-thud of an army helicopter. It was not one of the big Wessex aircraft that had carried them into position the previous afternoon, but a small airborne observation platform to keep watch at a distance and warn of any hostile activity nearby. Almost simultaneously the unit's radioman murmured a few short words to Captain Ward, who had been assigned the task of conducting the search by his company commander.

"Eagle, Two Three Sierra," the prearranged signal to indicate that their operational area would be supported by aerial reconnaissance for as long as it was needed. Ward nodded his response and a coded acknowledgement to Eagle, the helicopter's callsign, was returned. They all knew that the audio frequencies were monitored by unseen men using Bearcats, the latest American scanners. Three transmission squirts told the soldiers on the other side of buildings, already alerted by the presence of the Lynx, to emerge from the undergrowth and begin their sweep. Each checked his weapon and then, at a slow jog, zig-zagged across the open country to such cover as was available behind the water tank, barns and stables. The absence of any animals in the fields added to the tension. This was bad news, and the soldiers steered clear of the gateways, especially popular sites for anti-personnel devices. No movement registered from inside the house itself. Moving with caution, the patrol converged on the main building, a crumbling two-storey drystone structure that, like so many in this part of County Armagh, had probably been abandoned by its Protestant owner at the outbreak of "the Troubles" some six years earlier.

The patrol knew the routine: two other sections of eight riflemen each had covered the perimeter. This reduced the chances of being ambushed once inside, perhaps by a concealed mortar, and left the section under Ward to undertake the final search, ever vigilant for the tell-tale signs of a booby-trap. Someone had made the call to the RUC for a purpose, and this would prove either to be a time-wasting exercise to divert the army's attention away from some illicit activity elsewhere, or an attempt to draw them into a trap. Either way, bandit country was too dangerous for the police, and it was up to the army to cope.

Like the rest of his platoon, Captain Ward was no novice. He was just twenty-eight, and the exhilaration of command had given way to the burden of responsibility for the safety of his squaddies. At this hour of the morning most of his school contemporaries were probably barely awake, perhaps contemplating a day in the City wrestling with the implications of the Chancellor's budget and the new financial year. In contrast, Ward had been up all night, and was ready to kill a terrorist at very short range. His pips and badge had been covered, and he was cradling a self-loading rifle which made him indistinguishable in rank from his men. Using barely perceptible movements to communicate with his sergeant while at close quarters, he crouched low and circled the derelict house. At the back he removed the magazine from the SLR, cocked it to eject the round in the breech, replaced the round, and then handed the weapon to his sergeant, who had watched his every movement. He would have it ready to hand if Ward had to get out of the house in a hurry. Having unholstered his 9mm Browning, and cocked it, Ward hammered twice on the back door. It was unlocked. Accompanied by Corporal Underwood, he pushed his way inside and gingerly checked the three rooms on the ground floor. They were all empty, devoid of furniture or decorations. Meanwhile two other members of the squad moved upstairs. The words "All clear up here, boss" were received with relief. Ward holstered his automatic and turned to call out to his sergeant, but at that moment a blast of tremendous ferocity ripped through the enclosed space of the hallway, bringing the central part of roof down on the four soldiers inside.

"Jesus Christ!" exclaimed the observer aboard the helicopter circling at four thousand feet, as flames from the explosion shot into the sky. "Nobody's going to make it out of there."

1

The little group gathered around the sailing-club bar in the spring of 1978 provided Terry Duggan with a rapt audience. He knew the story well because he had already had a lot of practice in the pubs of Cowes.

"So instead of cutting the line," he continued, "I put on the bottles and went over the side to recover the anchor. I followed the rope down to the bottom and found that it had fouled on something in the mud and just wouldn't budge. I cleared away some of the mud with my hands and even through the disturbance I could make out what was holding the anchor."

The attention of the weekend sailors heightened as the twenty-one-year-old diver revealed what he had found in just forty feet of water in Gurnard Bay . . . a Messerschmitt 109 fighter, complete with the body of the pilot still locked into the cockpit.

Terry, whose usual diving work consisted of contract work for the harbour authorities and occasionally some underwater salvage, had been understandably excited by the find. The aircraft had shifted little from the day in 1940 that it had been shot down, in spite of the strong tides that sweep along the Isle of Wight coastline. Indeed, it seemed that the currents had only served to cover the plane with a thick layer of mud, preventing it from being broken up.

Some of those present around the Island Sailing Club's bar, overlooking the Medina estuary, knew part of Terry's story already. The Admiralty in Portsmouth had been informed of the wreck and had given Terry the necessary permission to stake his claim and put one of his diving marker buoys on the surface. The next step had been for the Navy to come and remove what remained of the German pilot from the cockpit so that he could perhaps be identified and sent back to Germany for proper burial. The Navy had sent a team of divers the previous Thursday, and Terry now gave the people assembled around him the latest instalment on his discovery.

"The Navy boys went down early in the morning with their own suction tubes to clear away the mud, and opened up the canopy. There was a hell of a

lot of mud actually inside because of the flak holes
through the aircraft skin. There wasn't really very
much of the poor old pilot but the instruments and
equipment inside were in very good condition . . .
even after all this time. But the most interesting thing
of all," said Terry, "was that there was a second body
in the plane. The pilot must have crashed with an
observer on board."

"But surely," protested someone in the audience,
"everyone knows that the Me 109 was a single-
seater fighter. It must have been a different type
of aircraft."

Terry grinned. Now he was really in his element.
"This aircraft was definitely a 109. There's no doubt
about that because we've lifted the engine now. And
there were definitely two men on board . . . a second
seat had been squeezed in behind the pilot's. He
must have been some kind of an observer. We're
going to try to bring the rest of the plane up on the
neap tide on the 26th."

The little group broke up, downing their beer and
discussing this strange turn of events. One of the
listeners remained to talk longer with Terry. He
was a tall, spare man, wearing jeans and a blue
sweater with "Finesse" picked out in white letters,
the name of the Dragon he was about to crew. He
was Captain Michael Ward, formerly of the Royal
Green Jackets.

Unlike Corporal Underwood, who had left a young widow and child in Gloucester, and Privates Fadden and Naylor, who had been literally blown to pieces as they had returned down the stairs of the farmhouse in South Armagh fifteen months earlier, Ward had largely recovered from his injuries. Now he could recall nothing about being pulled from the ruins by his sergeant, or the helicopter flight back to safety. He had not regained consciousness until fourteen hours later, after surgeons had operated to remove dozens of wood and stone splinters from his face, and made a vain attempt to save the sight of his left eye.

Ward had been protected from much of the blast by the thick wall of the kitchen, and his flak jacket had reduced his injuries, but his face had been badly burned by the intense heat of the flash. When, five weeks later, he had been allowed to look in a mirror, he thought himself terribly scarred but now, with his wounds healed, his face just looked lumpy and pockmarked. His leg, which had been crushed by a falling beam, had mended, and the steel pins that had been inserted above and below his knee had been removed.

Since being invalided out of the Army he had had little to do. One or two offers had been made to him but none really appealed. With the country going through the throes of recession, even the more charitable of his contacts were unable to give him the helping hand he needed to readjust to civilian life. His training since leaving school had been the leadership of men and he had done his job well. He had been looking forward to getting his Major's Crowns and, with promotion, the job he was after, a secondment to the Gulf. But now he was through with all that and the future didn't look too bright. The pension he received was enough to keep the wolf from the door for the time being but sooner or later the compensation that he'd been promised, but which had not yet materialized, would come to an end. Nowadays he spent the weekends crewing Darings and Dragons in Cowes and the rest of the week avoiding the chore of reading all the "Situations Vacant" columns.

Terry grinned a welcome to Ward. "Hello there, how's tricks?" Both had occasionally crewed on the same boats, and could usually be found in the Island's bar on Saturday mornings during the season.

"Not so bad. You must have been busy with this plane business. What's going to happen next?"

Terry enjoyed talking about his find. "Well, we've done as much as we can for the time being. Now we have to concentrate on bringing the aircraft to the surface intact."

Ward nodded to show his growing interest in the Messerschmitt.

"The Navy in Portsmouth have given us permission to make the final lift and that's all being planned at the moment."

"How are you going to do it?" asked Ward.

"We rely on nature to do all the work for us," explained the younger man. "If we were to use lifting gear we would run the risk of shattering the airframe. Our plan is to put slings under all the vital points and attach them with guys to floats on the surface. Then we wait for the neap tide. As the tide goes out, and the sea level goes down, we shorten the guys. Low tide is around 0600 when we make the final adjustments. After that, the sea does the rest. As the tide comes in, the floats will rise and lift the plane gently off the bottom. At least, that's how it should work in theory. Provided the weather holds, it's pretty much standard practice. There shouldn't be too much trouble because we've done the preliminary work already. Most of the mud has been vacuumed away and the plane is resting happily on the bottom. Why don't you come and watch the final lift?" invited Terry. "You should be able to see everything from the beach, we're not that far out."

"I just might at that," murmured Ward. "Who's going to pay for all of this? You must have laid out a fair penny already."

"It's not so bad, you know. I obviously won't be

paying for the use of our diving boat, the *Snow Goose*, and with our compressors it's not very expensive to fill the bottles. The rest of the gear is ours too, so our only real investment has been time and the hire of the vacuum pumps."

"What'll you do with the aircraft, assuming you get her up onto the beach in one piece?"

"Well, we haven't really decided that one yet. We thought of displaying her during Cowes Week, but I think that'll be quite difficult to organize. I expect we'll sell her to a museum. We've had some publicity in the *County Press* so no doubt there'll be some offers before long."

"Have you tried selling the rights for the story?" asked Ward. "There might be some good photographs in it."

"We've already been to see a postcard manufacturer on the island and they may buy any good pictures that we take, and there's some German magazine here for Cowes Week that might be interested. They're going to be staying over in Newport and I thought of going to see them."

"What about the television?"

"Bugger the television," said Terry. "They're always more trouble than they're worth . . . always getting in the way and once they're in on it they won't be content to stay on shore. They'll be all over the place in boats and suchlike and they're just a pain."

Ward smiled. He suspected that Terry had come into contact with television crews before whilst diving.

"Is there anything else that can be used commercially . . . that you can make money out of? The engine, perhaps?" he suggested.

"There are one or two things that I reckon are worth a bob or two," said Terry lowering his voice conspiratorially, "but they're nothing to do with the engine. When the Navy took out the bodies they sucked out all the loose material inside the cockpit. They picked up a few odds and ends that must have belonged to the crew."

"Such as?" prompted Ward.

"Such as," continued Terry, "a couple of watches, a silver cigarette case, a gun, some coins . . . and twenty-five gold sovereigns."

Ward whistled. "They should make the whole operation worth while if nothing else doesn't. Who will they belong to?"

"I'm hoping it'll be me," answered Terry, "but at the moment the Navy have got them and all the rest of the things they recovered. It all rather depends on who owned them in the first place. They might have been the Luftwaffe's, or there again, they might have been the pilot's."

"But why on earth would a pilot on a dangerous flight take up anything so valuable? He'd have to be crazy. I suppose there's no chance that they got into the aircraft after she crashed for some reason?"

"Impossible," replied Terry. "They were definitely on board at the time of the crash and if I can prove exactly who they were being carried by I might get them, or their value."

Ward nodded. "It certainly seems worth a try. The sovereigns could fetch a small fortune . . . at least to the likes of you and me!"

"You give me a hand in finding out where they came from, and in persuading the Navy, and I'll let you in for some of the proceeds. I can't cope with those Service fellers. They tie you all up in their forms and red-tape and I think they want to keep the sovereigns for themselves if they can. You see if you can get any sense out of them, and we'll talk money afterwards."

The deal was struck and that night Ward went to bed weighing up all the possibilities. Two dead Germans in a plane that usually only carried a crew of one, and a small hoard of gold sovereigns. Even if there was no money at the end of it all he reckoned a little research would beat scanning the newspaper columns over and over again.

On Monday morning, as he had been instructed by telephone, Ward presented himself at the front entrance of HMS *Dolphin*, a huge, dull, fort-like structure perched beside the mouth of Portsmouth Harbour.

At the main sentry post Ward asked the rating on duty for the officer he had spoken to the previous day and was quickly shown up to Lieutenant Shaw's rather sparse office.

"Aah, Captain Ward," greeted the uniformed figure behind the desk. "Please do come in. I've brought out the Germans' possessions from the stores in case you wanted to verify what we're holding. Not much, I'm afraid, but I suppose it's something that even this much was left down there. Nasty business."

Ward nodded in agreement. "What steps have you taken to find out the identities of the bodies?"

"Usual procedure in matters of this kind. The Admiralty have contacted the German authorities and given them all the information we have." He glanced down at the file he was holding. "I'm afraid that it's not much but at least we do know the serial number of the aircraft. The Germans should be able to check their own archives and trace the names of the crew assigned to that plane. Not too difficult really."

Ward walked over to the trestle table at the side of the room and glanced over the bits and pieces laid out. "What happened to the gold sovereigns?" he asked.

"Oh, don't worry about them. They're in the strongroom, just to be on the safe side. Better that they're there until it's decided what should happen to them."

"What usually happens in cases of this kind?"

"Well, we've never really had one quite like this and the law is rather complicated. It may be up to the Coroner to decide on whether it's treasure trove, in which case the Treasury will have an interest, or it may go to the Admiralty Court. I'm afraid I'm a bit new to this sort of thing."

Ward muttered that he quite understood and looked over the items on the table again. The Naval officer must have read his thoughts because after a few moments he commented, "I thought you'd be interested by one or two of those so I've had a complete inventory drawn up. They're rather odd, aren't they?"

Ward certainly found the display on the table before him odd. Apart from a cigarette case engraved with the initials BDSM, two wristwatches and a Luger, there was a small quantity of coins. What seemed incredible was that some of the coins were English.

"Strange, isn't it?" said Shaw. "I didn't know that German fliers were issued with foreign currency in case they were shot down. Seems rather a waste of time to me."

Ward started to agree, but suddenly became absorbed by the silver cigarette case. After a few moments he put it down and turned his attention to the two wristwatches.

"I know what you're thinking," said the young lieutenant as Ward held a small pocket magnifying glass to the Luger. "The serial number might be recorded and give a clue to the owner. Well, that won't be necessary because I'm told that the Luftwaffe were meticulous in keeping details of all their sorties, so we should know who the two blighters were in a day or so."

"Oh good," murmured Ward, clearly absorbed by his study of the gun. "Would it be all right with you if I borrowed one of the watches and the cigarette case for a few days?"

"I'm very sorry, sir, but that's out of the question. I can't let any of those items out of official hands until it's known what's to be done with them. You could say that at the moment they're Government property. I couldn't let them go even for a few minutes. I'm awfully sorry, sir."

Ward thought for a moment and then offered an alternative. "Suppose you accompanied me for just a short time? You'd be back by lunchtime."

The Naval officer looked perplexed. "What have you got in mind?" he asked.

Ward picked up the gun. "You've tried to clean

up the Luger a bit haven't you?" The younger man nodded in agreement. "Well, all I want to do is try and clean up the cigarette case and this watch here. If we take it to a local jeweller they can do it in just a few moments. It won't take long and you may find the exercise very interesting."

After a little hesitation and a brief telephone call to request permission to go ashore, the two men closed the deal and went off in search of a jeweller. Within minutes they had located a watch repair shop in Fratton Road and had asked to see the manager. Although he was a little puzzled by Ward's request he agreed to examine both the items before him, and with the reward of £10 being offered, asked no further questions. The Naval officer to whose charge the two valuables had been entrusted was equally mystified, but he kept quiet.

When the craftsman returned he was wearing an expression of even further amazement. "I'm not sure what you are both after," he said, "but I will do my best. I will not bore you with the matter of the interpretation of hallmarks except to say that the cigarette case is made of solid silver and was minted by Garrards of London in 1937. I have taken the liberty of cleaning up the case which, if I may be permitted to say, was in a shocking condition, and beyond that I can make little comment. The initials BDSM may well have been the initials of the original owner but I can tell you little more.

"The watch, however," continued the jeweller, "is more interesting. It is an English make with a Swiss movement but I don't think it has been sold in this country for a long time . . . certainly as long as I can remember. The mechanism itself is in fairly good condition but it will never function again as this type of watch required a certain amount of lubrication and from the look of it I would say that there has never been a service and the necessary oiling has been completely neglected. Furthermore, the mainspring is intact which would indicate that the watch has not suffered from overuse but some kind of unusual environment . . . and that would account for the lubrication congealing."

The watch-repairer looked up at the two men before him and all three grinned broadly.

"Thank you, Sherlock Holmes," said Ward, "I think you've given us more than enough to think about."

"Would you care for a valuation of the cigarette case?" asked the jeweller.

"No," said Ward as he hustled his Naval companion out of the shop. "You've been most helpful."

Once they got outside and were headed back to HMS *Dolphin*, Ward was bombarded with questions. "I think it's time you told me exactly what is going on. You knew bloody well what that old man was going to find long before we got here. What the hell are you after, and who the hell were the German airmen?"

Ward hesitated before answering but decided to share his suspicions. "It was only a hunch, but you're quite right . . . the watch at least was English and, combined with the gold sovereigns, the temptation was too much. As soon as I noticed that there was a hallmark stamped on the case I was determined to find out what this is all about."

"And what *is* it all about?"

"I'm not sure, but I think it's fair to say that the circumstantial evidence points to the second member of the Messerschmitt crew being a one-way only passenger. I will take some convincing that it was standard practice for Luftwaffe pilots to carry gold sovereigns over enemy territory or for observers to own solid silver cigarette cases from Regent Street, wear English-manufactured wristwatches and carry quantities of English money on them. It's just not possible."

The Naval officer quietly considered what he'd been told. "According to my way of thinking," he concluded, "one of those two bodies either belongs to a German who had been about to masquerade as a blue-blooded Englishman, or it's a traitor on his way to – or from – the Fatherland."

Ward turned to his new friend and agreed with him. "That's exactly what I think, and I intend to find out which. Let's talk about it over lunch."

The following day Ward went up to London armed with the cigarette case that he had managed to borrow from Lieutenant Shaw over a long pub lunch the previous afternoon. He had taken a lot of persuading and in the end would only be parted from just one of the items for that day. Ward had promised to return it within twenty-four hours without fail, and so had made an early start.

His first port of call was the showrooms of Garrards, the Crown Jewellers, in Regent Street, where he left the cigarette case with the chief silversmith, Mr Leonard, instructing him to make as detailed enquiries about the case as he could.

Ward then took a tube to the Imperial War Museum and asked to be shown up to the reading room on the second floor. When his request was granted, he found a place already prepared for him and several large green volumes piled up around the seat. The previous afternoon he had explained to the staff in the Museum Library what he was after and he had been promised full co-operation. They were as good as their word and after a few minutes the Museum's resident expert on the Luftwaffe, Mr Hine, came over and took the neighbouring seat.

"Good morning, Captain Ward," he welcomed. "I've made a search through the German records for the plane you've found and I think these are all the relevant details here."

He opened one of the larger books at a page marked by a slip of paper and indicated the Messerschmitt number.

"This is the German entry for your aircraft. Each plane had a works number which prefixed the serial numbers of most pieces of equipment carried on board, and the 4782 figure given to you by the Navy would be quite correct. As you can see," he said, pointing to a long entry stretching across two pages, "this number is under the fourth column, next to the 'type' space which shows that the aircraft was in fact a Messerschmitt 109E, an adaptation of the famous fighter, and usually used for low-level bombing operations. Actually," he continued, looking up from the book, "a two-seater version is not as unusual as you think. The 109 series were used for a whole variety of tasks including fighter training in twin seaters. Of course these aircraft with the observer facility became much more common later in the war, but at the date of this loss – and incidentally it's logged at 26 August 1940 – they were about, but I must admit I had no idea that they were actually flying operationally."

He returned to the text in front of him. "This

first column shows the unit the aircraft belonged to, in this case, 4 11 (S)LG2 which was a wing based at Etaples in Normandy at the time. The second column, which is blank, is used to show the cause of the loss and these last two spaces are to show the crew and their fate, if known."

"Why is there only one name down under 'crew' when there were two bodies, or what remained of them, recovered from the site?" asked Ward.

"That, I'm afraid, will have to remain a bit of a mystery unless you can get some eyewitness accounts from people who served with that wing. I agree with you that if two fliers had been in the crash, then yes, both names should appear. As it is, only Hauptimann Scherer is listed as having been aboard. I can't really think offhand of a reason for the omission, except to suggest a clerical error, but the Luftwaffe were usually very meticulous about keeping their records. I don't know what the answer is. No chance, I suppose, that the second body was that of a diver or swimmer who got trapped?"

Ward shook his head. "I haven't been down to the wreck myself, but I gather that it's unlikely in the extreme. I think we just have to assume that either someone made a blunder, or the Germans had some good reason to keep the identity of the second man quiet."

"Deliberate falsification?" wondered the expert.

"It's possible, of course, but that would be unusual for the Luftwaffe. I can't see that there would be any reason to go to those lengths unless they had something quite important to cover up, and the death of an observer would hardly merit that kind of treatment. And even if the flight was some sort of unauthorized jaunt it would have been strange behaviour by the Luftwaffe, to say the least. I expect it will just have to remain a bit of a mystery until you trace some survivors from that wing. I hope you'll let me know if you succeed." And with that the librarian made his departure.

Ward was now faced by an apparently insoluble problem. The aircraft had definitely carried a passenger, but the passenger didn't appear on the records. The obvious answer, he reckoned, was that the extra man had been aboard when the plane crashed, but hadn't been in the aircraft when it took off from Etaples. The implication of this was that the passenger had been picked up after departure from France . . . The Messerschmitt must have landed at a rendezvous in England and collected someone who was ready and waiting. The whole thing seemed preposterous, he knew, but that would at least tie in with the English coins found in the wreck; it might well have been loose change in the mysterious passenger's pockets, not unreasonable if he really had been scooped up in an English meadow.

After a few minutes he went into the small room adjoining the main reading-room and put the proposition to Mr Hine, who listened patiently to the explanation Ward suggested, but shook his head. "Not possible really. I admit it's an ingenious solution, and in theory it might have been practical for an enemy aircraft to land and take off quickly beneath the radar in some remote part of the countryside, especially at dusk, but it's still not possible. What with Allied analysis of captured documents since the war and all the historical research that has gone on in recent years we now know that every German agent who ever arrived in this country either gave himself up immediately or was caught pretty quickly, usually within a matter of hours. The Germans had a wealth of spies in Britain, or thought they did, but in fact they had all been 'turned' by MI5 and the famous Double Cross Committee. We'd know if there had been any successful espionage rings left, and I can assure you that there weren't. I'm afraid your theory just doesn't hold water."

"How can you be so sure that every single one was identified and arrested?" asked Ward. "Surely there must have been one or two who managed to slip away without us even getting to know about it at all?"

"Again, not possible. A check through the Abwehr records shows that they were completely taken in by our counter-measures under the supervision of MI5. And even if there was perhaps one solitary spy who did manage to get here, the Germans wouldn't have risked picking him up by plane in broad daylight or even at dusk. They only used the regular channels to Britain via the neutral countries, submarines and parachutes to deliver their 'V-Men'. Actually landing an aircraft never happened."

"But you can't know for certain, can you?" countered Ward. "We managed to land agents all over occupied territory in the war without catastrophic results. Why not the Germans? You said yourself that the 109E had been specially adapted for low-level work – perhaps that's why."

"First of all, you can't just land a plane anywhere in the dark or even at dusk. All our Lysanders that dropped off SOE agents and the rest of them were properly organized by reception committees with flares and radios. The Germans in England didn't have that capability on the ground. We would either have known about it then or it would have come to light later on, since the war, and I've never heard of such a thing."

"But would you necessarily have heard of it? Suppose for a moment that this event was just a one-off attempt that failed. It was early enough on in the war . . . couldn't it be conceivable that it was only on the results of this try that they decided that it was too risky to use pick-ups with aircraft?"

"I can see what you're driving at, but how do you explain the lack of any reception committee?"

"Perhaps, if this was a unique occasion, there wouldn't have been any need for a committee of helpers. Imagine for a moment that this chap, our spy, slipped into the country some other way, perhaps by submarine – or even had been living here long before the war and wasn't suspected or interned – and then had to be got out at short notice, but at any rate by plane. He could handle all the arrangements himself and not need to involve anyone else at all. If he put down the flares or windsock or whatever one needs, himself, then he could just clamber aboard and leave everything behind. Not impossible, surely?"

"Not impossible, I suppose," replied the expert, a little puzzled. "Can you also explain why nothing appears about any of this in captured German documents which were pretty comprehensive?"

"Now there you've got me. That's something I can't speculate on, but I could hazard a guess why such an event, if it really did happen, wouldn't be over-publicized by our side. MI5 wouldn't thank anyone for showing them up in a poor light so that even if some time afterwards they did find out about it they would probably still keep it under wraps. And from the German point of view, the operation wouldn't have been anything to shout about as they lost their pilot, aircraft and agent, so there wouldn't be anybody bleating about making fools of the British after the war!"

The older man scratched his head and smiled. "Well, I'll say this for you . . . you've got a wild imagination . . . either that or you're dead right. The only stories that come from classified sources nowadays are all the triumphs of British espionage. You rarely hear of the blunders . . . at least not from our side directly. Could be that you're right."

"Good Lord," grinned Ward, "I never thought I'd hear you admit that. Thank you for your time, and I'll let you know what happens."

A short while later Ward strolled slowly up Regent Street from the Piccadilly Underground station to Garrards and went to find Mr Leonard for news of the cigarette case.

"You've arrived just in time," said Mr Leonard, "I was wondering how I was going to contact you before you came back this afternoon. You're quite right of course, the piece was assayed by the Goldsmiths and Silversmiths, in fact in 1937, which one can see from the hallmarks here on the outside." He pointed out the small, almost indecipherable squares on the side of the case. "The letter 'B' indicates the year that the Assay Office stamped it and the letter 'G' within the triangle shows that it was us who originally made the case. As you probably know, the lion rampant indicates that the case is solid silver."

"Do your records show who originally bought it?" asked Ward.

"No, I'm afraid our sales ledgers don't go back as far as that – we haven't got the room to store them all – but if it's of any help I can tell you that although this is our original work, another jeweller, and a very skilled one at that, has done further work to it. I am not quite sure why, as it doesn't appear to be repair work."

"What sort of thing has been done to it?"

"You see that in effect the case consists of two flat metal sides, hinged down one side with a clip on the other. Well, one side weighs more than the other, even when you take this extra little silverwork for the clip into account. It wouldn't show up unless the case was given a really thorough examination as you requested, but it's there nevertheless . . . an extra sheet of silver has been added to one side. I first guessed by the weight, but if you look more closely you can see that this lower part," he rubbed his finger along the bottom edge of the case, "has definitely been added on later. It certainly wasn't done by Garrards."

"Could you guess why it's there?"

"I can't really be certain until I've actually

removed the plate and then I'm afraid the piece may be very badly damaged. Once the piece was removed it might become quite expensive to replace it. Probably quite a long job."

"Don't worry about that," replied Ward. "See if you can take it off without too much trouble."

"Very well," he said. "I won't keep you for more than a few moments," and with that he disappeared back to his workshop. In the meantime, Ward reflected on the possibilities. Someone flying in a German aeroplane in 1940 had been wearing an English watch and was carrying a solid silver case from the English Crown Jewellers. And now it looked as though the case had received some rather suspicious attention.

Some twenty minutes later, Mr Leonard returned, looking triumphant. "I've removed the plate, which as you can see is terribly thin. And inside there was this piece of paper. Actually," he said, correcting himself, "it's not paper but something more like celluloid. It's covered with all these numbers. They don't seem to make much sense but perhaps they will to you. Use my glass."

Ward took the flimsy, yellowed scrap and examined it closely through the instrument. In his fingers it felt almost oily, just like celluloid, and the whole of one side was completely covered in numbers in five-figure groups. Even though the thing was quite small, Ward calculated that there must be hundreds of the groups. As he turned the celluloid over he felt the piece move slightly in his hand. His instinct was that it was about to collapse after such a sudden exposure to the atmosphere after so many years, but he quickly realized that there were no fewer than three thin sheets altogether. In total, the number of groups must be nearer a couple of thousand.

The bespectacled Mr Leonard watched the face of his customer light up with satisfaction, and offered to try and replace the silver plate on the case.

"No, that really won't be necessary, but thank you anyway," said Ward. "There is one final way you can help me, though. I would like to trace the original owner and I wondered if you could give any guidance?"

"I can't tell you anything from our own records, as I've explained, but there may be something inside the case to help you, as well, of course, as the initials."

Ward had been looking so closely at the three slivers of celluloid that he hadn't spotted what else the fake plate had hidden: a crest of a lion rampant holding a crucifix.

"Just from the initials alone you might have had some luck, but with the crest I wouldn't be surprised if you could find your man quite quickly. Again we only keep the crest dies for a limited period of time, but I expect that a heraldry expert or the College of Arms would soon be able to lend a hand."

Ward thanked the craftsman again for all his kindness and set off to trace the dead Englishman whose initials were BDSM and whose family had a crest like the one that had up until moments ago been completely hidden. As he left the shop he realized that although the search might well be fruitless, it might easily become important. After all, he mused, the only people who carried gear like that were spies and the way the wartime history read, all German spies in Britain had been either arrested or turned. And now here seemed to be one, from under the Solent, who was neither. Even more significantly, Ward had got the man's last message . . . and surely that, he reasoned, was worth something.

Determined to take the bull by the horns, Ward walked through to Leicester Square and spent the rest of the afternoon reading up as much as he could from the Heraldry shelves in Foyles' bookshop and the Westminster Reference Library nearby, in St Martin's Street. By closing time he was still no nearer his goal, although he had learnt plenty about crests. He would have to go to the College of Arms and that would mean spending at least another day in London, if not several. Having taken that decision, he tried to telephone Shaw at HMS *Dolphin* but was told that he was out of his office. He left a somewhat vague message, promising to drop "something" off with him as soon as he could, neglecting to mention what he had discovered inside the cigarette case. He was reluctant to be specific in his message, for Shaw's sake: the Navy might not be too pleased to learn that the lieutenant had allowed any of the finds to leave his custody.

The next thing to do was to find a place for the night, and after a couple more calls Ward had negotiated a bed in his sister's flat in South Kensington. Lucy, his only sister, was two years younger: she led a life that seemed chaotic to Ward, but was devoted to her brother, even if she was not too keen on his Army friends. Lucy was not exactly a beauty, but she had an infectious sense of humour, and great charm when she cared to use it. Tall and strikingly pretty, with shoulder-length streaked brown hair, she was rarely seen wearing anything but jeans and casual sweaters – cashmere, of course, and worn with a confidence that boasted its own elegance – but there was nothing contrived about her relaxed attitudes.

Although she was younger than Ward, she was more academically orientated: while he had gone straight to Mons after leaving school, Lucy had read PPE at St Hilda's. But instead of coming out in London, as her parents might have wanted, she had taken off to Florence and then Venice to learn

the art of engraving glass, and was now beginning
to make a name for herself in the London galleries.
Over the years she had had a succession of boyfriends
– in much the same way that her brother had never
stayed long with one girl – although the latest,
Graham Cooper, seemed to have survived Lucy's
eccentricities, to say nothing of her notorious short-
comings in the kitchen, rather longer than most.

After a poorly prepared frozen dinner of lamb
chops washed down by a rather nasty Spanish white
wine provided by Cooper, Ward launched into his
story so far to a rapt audience. His sister clearly
thought the whole thing was a wild-goose chase and
anyway had other things on her mind, but her new
flatmate became more and more intrigued by Ward's
tale, from the original finding of the Messerschmitt
by Terry right up to the events of the previous
few hours.

"I had these photocopies made of the originals at
the print shop down the street," explained Ward,
as he handed over the three sheets. "They've been
enlarged quite a lot too, so they're clearer. I don't
suppose they'll mean much to you even if you are
an accountant."

"I don't suppose they'll mean much to anybody,"
said Lucy. "These things are thirty or forty years old,
and there are yards of books about all that stuff every
year. There can't be anything new, surely, after all

this time? The war's over. The washing up, on the other hand, isn't," and she began to clear away the plates and glasses.

Cooper ignored her – rather bravely, Ward thought: it was not for nothing that Lucy had been known, affectionately, to the family as "the boss" – and spread the photocopied pages out on the table. "No, they don't mean anything to me, but this has got to be the key to the whole thing. If you could get these numbers turned into decent English or German or whatever it is, you could really be on to something. The colour supplements alone would adore to pay a lot for this . . . and imagine what *Stern* would offer." He returned the copies to Ward. "How are you going to get them deciphered?"

"I wasn't intending to go about it like that, rather just trace our friend in the passenger seat. I've got his initials and crest and even if I have to resort to searching the 1940 telephone books I'll track him down. Then I thought I'd go on from there. If all these numbers really are a coded message of some kind – and I don't even know that – it would be almost impossible to crack it. I have difficulty doing the *Sunday Express* crossword."

"What about the Admiralty? Surely they would have the facilities for deciphering and all that lark?"

"Very possibly, but for a start they don't even

know of its existence and they certainly wouldn't be very pleased to hear where I got it from, and who would pay for all the work to be done? The message is over thirty-five years out of date and even in these days of computers it won't be easy to decode."

"Rubbish," said Lucy, as she reappeared through the kitchen door with a tray of coffee. "I'll tell you exactly what you should do."

As so often in the past, even when their parents had been alive, Lucy had taken command.

2

That dinner in Thurloe Street had been on Tuesday evening and now it was Thursday. Ward had spent much of the previous day down at the Queen Victoria Street headquarters of the College of Arms, and had fruitlessly made his way through huge volumes of family crests, each illustrated in colour and described in detail. He had still shed no light on the owner of the initials BDSM and had left the uphill struggle in the hands of a freelance researcher offered by the College.

At this moment Ward was in Oxford seated in a bright, cheerful room which was rapidly filling with pipe smoke. Opposite him in a very worn Gladstone chair was an elderly, wrinkled man with strands of thin, white hair falling over his forehead. One hand was steadying a steaming mug of coffee on the arm of the chair, the other was holding the three photocopies up to the light.

"Yes, of course I remember your sister," he repeated for the third time. "Such an intelligent girl, don't you know. Very attractive. We all thought she was going to marry that poet chap at Wadham. Funny she still hasn't got hitched. Soon will I expect. Damn pretty girl, I always thought."

Ward nodded his agreement. The older man before him poring over the numbers was J. D. Coleman, the historian. Apart from being a Fellow of All Souls and Dean of Queen's College, Oxford, he was also an ex-member of Britain's Secret Service, or rather, more accurately, MI5. He had returned to the city of dreaming spires as soon as the war was over, though of course the undergraduates always used to whisper that he had never actually been retired. In spite of the thousands of students who had gone down from the University since Lucy's days, the old boy still appeared to remember her with affection.

"Some trouble with the police up at Cumnor, wasn't there?" asked Coleman. "And didn't some chap nearly drown one May morning because of her? Damn waste of a fine brain I always said. Intelligent, but headstrong. Very pretty, though." He got down to business. "Want all this decoded do you? Quite sure it's German in origin, eh?" He gave all three pages another long look. "Quite sure about the date, eh?"

Ward nodded to all these questions. Before he became famous as a twentieth-century historian, Coleman had been asked to join a large group of lecturers and professors who had been gathered under the umbrella of MI6 in the late thirties. Some worked in the famous huts of the "Government Code and Cipher School" at Bletchley Park, the large estate and mansion some fifty miles from London and scene of Britain's wartime cryptographic success. Eventually over seven thousand people worked and trained at Bletchley, snatching German signals out of the ether and sending them in clear English down the teleprinter cables to London. These behind-the-scenes boffins discovered the secrets of the German code machine known as the Enigma, and throughout the war were able to report daily on Nazi movements and intentions.

Now that so much had been allowed to be published about wartime codebreaking, not least by Coleman, who had highly individual ideas of the importance of cryptography, there was little the old man enjoyed more than a receptive and interested audience to whom he could recount his experiences.

"I keep in touch you know," Coleman said, "with many of my old colleagues. A lot of course were

Oxford men. Damn shame some of them died before anyone was allowed to know what they were up to during the war. I'll do what I can with this lot. Won't be as difficult as it looks. Quite like old times, except I'm a bit rusty. Get a bit of help, I dare say. Where did you say you got hold of it?"

Ward repeated the story that he'd prepared with Lucy. "I suppose it originally came from a German, though I don't quite know where," he lied. "I was going through my uncle's old wartime diaries and I came across it in the August 1940 section. Spoils of war, I suppose, but if it's interesting I'd like to add it to his memoirs."

Ward thought the explanation was fairly plausible, and so apparently did J. D. Coleman. "We read all their stuff, every bit of it, right up to the end of the war. Knew it all in advance. Problem was, we couldn't be seen to be too clever or they'd have caught on. Damn arrogant lot, the Germans. Some of them still don't believe it. Often been told by them that it was impossible. Absolute rubbish of course. Some of their signals came to us before they got to their proper destination. Don't underestimate it."

Ward promised not to, and made his way back to the High. The old historian had explained that he was going to look up his old papers and see if he recognized the cipher. From his days locked in with "turned" German spies at the MI5 cage at Ham

Common, and the hundreds of hours spent discussing particular types of ciphers with case officers at the MI5 headquarters in St James's Street, Coleman had accumulated a gigantic collection of wartime espionage tools. Often he made his files available for researchers delving into the secret war but best of all he liked to be consulted, as Ward had just done. If anyone in England, outside Government service, could crack the meaning of those three slivers of celluloid, it was J. D. Coleman.

Ward caught the two-twenty train back to London and remembered to buy Lucy her reward . . . a decent bottle of champagne. Just as he walked into the flat, the telephone started to ring and he answered it. It was the College of Arms. The researcher had indeed found the owners of the lion rampant with crucifix crest: it had been borne by the Messenger family since 1858 and the initials must have belonged to Benjamin David Sykes Messenger . . . a Captain in the Intelligence Corps killed in August 1940.

Ward had now put a name to the body found in the Messerschmitt, and a name to the owner of a cigarette case that concealed some kind of enciphered message. But what on earth was an "I Corps" officer doing in the wreck of a German plane? Had the body been that of a spy of the civilian variety it would have been extraordinary; but to find a serving officer was quite another matter. Two thoughts sprang to Ward: was the officer's presence on board authorized, thereby making him part of some previously undisclosed clandestine operation, or was the explanation altogether more sinister? Perhaps the man had simply been masquerading as a British officer? But if so, why take on the identity of an authentic individual who could easily denounce him?

Certainly Ward knew all about the I Corps, as it was known, a regular regiment now, but one that had been hastily recreated on the outbreak of war after it had been disbanded in 1919. It had provided the Field Security Sections with personnel, and given useful military cover to MI5 staff. But how could an officially gazetted member of the unit find his way into an enemy Me-109? Ward groped for explanations.

Perhaps, he thought, the aircraft was a duplicate. He knew that the RAF had secretly assembled a squadron of captured enemy aircraft, and had occasionally flown missions under false colours against the Luftwaffe. Could the wreck have been part of some similar operation that had gone terribly wrong? Perhaps the Messerschmitt had been attempting to infiltrate Messenger into enemy-occupied territory, and had been shot down accidentally by an unindoctrinated gun crew? But if so, how come the loss had been recorded officially by the Luftwaffe?

Nothing seemed to make sense, and Ward groped for plausible explanations. Could the man with Messenger's cigarette case merely have been a courier, someone carrying it as a recognition signal? In that event Ward was only a little closer to discovering the truth. What was the official explanation for Messenger's death? That surely would solve the mystery.

Sir David Messenger leaned over from his deckchair and offered another glass of home-made lemonade.

"Last year ruined the lawn and I'm surprised it's recovered at all. I know it's hard to imagine, but all of this was an absolute wasteland." Ward surveyed the finely kept flowerbeds and shrubs scattered around the garden. In the early summer afternoon, all the plants were looking at their best and the scene couldn't be more typically English. A group of four children were being encouraged by two older women to take their game of croquet seriously, and the farmhouse built in Cotswold stone at the end of the lawn seemed to exude a kind of secure warmth to those gathered in its grounds.

Ward had had little difficulty in finding one of the only two remaining relatives of Benjamin Messenger. Mrs Messenger, Benjamin's mother, was in a private home in Brighton, and was apparently too frail to receive anyone but family, and Sir David, knighted in 1964, was Benjamin's elder brother. *Who's Who* had readily given up the information that Sir David, a retired civil servant, lived at Tutton Hall, Denning, in Hampshire and a further telephone enquiry had been received with a certain amount of hesitation, but it seemed that Sir David's curiosity had been aroused when his late younger brother's name was mentioned. He had reacted oddly, Ward thought, but perhaps he was bound to after so long. Ward had lied that he would be in the Denning area that Saturday afternoon, and an invitation had, as he'd guessed, been immediately forthcoming.

"You mentioned that you had some information about my brother. Would you like to tell me about it?"

"I'm not sure, but I think it's possible that your late brother's remains may have been recovered. I wanted to find out as much as I could about the circumstances of his death, his wartime service and so on, so that he can be properly identified."

"If you don't mind my asking, why aren't the proper authorities making these enquiries?"

"Well, I expect they will be eventually, but there is a certain amount of confusion at the moment over identities. The authorities seem to think that the body found by a friend of mine may have been a German."

"Where were the remains found?"

"In the sea, but the Navy will be able to give you fuller details when they come to see you."

"And when will that be? I'm rather surprised that I haven't been informed already. Apart from Benjamin's mother, I'm his next of kin. Surely I should have been told first?"

"Well, yes, I agree," said Ward rather uncertainly. "In normal circumstances yes, but in this case, owing to the time involved and so on, it's been too difficult to make any formal identification. I have just been following up one or two clues in a private capacity, not official in any way. But so far it does seem likely that your brother has been found. I wonder if you could help me with a couple of points that occur to me."

"I'll do my best," replied Sir David.

"How were you informed of your brother's death? Can you remember the date?"

"Not exactly, but I remember I was stationed in Scotland at the time and I received the standard War Office telegram. 'Killed on active service.' I think I've probably still got it somewhere'.

"Do you know the circumstances of his death?"

"No, we were never told, but I believe he was killed decently, in the service of his country."

Ward nodded hastily. His questions were not being received as well as he had hoped. "Did you know what sort of work he was involved in?"

"No, he never discussed his work and we never expected him to. He was in the Intelligence Corps so naturally their activities were secret. We never pried."

"Did you ever meet any of his brother officers, people who served in his unit?"

"Not that I can remember. You weren't born then, young man. You couldn't possibly know what those days were like. People didn't ask questions all the time. One knew that perhaps someone was doing something hush-hush and one left it at that. Surely you can understand that?"

"Oh, yes indeed. I was in the Services myself until recently. But were you never curious about what had happened, or why there was no proper burial?"

"Not really. My CO at the time told me when I got the telegram that owing to the sort of work Ben had been doing it wouldn't be possible to hold a ceremony. Of course we had a memorial service for him later, but that was all. I'm afraid it happened to a lot of chaps."

"What happened afterwards?"

"I got three days compassionate leave to come down here and tell my parents. And that was all."

"You never made any enquiries later?"

"Not really. I think I may have asked around a

bit but I never received any official word. I suppose in a way I'm rather pleased that the whole thing is settled now. When will I find out for certain?"

"I don't really know, but I'll do what I can to speed up the processes and try and put the Navy on the right track. They're in charge because your brother's remains were recovered from the sea. I'm sure it will all work out in the end."

"I should hope so," said Sir David.

"Perhaps I could ask you one last question. How close were you to your brother, in age?"

"He was four years younger than myself which in those days, living in the country, was enough to keep us apart quite a lot. I suppose you could say that we were never really very close. Different regiments and all that."

"One last one, Sir David, and I hope you won't think this impertinent. When your brother was killed, had he said anything to you about problems, financial or otherwise?"

"Not that I ever knew about. He wasn't queer or broke, if that's what you mean, though I can't think how that could be of any interest to you, Mr Ward."

"What about his politics? Was he a member of any political parties or organizations that you can remember?"

As Messenger got to his feet, Ward realized that

he had gone too far. "Enough is enough, Mr Ward. I have answered your questions but you have given me little reassurance. You won't even tell me where my brother has been found, something I would have thought would be a basic courtesy, and all you have done is make insinuations. No, I have no idea if Benjamin was a Tory or a Socialist, but I can tell you that if you try to rake up dirt about him, dirt that doesn't exist, then I'll come down heavily upon you with the full weight of the law. He's been dead a long time and your digging won't do any good, mainly because there isn't anything to find. I don't know what your game is, but I don't like it. Good day to you, Mr Ward."

And with that, the interview was over. Ward was escorted across the garden and through the house and left standing on the front drive. As he made his way towards his hired Ford saloon in the lane, Ward wondered whether he had just witnessed the natural anger of an aggrieved relative, or whether perhaps he had touched a rather sensitive nerve with his last question. Of one thing he had no doubt: Sir David Messenger was a formidable person, and he was not the type to waste any time in getting on the telephone and placing a few calls to his old contacts in Whitehall. He had all the reserved confidence, perhaps even arrogance, of someone who was not easily intimidated, and was used to having his own way. He hoped that Lieutenant Shaw, back in Portsmouth, was prepared for the inevitable onslaught.

Ward spent the rest of the weekend on the Isle of Wight and attempted to bring Terry up to date with developments, but he took little interest in Ward's attempts to identify the passenger. He was pleased, though, that the cigarette case had now been returned to HMS *Dolphin*, and that its absence would not jeopardize his relationship with Shaw and the Salvage Department.

Monday afternoon was spent in Kensington Public Library's Reference Section finding out as much as he could about the Messenger family, but there was precious little to examine. He was soon exhausted with his research and was now itching to find out what Benjamin's last message might have been. Overcome with impatience, he decided to call Oxford.

"Yes indeed, I'm working on the ciphers at the moment young man," confirmed Coleman, "though I don't suppose I'll be able to get much work done if you keep pestering me."

Ward stifled a protest that this was his first enquiry, and asked what progress had been made.

"I've established one or two quite useful characteristics," replied the historian. "You may be interested. The first task of a cryptographer is a process known as discrimination. This is a matter of analyzing the construction of a text to see whether it contains the familiar characteristics of a machine-generated cipher, or a manual cipher. Confirmation that it is of German origin, and of wartime vintage, is a great help. The omission of callsigns and the other identifying preliminaries show that this example is not a regular signal, of the kind we regularly intercepted, beginning with such essential data as the addressee, time of transmission, number of groups in the main body, etcetera. This is all vital information for the recipient of a wireless signal, but in this case it has been omitted. That rather narrows the field. Clearly this is some kind of manual or hand cipher, and all one needs is the key which, as likely as not, is buried somewhere in the text."

"The key?" asked Ward. "Why would anyone put a clue to the code in the actual text itself?"

"So the recipient can recognize the text for what it is, and select the correct key or method to unravel it." Coleman returned to his subject undaunted by Ward's interruption. "The Abwehr's hand ciphers were the first of the enemy's codes to be solved by my colleagues at Bletchley, largely thanks to MI5's work with the double agents, each of whom had been equipped with a hand cipher with which to communicate to their German controllers. Even with the passage of time, I can spot an Abwehr hand cipher straight off. It's like recognizing an old friend with whom one has spent many long hours. No problem," chuckled the academic, "as you might say."

Ward knew better than to interrupt again.

"Having eliminated the regular services, such as the Wehrmacht and the Kriegsmarine, we are in more interesting territory. These groups are not, as one might have expected, a regular message in letter form with full-stops. Usually I go straight to the full-stops to identify the structure of the text because having established them, the rest is relatively simple, if time-consuming. In English sentences, nouns, as the subject, normally appear immediately after the full-stop. In German, the predicate often comes at the end of a sentence so the code-group immediately before the full-stop may well be a verb. Again, in this set of groups, the structure is different. At a guess, I would say that you may have a list of some kind. Perhaps a shopping list or an inventory . . . is that possible?"

Ward explained that he really didn't know, but encouraged the older man to press on.

"It may be that this is a RSHA cipher, perhaps one from the Sicherheitsdienst or Gestapo. If you could tell me a little more about its origins it would save time."

Ward explained again that there was no more tracking down of the source that he could do.

"Very well, you'll just have to be patient. At least we know what it isn't. I'm so glad you've brought this little problem to me. Quite like old times. Incidentally, I've brought in one of my old chums to give me a hand. Very experienced chap, Colonel Green. Used to be a case officer with Masterman and that gang. Spent most of the war in a country house in Hertfordshire, cooped up with some Nazi or other. Better at the old SD ciphers than me. Not much of their stuff left, you know. Lots destroyed in 1945. Lot to hide, you know. Must get on now. Give my regards to Lucy. All very exciting this, isn't it?"

Before Ward could agree, or dispute what had been said, the line went dead. No doubt the old boy was back at his figures already, he thought.

Later that evening, Ward was sent out by Lucy to buy the dinner for the three of them. Lucy and Graham were becoming accustomed to their new lodger, but had decided to make use of him. As he walked slowly along Thurloe Street towards the shops in the Old Brompton Road that stayed open late, Ward noticed two men leaning against the back of a Ford Transit that had apparently broken down.

"Can you give us a push, mate?" asked one. Without a second thought Ward walked over to the rear of the van and was just about to apply his weight when a violent blow crushed into the base of his skull from the left – his blind side. He felt four strong hands seize him and bundle him into the back. He went sliding across the floor of the rear compartment and fell in a heap. By the time he had regained his senses and realized what had happened, the two rear doors had been locked shut and the van was being driven off at quite a speed.

For a few moments, Ward couldn't believe that it was really happening. It wasn't even nine o'clock yet and there was plenty of daylight . . . and yet he had definitely been kidnapped. He tried banging on the steel partition behind the driver's seat, and on the sides of the van, but all to no avail. Nor was there any inside handle. Without any opportunity of gaining a purchase on the smooth metal sides, he had no chance of forcing the doors open.

Each time the Transit stopped, he renewed his efforts, but it was difficult to keep steady and he was unsure how much noise would be detected on the outside. Within a few moments the effort became futile because the van had picked up speed and the gaps between the stops became larger. Soon they were on the move more or less permanently and there was little change of direction. Perhaps they were now on a motorway, thought Ward.

After about an hour, the van's speed slackened off and again Ward found it more difficult to remain sitting upright on the hard steel floor. If they had been on a motorway before, they were definitely off it now. As time went on and they showed no signs of either stopping or appearing with an explanation, Ward tried to reason out who his assailants were. He could come to no firm conclusion other than that they were both big, and clearly professional. It was not a comforting thought that both men had obviously done this sort of thing before.

As he pondered his rather bleak future, the van turned off the metalled road onto a very rough track and Ward was thrown all over the rear compartment. The van then came to a sudden halt, though the engine was left running. Both side doors banged shut, and Ward could hear muffled voices outside and the sound of feet on gravel. He tried kicking the sides of the Ford again but he was ignored.

It was only when he stopped banging that he realized that the tone of the engine noise had changed somewhat and he peered through the darkness at the rear of the van where he could hear a scraping sound. Slowly it dawned on him what had happened. Someone had attached a rubber tube from the exhaust-pipe to the small vent in the rear-offside door, forcing carbon monoxide into the interior where he was crouched. It was then that Ward realized that he was going to die, and that he didn't know who his murderers were or why they were killing him.

3

Very gradually, a picture was beginning to form in front of Ward's eyes. It was blurred and not at all clear but he could certainly feel that someone was squeezing his hand gently and whispering to him. It was Lucy.

"Can you hear me?" she pleaded.

Ward grunted an answer but the words just didn't seem to form properly in his throat. His mouth was burning and very little seemed to make sense. "Where am I, Lucy?"

"In hospital . . . Reading General. What on earth happened?"

Ward struggled desperately to try and remember what had been going on. Slowly he began to recall going out to buy the dinner and then being bundled into the back of a van. Then it all came back to him.

He was being gassed. He blinked again and tried to lift his head.

"Is that really you, Lucy?" he demanded again.

"Of course it's me, silly. What happened?"

"I was rather hoping that you were going to tell me that. The last I can remember is lying in the back of a Ford Transit watching the exhaust fumes coming in. I thought I was dead."

"Why on earth were you there?" she asked.

Ward tried to explain but soon realized that what he wanted to say and the sounds coming out of his parched mouth were two different things. He gulped down a glass of water and immediately began to retch, but after a couple of minutes he felt a little better.

"Two men jumped me outside the flat and drove off somewhere. They just left me stuck in the back after they had connected the exhaust to the vent. I thought I was a goner. That's it, I'm afraid. How did I get here?"

"A gamekeeper found you. He thought you were a poacher and bloody nearly shot you. Apparently the van was slap in the middle of some squire's estate in a place called Yattendon. The keeper crept up on the van because the engine was running and there you were, unconscious in the back. He called the police and an ambulance. The police contacted me."

"Are they still here?"

"Yes, they've been here all the time. They want to see you."

"And I want to bloody see them. It was quite deliberate . . . they just left me for dead. Trouble is, I never really got a good look at their faces. I just wasn't looking. Bloody daft, but when someone asks you for a push, you don't expect to be walloped on the back of the head."

"It's a bit more complicated than that."

"What on earth are you talking about? What could be more complicated than that?"

"The police seem to think that you were trying to commit suicide . . . that you rigged up the van and everything."

"They must be mad. Surely it's obvious . . . I got coshed and they just left me."

"I'm afraid not. The rear doors weren't locked and they've traced the van back to the hire company in London."

"And . . . ?"

"And the van-hire people say that it was a Captain Michael Ward who hired the van yesterday afternoon. They've got your driving licence number and everything."

Ward sank back into his pillows with a gasp. "Those cunning bastards," he murmured. "They must have unlocked the doors after I had blacked out, and then pushed off."

"And that's not all. They've been on to the regiment and they found out all about the ambush in Armagh. They think you're off your head . . . excessive strain."

Following a long interview with Inspector Bushrod of the Thames Valley Police that evening, Ward brushed aside all protests and discharged himself from hospital. In spite of all the claims that he was in need of rest and would be well advised to stay in for a couple of days "for observation", Ward insisted that Lucy drive back to London.

He had made a statement about the attack but he could see from the Inspector's face that not a word of it was going to be believed. Chelsea Police had not had any reports of an attack in Thurloe Street and the van-hire firm were apparently adamant that it had been Captain Ward who had signed all the documents. The Licensing Centre in Swansea had confirmed that all the details of Ward's driving licence had been given correctly, so the police were satisfied that they had a nutcase on their hands. The fact that the Yattendon keeper hadn't seen anyone else at the scene, and was sure that the rear doors hadn't been locked, seemed to clinch it.

When Ward asked the Inspector why it was that he had apparently hired a car to do away with himself, the policeman merely pointed out that Lucy had

confirmed that he didn't own a car and that perhaps he hadn't wanted to use Lucy's Mini. "Carbon
monoxide poisoning is a very popular way of doing
it nowadays," added the Inspector cheerfully.

Lucy, however, did believe him and supported
him as much as she could. She pleaded that he
couldn't possibly have tried to commit suicide
because anyway Ward had only popped down to
the supermarket to buy some dinner, but the police
would have none of it.

"If there was anything to investigate, believe me,
we would," said Bushrod, "but there's nothing.
People do very strange things, especially after something terrible like what happened to your brother in
Northern Ireland. Sometimes it's just a spur-of-the-
moment thing. They are sparked off by some trivial
incident and they say 'That's enough'. It's not so difficult to understand. Happens every day. There's no
report of any fight, and your brother himself admits
that he can't think of anyone who would try to kill
him – apart from the IRA, which isn't very likely in
South Kensington. His description of the two men is
very unhelpful . . . 'medium build, medium height,
thinks one of them may have had a moustache'. We
can't start enquiries with that sort of information.
Besides which, the hire people say it was he himself
who rented the van and they can't be lying. They
could even quote his Driving Licence Number."

*

Ward's first stop back in London was to call at the offices of the van-hire firm in Barnard Road, Battersea. The receptionist behind the desk in the scruffy office gave the impression that she was thoroughly bored by the whole affair.

"Not *more* bloody questions," she exclaimed. "We've told all we know to the local coppers. We haven't even got the van back yet. And who's going to pay for that, I'd like to know?"

Ward produced his wallet. "I will, if you can answer just a few more questions. Did you see the man who hired the van?"

"No," she replied, "I was just down the road for a moment. Our mechanic, Billy, saw the geezer. He's seen the police as well, you know."

"May I see him for a moment?" Ward opened his wallet and this seemed to make the young girl's mind up for her. Moments later, Billy was led into the office, wiping his grease-covered hands on his overalls. He looked blankly at Ward and Lucy.

"You don't recognize me, do you?" asked Ward.

"No," he replied. "Should I?"

"Not really, except that you apparently rented me a van yesterday."

The young mechanic looked puzzled. "I don't think I've ever seen you before. Certainly not yesterday, any rate. I'd remember."

"My name is Michael Ward, and yesterday you told the police that you'd hired a van out to me."

"It wasn't you, mate," said the mechanic patiently, "but it was to Captain Ward. I saw him. He was standing in this very office."

"The man you saw wasn't in fact Captain Ward, but someone impersonating him. What we want to know is where all the details on the hire document came from."

"The man filled in all the form . . . I watched him do it. He said he had some furniture to shift. The rental agreement was filled in perfectly and he paid up. I couldn't have known that he was a fake."

"Did you actually examine the driving licence?" asked Ward.

The man hesitated. "Not exactly. He'd left it at home. He offered to go back and get it, but I didn't really see the point. He had all the licence numbers and so on written in the back of his diary. I saw them," he added defensively.

As Ward and Lucy made their way back to Thurloe Street, they discussed the problem.

"Even if I tell the police that the garage never actually had sight of the licence I don't suppose they'd start an investigation. It seems to me that I'd be better off out of the way somewhere for the time being . . . those two heavies won't be too pleased by the gamekeeper's intervention and they may try again. I don't want to endanger you."

Lucy smiled up at her brother. "So you're quite sure now that they really were after you and they didn't mistake you for someone else?"

"Pretty certain. Even my bank manager isn't *that* desperate. Those two went to quite a lot of trouble to make it look as if I had committed suicide. But for a nosey-parker they would have succeeded and I'll bet the Coroner would have given a verdict of 'while the balance of his mind was disturbed'."

"Any ideas on who's responsible?"

"In the last week only one man has actually threatened me, and he's a top civil servant, so I think we can count him out. More likely, Coleman has been telling too many people about the cipher and someone is very, very angry."

"But who? The war has been over for decades. Who on earth cares about some rotten old message that probably won't be unravelled anyway?"

"Coleman told me that he was on the way to cracking it and he'd already discovered that it wasn't an ordinary message. He said it looked like a list. Apparently it didn't conform to the usual sort of 'Dear Spy' and 'Yours sincerely' structure. Anyway, he should know."

"So what's next on the agenda?"

"You go home and give Coleman a ring. I think

you'd better tell him where the cipher really came from, and ask him to be careful who he tells. I'm going back to the War Museum . . . something Coleman said has given me a hunch."

When the traffic lights in Sidney Street turned red, Ward jumped out of the Mini, adding as an afterthought, "And for God's sake be careful." He then hailed a passing cab and instructed the driver to take him to the Imperial War Museum.

Mr Hine was having tea when Ward walked into his tiny office off the reading room. The bespectacled academic quickly put down his cup and greeted his visitor. "I didn't expect to see you back so quickly. More progress on that sunken 109?"

"I've managed to find out quite a lot and I've also identified the extra man in the cockpit."

"Good Lord!" he said. "That's a bit of a break-through for you. What nationality was he?"

"I'm not absolutely certain, but he was either a British intelligence officer or a German posing as a British officer, and I need your help."

Hine whistled. "You're not pulling my leg are you? This is utterly fantastic."

"I know it seems that way, but all the evidence is there. Furthermore, if the passenger was a spy it would explain why no other name was found in the German losses book."

"Now just hold on a minute. What is the evidence?"

"I successfully traced the bits and pieces found inside the Messerschmitt's cockpit to a British officer who was killed at about that time. No one seems to know anything about the exact circumstances of his disappearance, as he was in the Intelligence Corps and whatever he was up to it was hush-hush."

"And now you want to know how someone normally wearing His Majesty's uniform came to be found in an enemy aircraft? I must admit it's intriguing."

"It's also a bit dangerous, but I won't go into that now. I haven't quite told you everything . . . This chap, whoever he was, was carrying a ciphered message on him which I'm getting decoded right now."

"So it certainly looks as though he was a spy of some sort. How very interesting. And how can I help?"

"I wanted to know a little more about the SD, as they may have been behind the operation. I'm not going to get very far in England and I thought it might be worthwhile to attack the German angle. After all this time, there must be someone on the other side who would be willing to cooperate. I wondered if you had any ideas?"

"Your deduction of the SD is very astute. When

I said the other day that it was almost impossible for the Germans to have operated an unknown ring in Britain during the war, I was talking about the Abwehr, Canaris' military intelligence organization. They were the spearhead of the espionage assault on Britain and their activities are extremely well documented. Within days of the outbreak of war, all those thought by MI5 to be sympathetic to the Nazi cause were detained under 18B on the Isle of Man, and this put paid to a number of 'sleepers', long-term spies leading outwardly normal lives, but waiting to become operational. The round-up was generally thought to be a spectacular success. Canaris tried to repair the damage by infiltrating a series of agents over from the Continent or Ireland, but they were all thought to have been picked up sooner or later. Some made incredibly stupid mistakes and were arrested by alert citizens, others were betrayed by agents already working for MI5. The net result was that the vast majority of information reaching the Third Reich from established agents in England was in fact being supplied by the counter-espionage authorities."

"And that's confirmed by the Germans?"

"From German sources, yes. Intelligence officers were able to compare captured Abwehr documents after the collapse and there seems little doubt that even the men who were regarded by the

High Command as their most reliable were actually being controlled and forced to work against their masters."

"And where do the SD come into all this?"

"It was a completely separate organization from the Abwehr – in fact the one didn't trust the other. Eventually Canaris was arrested for plotting against Hitler, and all the worst suspicions of the SD were confirmed. But the difficulty is that we know relatively little about the operations of the SD, if only because it was an official Nazi organization and few people have come forward to give detailed reports on their activities. What is known is that much of its work was in clear breach of international law, ranging from mass murder to genocide and torture."

"The Abwehr must have been a secret body too. How come one is so well documented and the other is unknown? It can't all be down to captured documents."

"Certainly not. Postwar politics had a lot to do with it. The Abwehr, because it was disbanded by the Nazis, was trusted by the Americans and the British. When the Federal State was established, many of its top people were drawn from the ranks of the old German Intelligence Service. Add to that the fact that the SD was extremely efficient in destroying all its documentation, and you have the final picture. If there really was a hitherto undiscovered spy ring in Britain during the last war, the chances are that it operated under the umbrella of the SD's Foreign Intelligence Section."

"And how much is known about that?"

"Not a great deal. The ex-employees show an understandable reluctance to give interviews, and only a few ever tried to write about their experiences."

"But some did?"

"Just a few. I suppose Walter Schellenberg is about the best-known, but even he didn't last very long. He wrote his manuscript after being released on health grounds from a heavy war crimes prison sentence and died in rather mysterious circumstances in the Italian Alps before he could publish. His wife kept the book and eventually managed to get it into print."

"Is there anyone else alive who might have known of this Department's activities?"

"I wouldn't really know. I expect we could find the names of British officers who interrogated captured SD personnel after the war, but it would be quite a job to track them down, and even if you succeeded they may be bound by secrecy not to reveal anything. Don't forget that it's only in the last couple of years that researchers have been allowed to examine the more sensitive Public Records files, and there must be easily as many that remain restricted."

"How would I go about finding the Germans? They appear to be the obvious answer as they aren't covered by our laws."

"It would be fairly simple to compile a list of men who served in the Amt II department of the RSHA. Quite a lot could be gleaned from reference books, but having found one or two of these characters I'm not sure how you'll succeed where the professional investigators failed. Nevertheless I wish you luck."

"Once I'd got the names, how would I trace them?"

"I think your best bet would be to go for the really senior men, as they would have been in a position to know about something as secret as a spy ring, and I believe that there are one or two organizations that keep fairly comprehensive records on convicted Nazis. Simon Wiesenthal in Vienna is probably the most famous but I've heard of others, one in Bonn, run by the Federal Government and another in Tel Aviv. Perhaps they could help."

Ward thanked the expert for all his kind advice, and for the second time that week promised to let him know how his investigations went. On the way out, he bought a copy of the *Evening Standard*, and took a cab to Thurloe Street.

It was while the taxi was waiting in a traffic jam near Victoria Station that the driver noticed his passenger gasp and sit bolt upright. Ward's attention had been caught by a small paragraph on page five, headed, "Historian Dies". The famous Oxford historian, J. D. Coleman, was reported as having collapsed at his Queen's College home and had been taken to the Radcliffe Infirmary where he was found to be dead on arrival.

Once back at Lucy's flat he had tried to take stock of what had happened. He needed help, but things seemed to be falling apart fast. The duty officer at HMS *Dolphin* explained that Lieutenant Shaw was unavailable, and was not expected back at his office for some days. He declined to say more, but Ward sensed trouble. He then tried to call Terry Duggan at his home in East Cowes, but he was out. His mother promised to leave him a message asking him to telephone Mike Ward, or his sister, in London.

Events were moving fast, and Ward knew that he had little option but to pursue the only line of enquiry left to him. Accordingly, he placed a third call, this time to Vienna.

4

As a matter of policy, the Jewish Documentation Centre in Vienna does not encourage personal visitors. Run from Simon Wiesenthal's small apartment in the old quarter, it houses the records of thousands of Nazis, many of whom have never been caught and put on trial. Each time a suspected war criminal somewhere in the world is arrested, Wiesenthal's organization sifts through their files for the names and addresses of witnesses willing to testify to their crimes against humanity. With over six million potential witnesses dead, the task can often be a dangerous one, hence the security of keeping callers away. The Austrian police keep a discreet permanent watch on the flat and, with the cooperation of the Centre, maintain electronic surveillance on both the flat and its telephones.

When Ward had telephoned from London with his list of ex-members of the Reich Security Agency's Amt II, his instructions had been explicit. He was to come to Vienna and book into a hotel. Having done this, he should then telephone the Centre again with his address and wait to be contacted. He had been promised that the work involved would only take a short time and that he wouldn't be kept long for the information he required.

Ward had left that night for Paris, judging the French capital to be marginally safer than London, and the next day he had flown Air France to Vienna, checked in at the Plaza Hotel, and had made the call. Some two hours later, Ward had been roused from his light doze by the receptionist who had rung to tell him that he had a visitor.

To Ward's surprise, the visitor turned out to be a long-legged, black-haired girl of about twenty-seven, dressed in denim jeans and tee-shirt. Her tall, slender good looks seemed strangely out of place in the hotel lobby filled with middle-aged tourists. She spoke good English with only the slightest accent and introduced herself as Evita. She declined his offer to move into the hotel lounge and with a smile sat down in the busy entrance hall.

"Can you tell me a little about why you want the information, Captain Ward? The Centre is willing to supply almost everyone who asks for our assistance but we prefer not to encourage personal vendettas."

Ward told her he understood. "I'm trying to track down these men because they all served in the same SD section during the war. There's a possibility that one of them may know about a man whose body a friend of mine pulled out of the sea some weeks ago. I think the man was part of some deep-penetration plan that only a few people knew about. Those who do know in England aren't pleased, and tried to kill me. I'm getting nowhere making enquiries there so I'm hoping that one of these men may tell me what it's all about, what can possibly be so important after all this time."

The girl listened intently as he told his story, occasionally asking a question.

"Supposing we do help you and your Germans refuse to talk to you. What will you do then?"

"I'm not sure. Someone put me in the back of a van and tried to gas me and unless I can find out why, there's a very good chance that they'll have another go at me. The police in England think I'm a bit of a nutcase, and whoever these people are, they are well-organized. I doubt if I'll get away so easily a second time."

"Have you got anyone else helping you?"

"Not really. My sister has done what she can but I don't want to involve her too much and the only other man, the chap who was going to do some decoding, has died."

"Rather convenient." Ward wasn't sure whether this was a question or a statement of fact. Either way her interest had been aroused and she made him relate the story right back to his original discussion with Terry at the Island Sailing Club bar. By the end of it both were hungry and she accepted his invitation to lunch but insisted that they remain in the hotel. When he queried this she explained the Centre's strict security rules.

"The location of Mr Wiesenthal's flat is no secret, so every visitor, whoever he may be, is vulnerable. It's in our own interest as well as our contacts' to be discreet, so we deal on a personal basis. This obviously puts our personnel, and there are only a few of us, mainly part-time, at quite a lot of risk. If we dash about all over the town it's too difficult for the police to keep an eye on us and the Centre wouldn't know where we are. So we have to stay in the same place with plenty of people about. If I don't call in, or if we're out of vision, then everybody knows that there's trouble."

Ward was slightly saddened that such an attractive girl could be so matter-of-fact and hardened by these life-and-death procedures. "Are we being watched now?" he asked.

"I don't know. It's possible. The police don't tell

us their plans. They operate completely separately unless there's actually a threat or they've had advance warning of trouble. They tap all our phones so they know what's going on from day to day. Perhaps they are watching, I don't know."

Ward smiled and took her up in the lift to lunch. As they squeezed into the elevator car with a group of tourists, Ward felt her body close to his and for a moment he was embarrassed. In another moment he had caught his own feeling and gave Evita a grin. Her head hardly moved but he could detect the laugh in her eye. She was unconcerned by the crush and whispered in a mock admonition for the benefit of the overweight American beside him, "We shouldn't keep meeting like this."

Ward couldn't help but chuckle out loud, and suddenly he felt a whole lot better. Here was a girl, infinitely capable, confident, he had no doubt, in every situation, and at the same time, full of a very feminine charm. He had the urge to ask her so much about herself, to really get to know her, but he knew this was impossible.

Over lunch Evita briefed Ward on her researches. Of the names that he had dug out of the Imperial War Museum reference books, almost all were known to the Centre. The most promising lead was the ex-chief of the Amt II, Professor Dr Klaus Six.

"He was born in Mannheim in 1909 and joined the Nazi Party when he was twenty-one. In 1935 he joined the SD and was appointed the head of Amt II by Heydrich in July 1940. If anyone were to know about an unknown group of agents, or even one of them working in Britain at that time, he would have done. He later went on to distinguish himself as a murderer of civilians in Russia and was arrested after the war and tried at Nuremberg. He was sentenced to twenty years but this was later commuted to ten years. In the event, he actually only served five years and was then released."

"Why was he released after such a short time?"

"It's not unusual. Lots of Nazis were let out before they'd completed their term. Pressure from the Americans and political expediency, mainly."

"What happened to the good doctor after that?"

"We've got his home address on file and his job. He works for the Porsche car firm, or did so until quite recently. I gather he's not very keen on discussing his past so I don't know how far you'll get."

"Do you keep this amount of information on all your names?"

"Quite often. It depends how important they were and whether they were even brought to trial. Thousands got away scot-free just by staying at home and relying on friends and neighbours. Even now, they all close ranks when we find a really good catch. It's difficult to get the Germans to do anything about it, but sometimes our information finds its way to the newspapers and the authorities are embarrassed into taking action. The other method is to get a foreign government to extradite the suspect. Bonn hates that and they try various smokescreens, but at least we've found our man and exposed him."

"But you won't help private vendettas?"

Evita laughed again, but this time there was a slight edge to her voice. "They give us a bad name, the amateurs. They hunt a man down without enough evidence and then bungle it, giving the Nazi a chance to start again in a more impenetrable life. Fortunately it doesn't happen very often, but to let any get away is a crime."

"And what about men like Six, people who have apparently paid their debt?"

"Those are the worst. The so-called civilized world has compromised with animals and butchers. One or two revenge groups try to make the balance a little more even, but there are so many of them and not enough of us."

Evita faltered as though she had given something away in her enthusiasm but the moment was quickly covered up. "Obviously it's not our job," she continued quickly, "to encourage illegal acts, in fact we're opposed to anyone other than legitimate governments becoming involved. To let *ad hoc* committees serve out their own rough justice may in a moral sense be all right, but on another level it's stooping to their old terrorist Gestapo tactics. We cannot allow it. Too much of the world has suffered from a lack of civilized behaviour. We don't want to go back in time, merely to ensure that the crimes of the Nazis will never be forgotten as long as any remain alive."

Ward decided that the conversation needed a breath of fresh air. A tension had entered between them and he wanted to take the pressure off. He had a strange feeling that up until her flip of "them and us", she was bending towards him.

"Where did you learn your English?" he asked. "It couldn't have been here."

Again that lovely grin. "I went to university in England, London actually, and I've spent a lot of time there. Would you believe I once worked during the Christmas vac. at Harrods? I adore England . . ." she hesitated, "and the English."

"But your home is here?"

"I suppose so. My parents were displaced persons originally from Czechoslovakia, but they'll never return now. As a result, I have an Austrian passport and an Israeli one."

"An Israeli passport? But surely your name isn't Israeli – or Czech, come to that?"

"We all use cover names," said Evita, "and mine

can be useful in . . . in certain countries. And my husband was Israeli. He was killed in a terrorist raid in the Gaza Strip five years ago."

"I'm sorry," said Ward inadequately.

She stretched her hand across the table and gave his arm a squeeze. "Don't be. I loved him very much, but he'll never come back. In a way I'm very lucky; I could have been widowed with children, but I'm free. I've got my independence and that's what I value most of all nowadays."

She released her grip and started to withdraw her hand but Ward took it and held it firmly.

"Independent or not," he said with mocking force, "you're going to have dinner with me tonight."

Evita grinned with almost childish delight and replied, "It seems I have little choice."

Later on that night in bed, Ward questioned Evita more about how she came to be working for the Documentation Centre. Evita had phoned the Centre to keep them posted, and they had had a delicious dinner at the Drei Hussaren and had afterwards strolled slowly back to the hotel through the warm Viennese streets. It seemed only natural that he should ask her to come up to his room and share the night, and it seemed only natural that she should make the decision she did.

They had made love fiercely and then again with

a quieter passion and now their bodies lay entwined in a satisfied calm. Very gently he stroked her long jet-black hair and even though she was breathing shallowly and regularly he knew she wasn't asleep.

"How did you get this job in the first place?" asked Ward.

"I was working in Holon, a town near Tel Aviv, as a translator for the Trade Ministry when the time came for me to do my National Service. I went into the Army and that was when my husband was killed. I had had enough of Israel and a friend told me that Wiesenthal was looking for someone in Vienna. I jumped at the opportunity to come back to Austria and I've stayed here ever since. And I love my work," she added as an afterthought.

"It's rather a peculiar kind of job for a person like you, isn't it, sifting card-indexes and searching through files?"

"I enjoy it. " She laughed. "I get to meet interesting people like you from time to time."

"Fringe benefits," murmured Ward. "Tell me about the groups you mentioned earlier – the ones the Centre don't approve of, officially at least."

"We only give the information that we've accumulated to *bona fide* organizations like Interpol. If someone is suspected of being a war criminal and it needs confirmation, we can usually provide a fingerprint or a photograph. It's a service that's necessary but no one else seems very keen to do it."

"And what happens when, for example, the Israeli Secret Service say they've kidnapped some Nazi? Do you give them the goods then?"

Evita skilfully parried the question. "Fortunately it's not up to me to make those decisions. Anyway, I expect Mossad have their own sources of information."

"I'll bet they have," muttered Ward. "How effective are the do-it-yourself revenge groups?"

"The ones that are properly run are supposed to be very good. Sometimes they come together specifically for one job, like when Mrs Meir ordered the deaths of all the terrorists involved in the Munich Olympics massacre. That was a sort of semi-official group formed within Mossad."

"And what about the Eichmann kidnapping?"

"Yes, another group specially recruited for the job."

"Are there any permanent squads on the trail of the Nazis?"

Evita rolled over and lit a cigarette. "Why all these questions, Mike. Who really cares whether there are or there aren't?"

"I don't care, but I think the Germans themselves might. You see, I'm trying to figure out a way I can get somebody like Six to talk. If I roll up and start interrogating him about his past he might even call the police. There's not much I can pressure him with because he's already done his time in prison. Right now he's just an ordinary citizen of the Federal Republic and if he doesn't want to co-operate there's no reason why he should."

"Unless you threaten him with an Israeli fate worse than death. Is that the idea?"

"More or less," admitted Ward. "But it's got to look genuine, otherwise he still won't budge."

"And you don't even look Jewish," laughed Evita. "The idea is preposterous! He'd never believe you."

Ward smiled. "I know what you mean, but I'm working on a bit of authenticity."

"How?"

"You."

"What the hell —"

"If you explain how they operate I might be able to bluff him, just for a short time."

"Isn't all this rather hasty? He might not still be living at the address I gave you."

"He is," replied Ward confidently. "I called International Directories and got his number. He answered the telephone and I put the receiver down when he gave his name. He's there all right. He might even be a bit suspicious about that call already."

"You must be crazier than I thought. You can't just waltz up to him and say . . . 'Hello Dr Six, I'm an Israeli agent in disguise and something awful will happen to you if you don't tell me what I want to know.' The only thing you can be sure of is that he may die laughing."

"That's not quite what I had in mind. You seem to forget that someone has already made a pretty fair effort at trying to get rid of me. If I don't get to the bottom of this soon, I expect they'll have another go. You said yourself it was pretty convenient the way old Coleman keeled over. More than that, I had a call from my sister tonight . . ."

"What did she say?"

"Her flat's been ransacked and two photocopies of the cipher have been taken."

"What about the originals?"

"I've got them on me, but I don't know what good that'll do me. On top of all that my friend in Portsmouth has suddenly become unavailable and Terry has been ringing Lucy up asking me to pack it all in, because he's dropped his claim all of a sudden."

"Why do you think that was?"

"I can't get hold of him but no doubt he's found a benefactor. His parents say he has gone abroad somewhere on a big contract. They've been told not to say where. We must find out what it's all about."

"We?"

"Afraid so. I need your help, just for a couple of days. I can't handle this by myself . . . it's too damn complicated."

"What do you want me to do? You seem to have it all worked out already."

"Nothing much," replied Ward. "Just come and see Lake Constance with me tomorrow."

Evita sat up with surprise. "Now I know you're mad. I've only known you for a matter of hours and you're suggesting that I go right to the other side of the country with you. Crazy . . . you must be."

"So what else were you planning for the weekend?" smiled Ward.

5

The early morning rays of the sun had already started to disperse the mist sweeping off the lake. Ward took a deep breath, adjusted his tie, and opened the gate of the neat little villa on the outskirts of the hamlet of Kressgrunn. With his heart pounding in his chest, he pressed the buzzer beside the front door and looked out over the front garden. The flowerbeds showed all the signs of frequent, careful attention, and every blade of grass appeared to be trimmed to perfection. Although the good doctor had reached retirement age, he clearly didn't mean to be idle.

The front door opened and an elderly, bald man appeared on the doorstep, wearing a printed silk dressing-gown. Surprise registered on his face and he asked his visitor what he wanted, in German.

"Professor Six?" Ward asked.

"Ja," the older man replied, still expressing a mixture of annoyance at being woken so early and distrust of the man standing before him.

"Dr Klaus Six, late of the Sicherheitsdienst?"

The man's head jerked back and he motioned to shut the door, but he was too late. Ward grabbed his arm and at the same time, lodged his foot firmly in the door.

"You have made a mistake," thundered the professor, "leave me alone immediately or I will call the police."

Ward tightened his grip and said slowly and very deliberately so the bald man would understand clearly, "There is no mistake, Herr Standartenführer, and if you try and call the police your daughter and grandchildren will be shot."

The effect was electric and the face that only moments ago had been red with anger paled to a deathly white. "Who are you?" he spluttered. "Where are my family?"

"Your daughter and grandchildren are at home in Munich, and will be quite safe if you answer a few questions. Disappoint me, and they will be dead in ten minutes."

Six started to shake. "How do I know you are telling the truth? I think you are insane."

"Then call your daughter," Ward offered, "and check for yourself."

Six stumbled backwards and reached for the telephone on the table behind the hall door. Feverishly his fingers dialled an eleven-digit number and in a moment the other end answered.

"Anna, is that you?" he demanded. "Give me my daughter. Who are you?"

A woman's voice answered his questions calmly and the blood drained from his cheeks. Quickly he handed the receiver over to Ward. Ward listened for a few seconds and then gave his instructions. "Follow the plan and shoot all three in ten minutes unless I call back." He replaced the handset and turned to the slumped figure of Six in an armchair.

"How do I know they are still alive?" he gasped. "She wouldn't let me speak to them. You may have killed them already."

"Don't judge us by your own standards, Herr Doctor," replied Ward. "If you answer my questions they will be released unharmed. You now only have nine minutes so don't waste time."

"What is it you want to know?"

"First of all," said Ward, fishing Messenger's three pieces of yellowed celluloid from his jacket pocket, "what are these?"

Six looked at all three quizzically and looked up again. "I've no idea. I've never seen them before in my life. It's true, I promise you."

"Take another look," ordered Ward. "You may have seen it in a different form."

"I promise you, I really don't know. Some kind of message perhaps, in code. But I swear I don't know what it is."

The old man's forehead was beginning to show beads of sweat forming; Ward was inclined to believe him, but he pressed on. "These were found on the body of a British officer who was killed in August 1940. Does that jog your memory?"

"Mein Gott," exclaimed Six, "Die Blauliste. That's what this is . . . Die Blauliste. After all this time, it hardly seems possible, but I'm almost sure."

"What was Die Blauliste?" demanded Ward.

Six had recovered his composure and he handed the thin pieces back to Ward. "If I am to explain it may take longer than just a few minutes. Will you telephone Munich and stop them?"

"Just as soon as you finish. What is Die Blauliste?"

"The Blauliste is a collection of names. They were all people who were willing to support a pro-Nazi government in England. They were important people . . . politicians, diplomats, administrators and army officers . . . all prepared to help the cause of the Reich."

"Who made the list?"

"A special section in the Reich Security Agency. It

was responsible for planning our arrangements after Sea Lion."

"Who was the man carrying the list to Germany?"

"I don't know. It was compiled before the war and it was sent to England by courier just before the invasion."

"Who took it?" asked Ward, a little puzzled.

"I forget the name he used, but he was a Britisher, an officer in the Secret Service. He was our link to the pro-Nazi ring."

"You mean the Blue List was being carried by him *to* England *from* Germany?" Six nodded in agreement.

"Was his name Messenger?" demanded Ward.

"I don't think I ever knew his real name. A security precaution. It was a long time ago. Please . . . will you call my daughter's house? I am co-operating."

"Very well," said Ward, glancing at his watch, "get them on the line."

Eagerly Six dialled his daughter's Munich number and passed the handset over to Ward, who issued a few brief instructions. "You have earned another ten minutes, make the most of them."

"I will, I will," promised the old man, "I haven't lied."

"Why was your courier taking the list back to England?"

"Because there was no single complete list in England. It was essential if Sea Lion was to succeed that everyone on the list be told when to act his part."

"What were they to do?"

"They were to paralyze the command of the defence forces and eliminate all the War Cabinet on the eve of the invasion. By the time our troops landed, England would already have a new Government."

"But that would have been impossible," protested Ward, "however big your list was, they couldn't have engineered that."

"Oh, yes, they could, and they nearly did. It was not our fault that Sea Lion was postponed and then cancelled. All our preparations had been made."

"How would you have picked off the War Cabinet and got control of the Services? The idea is ludicrous."

"Not at all. In a way Churchill behaved as if he wanted us to carry out the coup. He made it all possible."

"Explain," said Ward impatiently.

"Even before the war, Churchill had urged that plans should be made to move the Government from London in the event of a massive bombing attack, which might leave the capital in ruins. By the time war had actually broken out, complete departments had been transferred to such towns as Harrogate, Bath and Cheltenham, but after a few months of war, the Cabinet had a change of heart. They decided that the dispersal policy should be reversed and that London be recognized as the seat of government.

"Buildings all over London were hastily converted, so that essential Ministries could withstand bombing raids. In Berlin, much the same had happened already with important branches being provided with accommodation in specially constructed galleries.

"In London, because of the lack of space underground, a 'War Room', rather like Hitler's Führerbunker, was built two storeys beneath the Cabinet Office, near St James's Park. We knew all about it. We also knew that in the event of an invasion, or the War Room being put out of action, another more secret location had been prepared, codenamed 'Paddock', in London's Hampstead. From this nerve centre, deep beneath the streets, the top echelons of the War Cabinet, the Chiefs of Staff Committee and the Home Forces GHQ would direct the situation. Our plan was simple. Once everyone was inside Paddock, we would seal it off and allow the men on the Blue List to go into action. Much of the British chain of command would be disrupted and our alternative government would denounce Churchill for the war-monger he was, and welcome a temporary German presence until order could be restored. Churchill's impregnable bunker would be transformed into a prison."

Ward was almost speechless at the plan. "Did you imagine the people on the list would have followed the call? It's unthinkable."

"I disagree. Millions of Britons voted against Churchill at the General Election, and many hundreds in top positions in the government, forces and business thought that their country was wrong to launch into a world war over a country such as Poland. Those men were patriots and they believed their politicians were all set to destroy the Empire. And of course they were proved right."

Ward grimaced. "So what went wrong?"

"Sea Lion was originally intended to take place on 15 September and we were ready but the Luftwaffe couldn't guarantee air superiority and the OKM took too long to gather all their boats together. The operation was postponed twice and then finally cancelled."

"But your courier bringing the Blue List to England was shot down. Surely that altered your plans?"

"Not much. We knew the plane had been brought down, and we were told the crew had perished. I suppose another pilot witnessed the incident. We didn't care. There were plenty of like-minded Englishmen in Germany we could have sent instead. In the event it was not necessary to send another copy of the list."

"What happened to all the people on the list?"

"They remained at their posts throughout the war, most of them unaware that anyone else was involved. We never made use of them again because they were not prepared to betray their country."

"But that's exactly what they had intended to do," protested Ward.

"As I said before, they were not traitors. I suppose a few might have given us information, if the right kind of pressure had been put on them, but most could draw a distinction between organizing a coup to save one's country from disaster and actually passing over secret military information. If all had gone according to plan, the British Empire would still be triumphant and those men would be hailed as heroes. Instead Churchill refused to allow the Reich to reclaim territory illegally confiscated at the end of the Great War, and now we all live in fear of world Communism. Now, of course, it's all too late."

"Do you know the names of the people on the Blue List?" Ward asked.

"No. There were only a few complete lists and they were classified as top secret. I know for a fact that our copy was destroyed along with a lot of other documentation when the Albrechtstrasse was hit in an air raid in 1943."

"Who else would have one?"

"I don't know. I suppose there might have been one at Hitler's headquarters, but I can't be sure. Of course, Müller would have had one, for the Gestapo and the NKVD. Other than that, I couldn't say. It had the highest classification so it wouldn't have been circulated very far."

"Why the NKVD?" demanded Ward. "Surely the *Russians* weren't a part of all this?"

Six nodded. "How little you know. The NKVD played a central role in the plan. They supplied the courier, as well as many of Die Blauliste's names."

Ward's stunned disbelief showed, and prompted Six to explain further. "We were committed together. Remember the Ribbentrop Pact with Molotov? Once it was signed the Gestapo took responsibility for liaising with the NKVD. Muller was in charge of that. And when the question of a coup in London was raised, the Soviets undertook to mobilize their underground networks to support it. In fact, the entire business could not have been undertaken without their assets. The courier was one of theirs, not an agent of the SD."

Ward's mind was reeling. A combined Soviet–Nazi plot to get rid of Churchill. Pro-Nazi sympathizers organized by Soviet moles. A potent combination indeed. Which meant that Messenger . . . Six interrupted his train of thought.

"It's surprising, considering how much has been disclosed about the war, that nothing has leaked out about Paddock," said Six. "I suppose it is because it would show your noble Churchill's true character."

Ward fingered his copy of the Blue List gingerly as he pondered the implications of Six's remarks. Suddenly it achieved an extraordinary significance, one that had been enhanced by the passage of time.

"Is there anyone you know still alive who could decipher this?"

Six shook his head. "None that I can think of from the original organization, but decrypting techniques are very sophisticated nowadays. Will you release my daughter now? I have helped you all I can."

"Very well, get your daughter on the line again." Six needed little prompting. He quickly reached for the telephone and dialled for the third time. Again the same woman answered, and Ward ordered the daughter to be released. As he replaced the handset, Six began to protest. "You haven't kept your side of the bargain," he complained. "I didn't speak to my daughter. I've no proof she's unharmed."

"Telephone again in five minutes and she'll tell you so herself, I promise you. Don't try to follow me or call the police. You know what will happen."

The professor nodded his head and watched while Ward opened the door. "Who are you?" he asked. "English?"

"And no questions," said Ward as he shut the door behind him and walked back down the path and through the wicket garden gate. He paused briefly to remove the valve cap from one of the tyres on the Porsche parked in the lane, let the air out with a twig from the hedge, and trotted up to where Evita was kneeling. She was hunched over a telephone junction box, screwing the steel cover-plate back into place. Ward quickly pushed the battery-operated engineer's handset onto the back seat of Evita's Fiat 128 and gave her a congratulatory kiss.

"Thank God that's over with," she said. "Let's get out of here before he really does ring his bloody daughter."

On the road back to Vienna Ward told Evita something of his conversation with Six, but he had decided against revealing the most sinister aspect of his story, the joint SD-NKVD plot to remove Churchill from the seat of government at Paddock. Six's tale seemed fantastic, and Ward had yet to be convinced that there really had been a second secret Cabinet War Room codenamed Paddock. Why "Paddock"? It seemed an unlikely cryptonym. And then there was the alleged Soviet involvement to take into consideration. This was surely a matter for the British authorities first, and not for the Israelis. Accordingly, Ward confined his account of the interrogation to how little had been achieved in getting the cipher decoded. Evita was nevertheless filled with the excitement of the confrontation and the success of the bluff.

"We may not know the contents of the list," she said, "but at least the background to it all has been explained. Your ideas have been confirmed from the one source that really should know."

Ward agreed, but his prime concern now was for her to concentrate on driving back to the capital so that the chances of Six finding out who'd duped him would be reduced. They also had to return the ITT telephone engineer's case to the Israeli Embassy before the police became involved, if anyone dared call them in. Evita had been closeted with the First Trade Secretary for most of the previous morning getting authorization from Tel Aviv for the loan of the equipment. The conditions imposed were that under no circumstances should the embassy be linked to the illegal use of the battery-operated set and that it should be returned immediately it had been used. Neither wanted to stretch the generosity of Mossad too far, so both were anxious to be rid of the lynchpin of the operation as soon as possible.

"I think the most important admission by Six,"

continued Evita, "was that Müller was one of the few men known to have access to the Blue List. It rather complicates matters."

"How so?" asked Ward innocently. "Don't tell me he's still alive?"

"Most probably not, but it would be a grave mistake to underestimate his influence over this affair."

"I don't understand," replied Ward. "Either Müller's dead or he's not. Make up your mind. If he's alive, then maybe he could unravel the cipher. If he's dead, it's just another brick wall."

"I'm afraid not," replied Evita. "I think I'd better fill you in about the famous Gestapo Müller. He was originally a conscientious detective in Munich but was destined to become chief of the Gestapo. What is so unusual about him is that he had a strong admiration for the NKVD, the forerunner of today's KGB and his behaviour during the investigation of the Russian *Rote Kapelle* or Red Orchestra network has led to a lot of speculation about his true allegiances."

"Is there any evidence?"

"Only a little, and that is rather thin. He was last positively identified in the Führerbunker in Berlin right at the end of April 1945. Most investigators assumed that he had been killed in the close fighting before the final collapse but when his grave was dug up in 1965, it was found to contain the bones of three much younger men.

"Immediately, the various interested organizations started an intensive search to find out where he had gone and several strange reports were uncovered. One was about a man fitting Müller's description who had been seen giving orders to two senior SS officers. The unusual thing that stood out about the report, which at the time was ignored and filed away, was that the man giving the commands was an unusually old second-lieutenant . . . dressed in a Wehrmacht uniform.

"That might have fitted a number of escaping war criminals, but there was a second report that revealed much more. Israeli agents broadened their sweep when rumours circulated that Müller had played the role of a double agent throughout the war, serving loyally the Soviet government. In return he had allegedly been rewarded with a senior position in an Iron Curtain secret service. Several countries, including the Albanians, were suggested as his hosts, but the stories were a little wide of their mark. The truth was eventually discovered by agents of an independent Jewish revenge organization, based in Argentina. Müller had in fact succeeded in escaping the approaching Allied forces and had made his way to Italy where the Vatican provided papers valid for travel to South America. All went well until

Müller tried to contact his fugitive helpers in his new home late in 1958. The ex-Nazi system, known as ODESSA, had been heavily infiltrated by Soviet agents and at a pre-arranged rendezvous Müller walked straight into a trap laid by the Czech Secret Service. Moscow ordered the snatch and within days the ex-Chief of the Gestapo found himself on a cargo ship bound for Stettin. Immediately he arrived behind the Iron Curtain, he was taken to Prague where he underwent a lengthy debriefing which resulted in the unmasking of many anti-Communist conspirators. What was never discovered, and is still unknown today, is just how much Müller co-operated with the NKVD during the war."

"But what you're saying," continued Ward, "is that if Müller knew the identities of all those on the Blue List, then there's a very good chance that the KGB know those names as well."

"Exactly. If Six's account of the list is anything to go by, then the KGB may have been presented with a whole lot of prominent people who had influential positions in 1940, and every last one of them a target for blackmail."

"A lot must have died since the war," countered Ward.

"That's true, but surely quite a high proportion must be alive still. If they were considered suffi-ciently well-placed or influential to have merited a place in the Blue List all those years ago, imagine how important they must have become in the postwar years. Perhaps even today."

Ward knew that she was right, and could see even greater implications than the one Evita had spoken of. The Blue List was no longer an out-of-date catalogue of people who had flirted with Fascism, or even conspired against Churchill many years ago, albeit in a plot that amounted to treason. Dr Six had put the List in its true perspective. It was actually a directory of fully committed Soviet agents, spies who had burrowed deep into the Establishment, and had been considered suitably positioned to assist in the threat to Paddock. Ward realized that the whole issue of vulnerability to blackmail was secondary. For many on the List, there would be no need to indulge in any coercion. They had already demonstrated their loyalty to Moscow's cause and no doubt had been presented with plenty of opportunities to serve the Soviets during the postwar era. Some might still be in positions of power, others might have recruited replacements to carry on the work after their retirement. But these were not matters that Ward felt he should share with Evita – yet. The first priority remained: to get a clear-language copy of the full Blue List as soon as possible.

The car sped on towards Vienna. They did not stop for lunch. Both passengers had been silent for several minutes, absorbing the new possibilities thrown up by their speculations.

Ward interrupted the silence. "Even if Müller never had anything to do with the Russians, and we can't prove it either way, there would still be a number of men, perhaps in the Government, who would be mighty keen to stop the contents of the Blue List from becoming known."

"They obviously know you've got your hands on it and if your Oxford professor was bumped off, then presumably they know that you still don't know the actual names on the list. And they may have given up after the raid on the flat . . . all the copies were stolen –"

"All except the one I have here," said Ward. "This original is still as important as ever and we must get it copied again and deciphered."

Silence reigned again while both racked their brains for a means of decoding the vital list. Evita started to think out loud. "The most obvious answer would be for you to return home and hand the cipher over to your police and let them deal with the matter, but of course we are still faced with the original hitch of whom to trust. The police already think you're off your head and they may decide to hand over the case to MI5 . . . "

"Which would never do," added Ward. "It looks, from the way things stand at the moment, as if they are thoroughly compromised, if not currently penetrated. I'll bet at least half a dozen names on the Blue List are senior MI5 men. They'd be only too happy to be given the list."

"Would the police surrender the whole thing to them so easily?"

"They'd have no choice to start off with, because the police would have to get the list deciphered and to do that they'd have to involve one of the specialist services. MI5 would have ample opportunity to step in and monkey about with the names if they felt so inclined, and perhaps the poor old CID might never find out."

"By substituting dud names?"

"Perhaps, or even reporting that the list doesn't make sense and that the whole thing was a hoax. If they say that, I can certainly see old Bushrod accepting their word against mine. Fat chance I'd have."

"What about giving it to different people, people you could be sure of trusting?"

"Such as?"

"What about the Press or an MP?"

"Even if we knew that they could definitely be trusted and," he reassured her, "I am not becoming paranoid about this – they'd still have to go through the same sources as the police. It would all end up eventually on the desk of some chap at MI5 who'd be asked to get it deciphered. In England, practically everyone believes in the Security Services. If they reported that the list was a load of bunkum, few people would question them. We don't even know who the hell they are. The Press and politicians have their contacts but it's supposed to be a secret where MI5's headquarters is! The point is, we all trust them because we bloody well have to."

"What about the German end? Why don't we move on down the Nazis known to have been in the Foreign Information Department?"

"Six ruled that out. He said he couldn't think of anyone else and I'll bet he was telling the truth. The Blue List had the absolute top security classification. We'll need the resources of a government to find out its contents, unless your organization can help."

"Unfortunately the Documentation Centre doesn't have those facilities; we can only provide information on individual Nazis and their wartime activities. The Federal Government's Nazi Crime Investigation office at Ludwigsburg probably wouldn't be equipped either. At any rate, you probably wouldn't get much co-operation from either them or the BND, the West German Intelligence Service. Both have employed very dubious staff in the past, whose backgrounds haven't been investigated very thoroughly, and I can't see them falling over themselves on this one . . . not unless it was an official Government request."

"Which rather rules me out."

"If only you knew someone in the American NSA then maybe they'd run it through their computers and get the work done in a matter of seconds."

"Unfortunately I don't, but since you seem to get on so well with the Israeli Embassy," he smiled at her grimace, "no doubt you could fix something up?"

"If you think it's worth a try, I'll ask," she volunteered, "but it rather depends how far you want the list publicized. I expect the security people in Tel Aviv are quite experienced in code-breaking, but if they can't handle it, I suppose they'd pass it on to the Americans. And if they knew what it was and managed to break it, I'm sure they'd feel obliged to pass a copy of it over to the British . . . and there you are, back to square one."

Ward sank back into his thoughts, and turned over in his mind his conversation with J. D. Coleman on the telephone; he remembered something he had said . . . a name that Coleman had mentioned.

"That old boy from Oxford, Professor Coleman, said something rather interesting to me when we last spoke . . . he told me that he asked a wartime colleague to help him with the cipher . . . a man called Green. It may be worth contacting him to see if he could do the decoding on his own."

"Is it worth the risk?"

"Are you suggesting that Green might betray us . . . or even that he killed Coleman? That would be impossible. He had been a fellow-officer in MI5 during the war and apparently was trusted by Coleman. I can't really see the risk."

"Well, someone must have found out that it was the List that Coleman was working on, if your theory that he was murdered is correct. Who told the List's protectors what he was up to?"

"I see what you mean, but the professor may have mentioned it to others. If there is a risk, and I don't concede completely that there is, then I reckon it's one we can afford to take. Forewarned is forearmed . . . and Green seems the only way out."

"So you'll go back to England straight away?"

"I suppose so. I've got to find this Colonel Green – and I've got one other chore to complete."

"What's that?"

"I promised the brother of the man found in the Messerschmitt that I'd tell him what I found out. When I met him I wasn't sure that it really was his brother. Now that Six has virtually confirmed his identity, I suppose it's only fair to tell him. Actually, he turned quite unpleasant when I went to see him, though I suppose I can't really blame him. His name is Messenger, Sir David Messenger."

"A knight . . . an important man?" she asked inquisitively.

"I'm not quite sure what he does . . . a civil servant, I think. I looked him up in *Who's Who* to find his address. Wasn't much of a biography there, as I recall."

"And when are you leaving, tonight or after the weekend?"

Ward grinned and put his hand across her shoulder, giving the nape of her neck a gentle squeeze. "Perhaps I won't go back straight away."

The Fiat was now speeding through the suburbs of Vienna and it wasn't long before Ward was deposited back at his hotel, leaving Evita to call in at the Embassy before picking him up again later that evening for a quiet dinner.

When Ward and Evita met again later that same evening, both were refreshed after washing away the dust and grime of their long car-journey. Ward had also taken the opportunity of telephoning London to put Lucy in the picture. Having told her all about his clash with Six, he asked her to try and track down Colonel Green. "Do your best," he had told her. "Use some of your university contacts. He was a friend and ex-colleague of Coleman's. And see what you can find out about Paddock."

"I haven't been too efficient about finding people

recently," said Lucy blandly. "Shaw is still unavailable and Terry hasn't rung me. His parents passed on a message, but they won't say where he is."

Ward told her not to worry but, as he admitted to Evita during their dinner, he was beginning to wonder just how big the conspiracy was. "I can hardly believe that this is really happening," said Ward. "It couldn't be wholesale murder. Somebody would be bound to notice."

"Don't worry," she reassured him. "I'll bet they've only sent young Terry on a long holiday. You said yourself you thought he'd been bought off. He's unimportant to them . . . he doesn't know anything about the List, does he?"

"No, I suppose he's safe, but Shaw vanishing as well is too much of a coincidence, especially when you think of poor old Coleman."

"Perhaps it was just the excitement that killed him," offered Evita. "Wasn't he an old man?"

"He was, but I'll find out more when I get back."

They finished their meal and made their way back to Ward's hotel room. They had known each other for only a matter of days and yet they were utterly compatible in bed, she succumbing to his almost ruthless lovemaking, he making sure that their moments of climax were experienced together.

It was much later that night that Evita gently

kissed Ward's cheek and asked if he was still awake. He grunted his reply from a state of half-sleep. "Only just."

"Then wake up a little more. I want to explain a couple of things."

"Go ahead," he murmured, putting his arm round her. "Apart from chronic exhaustion, I'm completely *compos mentis*."

"I wanted to try and tell you a little about myself. I wasn't completely truthful when you asked me the other night."

"Oh?" His voice betrayed no surprise.

"I suppose you've already guessed that as well as working for Simon Wiesenthal, I work for Mossad?"

"It had crossed my mind," admitted Ward. "You organized that telephone engineer's kit pretty swiftly. The Embassy certainly give you good service."

"Everything else I told you . . . about my husband and so on . . . all that's true."

"Except it wasn't the Trade Ministry you went to work for before your military service?"

"Oh no, that was true. But I didn't stay long there. I had only been there a couple of miserable months when I was visited by my old unit commander in the army. She asked whether I wanted to join a special GHQ Reconnaissance group that was being formed for fringe intelligence work and I accepted. It was only after I'd passed an arduous six months training that I was told I was destined for Mossad. A year after my initial recruitment I started work properly, going on operations overseas."

"Does Wiesenthal know you're a Mossad agent?"

"He's not supposed to know, but he may have guessed. He's commented a couple of times that the Israelis must have an excellent intelligence-gathering network as they rarely seem to need his services."

"And you've reported back about the List?"

"I had to. And in a way it's just as well."

"How so? And why are you telling me all this?"

"Because when you told me Messenger's name earlier this evening, I was almost sure that I'd heard of him before, and I wanted to check before telling you for certain."

"And what was the result?"

"It seems that your Sir David Messenger, knighted in the 1964 New Year's Honours List was, to give him his full title, the Deputy Director-General of the British Security Service. He used to be second-in-command of MI5 until his retirement in 1963."

Ward was bolt upright. "Are you absolutely sure?" he demanded.

"There's no mistake. He was quite well-known to Tel Aviv . . . he was a career intelligence officer who joined MI5 just before the war. He once ran an anti-Fascist section and used Jewish agents to penetrate anti-Semitic political parties. That's how we first learnt of him."

Ward was silent for a few moments to let the news sink in. "The bastard! All that rubbish about not knowing what sort of work his brother had been doing. He's in it up to his neck. This bloody affair's getting worse and worse." Privately Ward wondered what Messenger's role might have been in the Paddock plot.

"The implications are really appalling for your country, and for the West generally," agreed Evita. "There must be a strong possibility that Messenger's name is on the Blue List. If so, we have to seriously consider the possibility that he may have been working for the Soviets for years . . . under pressure of blackmail. Exposure of his Fascist sympathies before and during the war."

"That seems a little far-fetched," said Ward unconvincingly. He knew only too well that Messenger's duplicity was more a probability than a possibility.

"It's certainly a likelihood. There have been so many cases of that kind over the years. Look at Vassall in the British Admiralty. He betrayed secrets because he feared exposure as a homosexual. That is a trifling matter compared to what may have happened here. Dozens of well-placed Nazi sympathizers in touch with Berlin at the height of the war . . . I think that's worth a little co-operation on the side. After all, put yourself in the shoes of a KGB controller. You'd never be able to resist exploiting such a potent instrument."

"Christ," murmured Ward, sinking back onto the bed. "That bloody cigarette case really turned out to be a Pandora's box. What the hell do we do now?"

"My instructions are to help you as much as I can while you remain in Vienna. Tel Aviv say that your lot in London would definitely be best for deciphering the List. They don't want to risk alerting the Americans and if all the names on the List are possible KGB agents, they don't know who to trust in either MI5 or MI6. It's an intelligence man's nightmare. The Nazis may have been using a one-time pad instead of a regular code so that it would be virtually impossible to decrypt the List without the key . . . and the only people known to have recorded in detail all the ciphers and keys are the British wizards from your Secret Service. Mossad won't approach the Americans, so it looks as if you're going to have to do it all yourself."

"That's really great," replied Ward sarcastically.

"We know MI5 are after me, the KGB is probably after me, one of them's already tried having a crack at me, and no one's willing to help. It's mad."

"I agree, but there it is. Every one of the names on the List may have been pressurized into doing something against his or her will, perhaps without even knowing that it was the KGB who was taking advantage of Müller's list. If that has happened, we must make sure that they're all isolated from any important decision-making as soon as possible."

"But we don't know how many there are on the List. There could be any number."

"We discussed this before. There can't be too many left now, but the danger is that those who are still in positions of prominence will have reached some very dizzy heights by now. Messenger's example – if that's what he is – rather serves to bear that out. In 1940, he must have been just a middle-ranking MI5 officer. Now he's got to the top and retired, leaving heaven knows how many agents in his place."

"My name is Cooper," lied Ward. "Graham Cooper. I am here to collect an overnight document which was being sent out from London."

The young receptionist behind the counter in

the lobby of the courier company's office asked Ward to wait a few moments while she checked the packets due for collection. She dialled an internal number.

"I have a Herr Cooper here," said the girl. "Is there anything from London for him?"

A couple of moments later, she replaced the receiver in its cradle and told Ward that someone was on his way down to see him . . . with his delivery. Ward had been in touch with Lucy to explain his predicament and she had come up trumps. As soon as he'd called she'd told him to ring back on a different number within ten minutes. Her brother hadn't recognized the number but from his experience in Northern Ireland he'd caught onto what she was up to. Just for good measure he'd rung the South Kensington tube station coin box reverse charges, and after a quick giggle Lucy had accepted the call.

"Terry's called," she told him, before he'd had a chance to say a word. "He's in Mauritius, of all places. He says that he's been forced to land you in the shit . . . the police have got a warrant out for your arrest for theft."

"For *theft*?" repeated Ward incredulously.

"Yes, of the cigarette case. Apparently Shaw and Terry have made a statement to the Portsmouth police and a magistrate has issued a warrant. I haven't had a visit yet but I think the police may be intercepting all the calls to the flat . . . hence this charade. You did return the ruddy cigarette case, didn't you?"

"Of course I did, but I only left it with the guardroom desk at HMS *Dolphin*. I never got a receipt for it. Shaw wasn't in and I didn't have much choice. No one offered a bloody receipt."

"It's too late now. What news from your end? You'd better make this quick."

"I've made quite a lot of progress, but things aren't getting any better. I need to come back to London, now, but I mustn't be arrested at the airport."

"What have you got in mind?"

"It's a bit drastic, but could you persuade Graham to lend me his driving licence for a couple of days?"

"I expect so. What do you want me to do?"

"Ring up a firm of international couriers. Tell them that you're Mrs Cooper, my wife, and that I've stupidly gone to Austria without my driving licence and that I need it desperately to hire a car. Tell them I'm on an export drive or something. I really need the licence in a hurry."

"Consider it done," she replied. "Call me again at the same time tomorrow at the flat and I'll let you know how I've got on."

Like most things that Lucy attacked with enthusiasm, she achieved success, and that resulted in Ward's call to the courier's local representative in Vienna. After signing an indemnity and a receipt, "Mr Cooper" was able to reach the airport by eleven, in time to catch his British Airways flight to Heathrow. Passport control at Vienna read his licence and, with a shrug of the official's shoulders, told him to continue on into the departure lounge. How unfortunate it was, he had been told, that both his passport and all his traveller's cheques had been stolen.

At Heathrow, Ward followed the stream of fellow-passengers towards the immigration desks in Terminal One, but instead of continuing through the queue, he made for the toilets and spent half an hour reading the *Telegraph* until he reckoned it was time for the Paris British Airways flight to be landing. When he had seen several passengers form up in front of the immigration officers, carrying "Aéroport Charles de Gaulle" duty-free bags, Ward joined them.

The Indian perched on a stool behind the desk briefly examined the driving licence and turned to Ward. "No passport, sir?"

"Afraid not," he replied. "Got stolen yesterday. This is all I have left."

"Where have you come from?"

"Paris."

"Very well. Thank you." He motioned Ward forwards and took the passport handed to him by the traveller behind Ward. So far, so good. If any alerts had been put out, thought Ward, he had successfully evaded them. Even if it was now known that he'd paid a visit to Vienna, and even if every flight from that destination had been scrutinized for him, no organization in the world would be able to screen every person who'd been to the Continent recently – especially not to the extent of catching a man using a genuine document within the EEC. Perhaps, concluded Ward with a smile, he should write to his MP demanding that photographs be used on British licences, like much of the rest of the Common Market.

Most importantly, he was back on the warpath . . . unknown. If anyone had taken the trouble to check on his movements, he was confident that he would have lost them through his simple but effective manoeuvre. Now he had to obtain the help of Colonel Green before anybody realized he was back in action.

Once back at his sister's flat, Ward was brought up to date on her research.

"Colonel Green was easier to find than Terry

Duggan or that naval chap," she recounted. "He's in *Who's Who*. He lives in Woodstock but at the moment he's clearing up J. D. Coleman's affairs in Oxford. Apparently he's his executor. Anyway, he's agreed to see us tomorrow at Queen's.

"The Paddock business was not so straight-forward. I really didn't know where to begin. I tried the Cabinet Office Historical Section, and they put me on to the curator of the War Room under Great College Street. He didn't seem to know anything about a *second* Cabinet War Room, up in Hampstead or anywhere else. The Imperial War Museum had never heard of it and I even tried Churchill's wartime secretary, Sir Jock Colville. He was very helpful and put me on the right track. He thought there *had* been a secret emergency bolthole, but he couldn't remember much about it. However, he did suggest I try Churchill's history of the Second World War. That was brilliant. It's in the index to Volume II. Churchill describes a still-classified underground site code-named Paddock. There's a brief account of him going down it with all his entourage during a flap in 1940. There's no doubt the place existed – probably still does. A chum at the BBC has recommended the Public Records Office at Kew for a trawl through the Cabinet records of the time for more clues. Is it worth pursuing?"

"Definitely," replied Ward emphatically. "According to Dr Six, the Soviets and the Nazis got together to stage a coup just as the invasion was about to begin. Churchill and the Cabinet were to have been isolated in Paddock, powerless to react, as a group of Nazi sympathizers took over the reins of government."

"But it would never have worked," protested Lucy. "They would have fought on regardless, surely?"

"Maybe so," replied Ward. "But it is not really a matter of what could or could not have happened at the time. It's more a question of what the Germans and the Soviets *thought* would happen. Look at their own experiences in 1940. Both regimes had achieved incredible military gains through the collaboration of Fifth Columnists. Stalin walked into Latvia, Lithuania and Estonia, all on ridiculous pretexts, aided by sympathizers. Poland was carved up by Berlin and the Kremlin, and the Wehrmacht took over France, Denmark, Norway, Holland and Belgium. Their method had worked well enough already. Why not in Britain? It's swift military action combined with political chicanery. The result? Enemy occupation. You can just imagine how keen a man like Gestapo Müller must have been on the idea of a joint enterprise with the NKVD. A simultaneous move by pro-Nazis, co-ordinated by deep-cover Russian moles, must have been irresistible."

"So what does that make Benjamin Messenger?" asked Lucy.

"Allegedly, a Soviet agent. Lord knows, there were enough of them recruited at university before the war – probably his contemporaries, Burgess, Maclean and Philby. Messenger's job was to carry the Blue List to England and mobilize each person on it. Paddock would have been sealed off at the appropriate moment, leaving no one in authority to cope with the invasion. It was an ingenious scheme. And even if they hadn't managed to pull it off, just the attempt would have caused chaos, thereby assisting the invaders."

"And what about Sir David? Do you think he was in on all of this?" There was a chill to her voice.

"It's hard to tell, but he did his best to put me off the scent when I went down to see him. He never said a word about MI5, although perhaps that was to be expected. But there was all that innocent bullshit too. I really can't be sure whether Messenger simply didn't know about his brother's treachery, or whether he was in it all up to his neck too. But if he *was* involved, think of his marvellous cover. He would have been in the best possible position after the war to conceal the truth and steer away people who got inquisitive."

"In which case," added Lucy, "the Blue List would have been a useful cover itself. If it were discovered accidentally, as you did, it could be considered as a list of potential pro-Nazis, compiled by ill-informed zealots in Berlin. But in reality it's something much more dangerous, and entirely relevant decades later – a list of probable Soviet spies."

6

The day after "Mr Cooper's" return home, Ward and Lucy drove down to Oxford and paid a visit to Professor Coleman's house in the hope of recovering whatever they could from his work on the cipher. Both realized there was only a slim chance they might find anything left at all, but they were optimistic that at least they would discover Colonel Green's traces. In fact they did even better . . . they met Colonel Green.

"How do you do," said the tall, ruddy-faced man in Coleman's library, introducing himself. "I'm Geoffrey Green, Professor Coleman's literary executor. Can I help you?"

The housekeeper, who Ward had met some ten days earlier, excused herself by getting the two visitors coffee, and Ward began, with Lucy's occasional interruptions, to explain about the cipher he'd given Coleman.

"I had a feeling you might turn up," said the Colonel, "but I didn't know where to find you. John told me all about the cipher but he didn't give me your name. He was very excited about it, as I suppose you know. Damn interesting find."

"We wondered how far he'd got in decoding it," said Lucy.

"I'm afraid I can't honestly tell you," replied Green, "for the simple reason that I can't find any of his work on it in the house. No trace at all."

"Isn't that rather strange?" asked Ward.

"I suppose it is," he replied. "There's so much work to be done here that I hadn't really thought about it much, but it's going to be a bit tricky for me to give it back to you if it ain't here."

"It doesn't matter so much about the actual cipher," explained Ward, "I've got another copy. What is important is to know whether he'd succeeded in decrypting it. Just before he died, Professor Coleman told me that he was going to consult you about it."

"That's right, he did. He'd certainly worked out what the cipher was, though when I spoke to him he had not got as far as the nuts and bolts of the thing. I was pretty sure that he was right in his interpretation and I was going to come and spend next weekend with him to make sure it wasn't a hoax."

"A hoax?" said Ward with surprise.

"Yes, it does happen from time to time. Apparently you hadn't been very forthcoming about your source and he wanted to make sure the List was genuine before giving it back. I'm sure you understand."

"Then he'd definitely got as far as that," muttered Ward. "When I spoke to him he was on those lines but he said he needed you."

"I see," said Green. He hesitated for a moment. "Do you in fact know what it was you'd got?"

Ward and Lucy exchanged looks and realized that it was now that they had to decide whether they could trust the man opposite them. He was an elderly, rather paternal-looking figure who certainly had all the appearance of being what he was, an officer and a gentleman . . . but both knew that there was a lot at stake. In the end, they didn't have to make the decision, because Green seemed to sense the situation and tried to put them both at ease.

"Perhaps," he said quietly, "I'd better tell you what I know already. That list never came from any military man's diary. From what John described to me, it could only be one thing and it must have come from a German source. He knew for certain that the cipher was a list of names and addresses of people in England. We also knew that it wasn't just another copy of the famous Gestapo Blacklist, the *Sonderfahndungsliste*, because the format was completely different. In that document each name and address is followed by the number of the Reich Security Agency's department that was interested in the arrest of that particular person. There was no such repetition on this list. We both agreed that it certainly appeared to be a very different list . . . a White List . . . the names of a German Fifth Column in England. Naturally we wanted to be absolutely sure there wasn't any fraud involved before you came back to collect it, as the consequences of that cipher were colossal. For a start, the courts would be choked with libel suits. It was damn dangerous."

"And are you satisfied now?" asked Ward.

"I still don't know where the list came from. You might like to know that a similar sort of thing was found a few years ago, in a steel container resting on the bottom of an Austrian lake. That turned out to implicate quite a number of prominent politicians in the West, but after a little investigation the list was shown to be a fraud, dreamed up by a KGB disinformation section. Caused quite a stink at the time when people assumed that it was genuine. Quite a lot of embarrassment as well, but fortunately it was exposed in time.

The professor and I wanted to be quite sure on this one."

Ward started to tell the Colonel about the Messerschmitt and concluded by giving a slightly watered-down version of his interview with Dr Six. By the end of his explanation, Green appeared to have lost his doubts.

"And now you reckon that the KGB have a copy of this Blue List?" he asked.

"It's possible. In which case our Security Service may have been compromised."

Green looked sceptical. "As the worst the KGB could threaten is to publish the List, I don't think there would be a lot to fear. Everybody could simply deny that they were ever collaborators and point out that the KGB were trying to discredit them. That rather speaks for itself."

"But that's not all," replied Ward. "According to Six these people were more than just Nazi fellow-travellers. There was a Soviet plot to arrest Churchill and take over the government, all timed to coincide with a German invasion. The names on the List were going to form a sort of Quisling government. Not only was the courier carrying the List an MI5 man, but his brother became the Deputy Director-General."

"Sir David Messenger?" said Green, astounded. "It's not possible."

Ward went on to give an account of how "Paddock", Churchill's secret war room was to be the scene of the coup. "If you read Volume Two of Churchill's *Second World War*, he actually mentions Paddock by name. The people on the List didn't just get there because the Germans thought they were likely friends . . . they were actively involved in a monstrous plot that nearly happened."

"It all seems quite incredible," said Green, recovering from his surprise, "but I for one can vouch for Paddock. It existed all right, though few people were supposed to know about it. The official line is that the War Room under Horse Guards is where Churchill directed the Allies from, and very well-protected it was too. Paddock was only there in case of an invasion or if the War Room was put out of action. Many of those who knew about Paddock were not told exactly where it was. I never found out where it was sited, but it must have been very secure."

"Would it have been possible for the Prime Minister and his Cabinet to have been caught down Paddock by a disaffected group?" asked Lucy.

"At first it strikes one as out of the question, but when one actually comes to think about it, one has to admit that it's not so improbable after all. There were several Anglo-German friendship societies going shortly before the war with plenty of important and influential members, to say nothing of Mosley's Blackshirts. There were many around who thought Hitler should be appeased; that debate divided families as well as causing a lasting division in the Tory Party. You have to remember that Churchill wasn't all that popular shortly before the war and his climb back to power alarmed quite a lot of people, especially those who could remember the First World War and the Dardanelles offensive. It's not a completely outlandish idea, assuming that the exact location of Paddock had been betrayed."

"When you were at MI5," asked Ward, "did you ever hear of any kind of active plot?"

"We heard about the occasional death threats to Churchill, but they're received by every head of Government. There was never a whisper of any plot, not that I heard anyway."

"Nothing at all, then?" persisted Lucy.

"Not really. I remember there was an invasion alert once, that's all. The codeword for a German landing on the South coast was 'Cromwell' and some idiot once started a panic alert by mistake. I can't see that that would be connected but," Green looked thoughtful as he racked his memory for any clues, "I do seem to recall that Hess might well have said something that mystified some of us."

"What was that?" asked Ward.

"It was later on in the war, the next year I think.

Hess turned up in Scotland demanding to see the Duke of Hamilton who was then, as I recall, an Air Force officer. He was arrested and brought down to us at our cage in Ham for interrogation. He was a little mad, but he did keep demanding to see what he called 'the opposition' so as to work out a peaceful settlement to the war. Nobody at the time seemed to know what he was talking about. Perhaps he was after this Fifth Column."

"Why the Duke of Hamilton?" asked Lucy.

"He seemed to think that the Duke was a leader of some kind of opposition party. Apparently the Duke had gone to the 1936 Olympics and some sort of contact had been made with the Nazis. It was enough for the Deputy Führer to fly right across the North Sea to find him anyway. He baled out within twelve miles of the Duke's home."

"And what about the so-called opposition party?"

"I don't know. I wasn't involved in the investigation. I was at Ham at the time because one of my 'turned' Germans was also in the cage."

"If the Fifth Column really did exist and the names on the List are genuine, then MI5 must have been involved," said Ward.

"I don't think Hess's story is evidence of a cover-up," defended Green.

"Perhaps not, but when you link it with Messenger's involvement, it rather seems to fit together.

Surely a young MI5 officer couldn't swan off to Germany in the middle of 1940 without someone at HQ knowing about it? And if he did just disappear there would have been an investigation. Messenger's brother, who was in the same outfit, should have known something, and he himself said that he'd received official notification of his brother's death. Add to that what's happened in the last few days and I reckon you could convince any jury. MI5 must have been in the plot right from the start."

"What better way," agreed Lucy, "to keep the lid on the *coup*. If the counter-espionage service itself was collaborating with the plotters there would have been little chance of exposure. On top of that, you have the perfect cover for contact with the enemy. Who would challenge MI5? They'd just say it was some secret operation or a bit of deception."

Colonel Green now began to look worried. "I suppose stranger things have happened," he ventured. "There might have been one or two senior men who knew what was going on, but there couldn't have been many. It seems incredible."

"But it is possible?" demanded Ward.

"Yes, I have to say it's possible because of the way we worked. The 'need to know' principle was our rule and one simply wouldn't have found out what a colleague was working on unless one actually had to be involved. For example, I was never allowed to talk about turning German agents and feeding their masters with false information, which is what I did throughout the war. Similarly, only a few of us knew anything about Ultra. John worked at Bletchley, but until his last book he never said just how extensive our code-breaking achievements were. He and the rest of the team were able to give Monty a complete summary of Rommel's orders and intentions before El Alamein, but you don't read that in the history books. One just never knew what the rest of the Secret Services were up to . . . and there were thousands of us."

"Did you never try and find out what was happening in other departments?" asked Lucy.

"Not if it didn't concern one directly. Even after the war we all kept fairly quiet about our espionage activities. It's only recently that people have been allowed to publish and reveal some of the secrets."

"But among yourselves you must have known?" insisted Lucy.

"Not so. In a way we actually knew less than the general public because we made a conscious effort not to find out too much."

"But at the end of the war, didn't any of you exchange notes?"

"To my knowledge, the career officers like myself didn't, but I can't speak for the university people recruited just for the duration. Of course, John and I discussed various aspects of our work, but only in general terms. We never talked about individual cases or operations. Let me give you an example. I left the Service in 1961 but I had very little idea about the overall effect of Double Cross until Masterman's official version was published some ten years later. Similarly, the British let it be known that they had a deep-penetration spy right in the OKW, thus explaining the very high-quality intelligence that was being passed on to our allies (including the Russians) which always appeared hot off the German High Command teleprinters. In fact the idea of having a well-placed agent was an elaborate smokescreen to obscure the success of our decrypting at Bletchley. Even now, in some quarters, the lie is still believed . . . over thirty years later."

"So it is just possible that Six's version of how Messenger's body came to be in a German fighter could be true."

"It makes sense, but I'd be amazed if the plot was as extensive and well-organized as you're suggesting. There would have had to have been a couple of hundred names on the List."

"Which only means that there are very few people

who can be trusted. First and foremost we must have the List deciphered."

"I couldn't do it alone," said Green, "but if John had done all the groundwork and discovered the key then I could probably do the rest. The problem is finding out how far he'd got."

"It seems a very fortuitous coincidence that the Professor should die and lose all the papers at the same time," commented Ward.

"Nobody has said anything to me about being worried about the circumstances of John's death. His housekeeper came in on Thursday morning and found him dead in his armchair. No signs of a struggle or anything that might make one suspicious."

"Had he received any visitors?"

"None that were known. He had dinner across the High at All Souls and walked back alone. There was nothing out of the ordinary."

"Except that all the Blue List papers were missing."

"They may turn up yet," said Green hopefully.

"You couldn't start from scratch?"

"I only wish I could, but John was the expert and his own files easily rival MI5's Registry when it comes to Abwehr and SD codes. As a case officer I dealt with the day-to-day application of the codes with whoever it was we'd turned."

"So we're really no better off," said Lucy mournfully.

"Oh, I wouldn't say that," replied the Colonel. "I can try and get some confirmation about all of this from some of my old contacts."

"Can you trust them?" asked Ward, still aware of his experience in the back of the Ford Transit.

"One or two of my colleagues were weeded out of the Service at about the same time Burgess and Maclean defected. Dick White, who became our Director-General, was determined to purge anyone who ever harboured left-wing sympathies so that we could point the finger at SIS with a clear conscience. One man that I know was posted to MI5 Registry for part of the war and he might be able to tell me if there had been an investigation into the 'opposition party' following Hess' visit. If he was taken seriously – and I can't remember whether he was – a report would have had to be sent to the Registry, which was then based in Wormwood Scrubs Prison. He might be able to help out, or at least find out who headed the investigation."

"And in the meantime?"

"Keep safe. I'll ask Dr Blackie to make the *postmortem* examination really thorough; I'll contact you as soon as I can."

"Where?"

"Try the Randolph, if you can get in. They're pretty busy with the tourists now, but Oxford must be safer than London. I'll be in touch tomorrow if I have any news."

Green didn't contact them the next day. They had to wait thirty-seven hours in the confines of their two adjoining rooms before the Colonel telephoned them with some news.

"Sorry for the delay," he said, "I've had visitors. Most of yesterday there were men in macintoshes rummaging about the house. They've turned it completely upside-down and taken quite a load of papers away with them, but they were mostly ones I had already sorted through."

"Who were they?" asked Ward.

"Officially they were police, but several other characters turned up later who didn't get introduced. Security Service, I'm afraid."

"Were they looking for the Blue List?"

"Probably, but it was never mentioned. They just said they were making a routine search for any official documents that may have been overlooked before Coleman's death."

"Have you ever heard of that being done before?"

"Oh yes, it's not so uncommon when one's been involved. I remember there was a hell of a stink when old Stewart Menzies died. The MI5 boys absolutely ripped his house near Badminton apart. Caused a lot of bad feeling."

"But they didn't find anything useful from Coleman's?"

"I shouldn't think so; they said they'd probably be back again. There's still a hell of a lot to sift through."

"And what about the *post-mortem*?"

"I've been on to the good doctor, who tells me that he's already made an examination and sent in a report. He says there's no evidence of foul play. Death through natural causes."

"And what exactly were those 'natural causes'?"

"Cardiac arrest."

"Bullshit," said Ward vehemently. "Everybody dies of cardiac arrest because when you're dead your ticker stops. There must have been more than that."

"Apparently not," replied Green somewhat tartly.

"Excuse me," apologized Ward. "It's something I picked up in Northern Ireland. If you suffocate a man with a pillow, his heart stops; if you don't leave any marks on his body, that's exactly what everybody will assume – cardiac arrest. A good old-fashioned heart attack."

"But there's no evidence."

"There's none to find, but you can believe it's true. What other luck have you had?"

"I had a chat with my chum from MI5 Registry and he confirmed that a report and investigation was made following the Hess landing."

"Did he say who was in charge?"

"Not in so many words. He said that from what he could remember he thought it was all done by F Division headed by someone who might still be in the Service."

"Messenger?"

"I'd put my money on it. But he wouldn't actually state the name. He also reminded me of a rather curious incident in the early part of the war that might be relevant. There was the most almighty row when there was a fire in the Scrubs and a good deal of the Registry files were destroyed. The MI5 Chief at the time had to resign. Most of what perished was the section that dealt with the 18B Regulations – suspects considered to have doubtful loyalty who would therefore have to be detained. In other words, a kind of English version of the Blue List."

"But there must have been copies? Records like that would have been far too valuable to keep all in one place."

"Oh yes, there were duplicate files on microfilm. Unfortunately, when the time came to replace the destroyed sections, it was found that they were too blurred to be of any use. The focus on all the micro-film made them unreadable."

"But that's incredible, especially if it was the work of someone erasing a few awkward details."

"Sir Vernon Kell was forced to resign, and an investigation was carried out, but no evidence of sabotage was found – chiefly due to the fact that only MI5 officers had access to Registry information and the human error explanation was more palatable than finding traitors within the counter-espionage organization."

"It all fits in, doesn't it?"

"I'm afraid so. We should discuss our next step."

But they weren't able to. At that moment there was a knock on the door and Ward exchanged looks with Lucy. There was another loud knock and a voice said: "Open up, we are police officers."

Ward quickly replaced the receiver and motioned to Lucy to return to her room. As soon as she'd disappeared behind the adjoining door, he went and admitted the three impatient men in the passage.

"Captain Ward?" asked the first.

"Yes?"

"I am Detective Chief Inspector Woods of the Thames Valley Police and I have a warrant for your arrest under the Theft Act. I must caution you that anything you say will be taken down and may be given in evidence. Is that clear?"

"May I see your identification?" asked Ward. The

first man reached inside his brown sports jacket and fished out a plastic warrant card, holding it up briefly for Ward to see.

"And what about yours?" said Ward to the other two men standing behind Woods.

"These gentlemen are Home Office observers," said Woods. "They don't have warrant cards."

Ward smiled. "Where are you taking me?"

"You'll appear before Portsmouth magistrates first thing in the morning."

Ward was given barely time to prepare an overnight case and was then escorted down to a waiting, unmarked, blue Austin, driver at the ready. A "U" turn across Worcester Street was swiftly executed and the car turned into St Giles', though, much to Ward's surprise, they went left at the traffic lights instead of continuing round towards St Aldgate's and Oxford Station.

"Where are we off to?"

"You'll see," replied Woods, who had taken the front passenger seat. After only a few moments travelling, the car pulled up outside a pair of wooden gates in the Woodstock Road, just north of St Giles'. Ward was signalled out and the two Home Office "observers" fell in alongside him as they crossed the pavement and entered the gateway. The three men, with Woods trailing in the rear, walked up a narrow gravel path lined with bushes and approached a large Victorian building that had suffered a modern glass and concrete extension. Once inside, they made their way up some wide institutional stairs to the first floor and along a badly lit corridor until they reached a solidly built oak-framed door. The larger of the two men took Ward inside leaving his companion to stay in the passage.

They were in a high-ceilinged, book-lined room comfortably furnished with leather armchairs and sofas. The view through the modern plateglass windows was south, overlooking a small, well-trimmed garden. DCI Woods had also apparently remained outside the room, so Ward asked his solitary guard whose custody he was in now. The man took no notice of Ward's question and motioned him to sit down. Ward murmured with mock approval, "Ah, the strong, silent type," and eased himself into an armchair, slightly nervous about his predicament.

After five minutes, the silence was broken by the entry of a grey-haired man in a pin-striped suit. Ward got to his feet with a smile on his lips. "Hold fast the Buffs, stand by the Greys . . . here come the gentlemen of the Intelligence Corps," he said facetiously.

"Captain Ward," began Sir David Messenger, "you are in a great deal of trouble. I strongly recommend that you become a little more responsible."

"What have you got in mind?" asked Ward. "Another trip to the country in the back of a van?"

"I suggest you try and be sensible," replied Messenger. "When last we met you told me, from out of the blue, that you'd found my brother's body. You promised to let me know how you got on, and I've heard nothing. What news do you have?"

"Nothing that'll please you. I know that your brother died as a traitor to his country. He was in the process of delivering a crucial message to a bunch of Nazi sympathizers in England when his Messerschmitt was shot down. I also know that you were in on it and so were a number of prominent bastards who reckoned they could run the country better than the elected government."

Messenger looked quite stung by this outburst. "Have you finished?" he asked sharply.

"No, I haven't," said Ward. "I want to know where I am and whether I'm under arrest. If I am, I want to be in police custody . . . not yours."

"If you'll give me a chance," said Messenger, "I'll put your mind at rest. You have been arrested by a Thames Valley Special Branch officer, and you will be charged with a theft offence shortly. You may also have to answer two charges under the Official Secrets Act."

"What charges?"

"We'll go into that in a moment. First of all, I want to assure you that by co-operating fully with myself, an officer of the Crown, you may be able to avoid further unpleasantness. Secondly, I want to remind you that you are in an extremely vulnerable position. Up until recently, you held Her Majesty's Commission and you should therefore know that the job of the Security Service is to protect the Realm. I know that you attended a course at Ashford and you should therefore remember that in the area of national security, our powers are justifiably unlimited."

"I have evidence to show that those powers have been, and are being, abused."

"Frankly, I doubt it. You have charged off on a one-man crusade against an organization that by its very nature cannot answer back. Its officers too are prevented, by the nature of their job, from making any public reply to your charges, however misguided they may be. Furthermore, many of the people on your famous 'Blue List' are dead and their relatives aren't in any position to clear your mud from their names."

"And what about my name?" asked Ward. "One murder attempt and several trumped-up charges later?"

"There won't be any charges if you will only listen to what I have to say. You cannot be in any position to judge the actions of men under orders some thirty-five years ago . . . "

"Meaning your brother, I suppose?"

"If you like, yes. He was involved in a highly dangerous operation, for which he volunteered. The only people who can deliberate on his work are those who are in full possession of the records of the time and the testimony of his colleagues."

"MI5 records are never released,' protested Ward. "But even that's not really the point. The Blue List proves that the Germans had an established Fifth Column in England, but worse than that . . . I believe the KGB have also got a copy of that List and people like yourself have been made targets."

"It's an interesting theory," smiled Messenger, "but it's pure fiction. Maybe the Germans did draw up a tentative Blue List, but it's utterly absurd to suggest that the KGB are making use of it now. What I do think is true is that you have been the unwitting accomplice of a disinformation campaign. There are literally thousands of intelligence men behind the Iron Curtain who spend their lives trying to undermine what we have achieved, what you have fought for and . . . "

"Don't give me that bullshit," exclaimed Ward. "You haven't got a bloody clue about fighting for anything. It's desk-bound bureaucrats like you, selling us down the river, that really make me puke.

Young men are told by the likes of you to go out and get killed for the sake of something we're all supposed to believe in, and all the time the Philbys of this world are sticking a knife in our backs."

"Ward, you may not believe it, but we're both on the same side. You fought on the front line in a conventional manner, my brother Benjamin chose a different path, but he was never a traitor . . . and neither am I. But I do have the Prime Minister's approval to use whatever weapons I choose in order to combat Soviet infiltration."

"And what if your own organization is rotten?"

"Then we wouldn't flinch. But if you think that everyone, including the Cabinet, are involved in some monstrous plot, then I suggest a holiday."

"Is that all you're offering?" said Ward sarcastically. "A holiday, a rather vague KGB disinformation plot and an affirmation of faith in the counter-intelligence service?"

"If you want to put it that way, then yes. If you co-operate with me, there will be no charges and no evidence will be offered in the court tomorrow. Case dismissed and that's that."

"No guarantees?"

"Of course, our terms are a little more complex than that. You must undertake to stop all further interference in what I am only permitted to describe to you as a 'current operation' . . . an important one and one that has taken many years for the Security Service to nurture. Your blundering about can only serve the very people you so vehemently oppose."

"Anything else?"

"You surrender your copies of the Blue List, both coded versions and the ones you got Coleman to decrypt. You also sign a statement admitting that you have been under mental supervision recently following a suicide attempt and that you admit wasting police time."

"Is that all?"

"Not quite. In order to give our guarantees some worth, you must admit yourself voluntarily to a nursing home, just for a few weeks. I'm sure you can understand the reasons."

"Don't worry about that," rejoined Ward. "I can see it all. I suppose that if I refuse then I'll just get locked up?"

"There will certainly be serious charges under the Official Secrets Act and the Crown will be obliged to ask for a trial *in camera*. We'll keep you out of harm's way for a long time."

"I don't really have much choice, do I? Have you got a nursing home in mind?"

"A private room in a very discreet clinic has already been prepared. You'll be under the care of a Doctor Schofield though of course you won't receive any psychiatric treatment . . . that is, not unless you actually want it."

"Oh, of course," murmured Ward.

"Three weeks should do the trick, just so that any wild stories that start after you come out can be discredited . . . but I hope that won't be necessary. We're both on the same side and I hope that one day I'll be in a position to give you all the details. For the time being, you'll just have to accept this bargain."

"So that's what it is," said Ward. "Very well, let's get on with it."

"I'd like you to write out the statement in your own writing. Brewer here," he indicated the "Home Office official" sitting silent and motionless on the sofa opposite, "will dictate the contents. Once that's been completed you'll be taken straight to the nursing home."

"How far is it? Can I make a couple of calls?"

"Later. Dr Schofield's place is in Scotland. There's a plane standing by at Kidlington Airport. When you arrive, you'll be allowed to make telephone calls, but you'll have to comply with whatever conditions the staff there impose. The security is quite strict."

Within half an hour of Ward's nod of assent, the statement had been signed and Sir David Messenger left the room, leaving Brewer in charge of escorting the prisoner to Scotland. As the two men retraced their steps down to the ground floor and the waiting car, Ward asked where they were.

"This is St Antony's College," replied Brewer.

"Good God," said Ward, "an Oxford college. Who'd have bloody thought it?"

"That's enough," his guard said as they were joined at the door to the building by Ward's previous escort who fell in behind. Ward looked round as the party walked back up the path towards the Woodstock Road entrance, but he could see no sign of Woods, the Thames Valley policeman. They reached the wooden gate and Brewer opened it for his two companions to pass. As he did so, the driver of the same blue Austin climbed out of the car, but Ward's attention was focused on Lucy's Mini that was just moving away from the kerb on the opposite side of the road. He knew that moments later she would be parallel to the little group and that if he didn't seize the opportunity, the next stop really would be Scotland. Either Dr Schofield's clinic, he thought to himself, or a dive into the Firth of Forth from 20,000 feet. The Mini appeared to crawl towards them agonizingly slowly as Ward pivoted on his heels and swung his elbow forcefully into his escort's stomach, catching him completely unawares. The man gasped with pain and bent double, one knee going to the ground. At that second, Brewer came through the gateway and took in the situation. Instinctively he parried the blow that Ward aimed at his chin and stumbled against the stone wall. Ward quickly recovered the initiative and landed a forceful kick onto Brewer's knee. The older man's face suddenly contorted with rage and agony as he mouthed an obscenity. Ward turned to deal with the driver who he thought he felt close behind him, but after he wheeled round to take an attack he saw that his adversary was practically riveted to the spot in front of the Austin. His deftly executed manoeuvre had found the man unprepared and he was acting as though his eyes were deceiving him. Without waiting for the driver to find his wits, he brushed aside the sprawling figure of his first guard and sprinted across the short distance to where Lucy was revving the Mini's engine. He'd hardly got one leg into the car when she let out the clutch and shot forward with the front wheels squealing on the hot tarmac.

"Right time at the right place . . . you're a bloody marvel," he said breathlessly.

"No sweat," she smiled as they careered into St Giles' heading south. "More importantly, where to? I can handle a nifty take-off, but I don't think I'm ready for a cops-and-robbers chase yet. Anyway, I can't afford to lose the no-claims bonus."

"Jesus," murmured Ward in admiration, "now I know you're mad too. We ought to dump the Mini for a while. Those gorillas weren't police but I've a feeling every bobby in Oxford is going to be on the look-out for us in a few minutes."

"How long have we got?"

"If Messenger decided to call in the locals again, then I reckon on about five minutes. Every batphone in the city will be giving our description and index number . . . turn into The Broad and we'll park there."

Lucy filtered left out of the wide traffic lane of St Giles and edged the car towards Broad Street. There were no parking spaces free so they agreed to leave the Mini on yellow lines outside Blackwell's, the bookshop.

"Was that Sir David you thumped?" asked Lucy as they got out.

"Just a couple of henchmen. They were going to take me to a funny farm in Scotland."

"Better than the back of a Ford Transit."

"Actually, he didn't seem to know what I was going on about when I mentioned that. It could be that a couple of his heavies got a bit over-enthusiastic. How did you find me?"

"I hid in my room while you were arrested and started to follow you. I thought I could get hold of Colonel Green and create a fuss. That theft charge is nonsense. You gave the damn stuff back, didn't you?"

"But where's Shaw to prove it?"

"Well, anyway, I thought it was a bit strange when they went in exactly the opposite direction from St Aldgate's so I just carried on until you got to St Antony's. Where are we heading now?"

"We've got to see Colonel Green. He's got the key and he doesn't know it. Messenger reckoned that I'd got the Blue List in clear. He made a deal with me, part of which was that I should surrender all copies of the List, both those in cipher and decrypted. For some reason he believes that Coleman did crack it."

"Then you think it's still in the house?"

"It has to be, but I think Messenger's got his characters watching the place. That's how they picked us up at the Randolph."

"We were followed?"

"That's my guess. Even if we can't find the List we've got to get out of Oxford. They'll find us here in no time."

As they walked briskly towards Queen's College, Ward told Lucy of his encounter with the former Director-General of the Security Service and the agreement they'd struck.

"What a bastard!" she commented. "Just supposing he did decide to let you out sometime, he could prove that anything you said later would just have been the insane ramblings of a nutcase. Nobody would have taken any notice of you."

"Too true. He'd got it all worked out. He was so damn sure he'd got a plane laid on specially for the trip up to this Schofield's place. Probably wouldn't have made the journey anyway."

They reached the corner of Queen's Lane and Ward suddenly pulled Lucy back. "Look at that Cortina. I'll bet that's more of the gorillas. We'll have to get rid of them."

They quickly retraced their steps to The Broad and telephoned Coleman's house. Briefly Ward explained the situation and gave Green a description of what had taken place in St Antony's. Green quickly agreed to lead the surveillance men away from Queen's College and put the front door on the latch. "I suppose you know what you're doing," said Green doubtfully, "but there's no guarantee that they'll follow me. It's you they're after."

"I know, but they'll have to make sure you aren't going out to meet me. Once you draw one of them away, it'll be much easier to get inside. They can't watch front, rear *and* you all at the same time. We'll nip in once you're away. Give us a ring before you come back to make sure we've made it."

Green was evidently intrigued by the whole operation and promised to carry out his instructions.

Minutes later he set off at a brisk pace, with a briefcase under his arm, causing one of the two men in the Cortina to jump out and follow on foot, just as Ward had predicted.

The one remaining observer was still a problem that Ward and Lucy had to overcome, because he had so positioned his car as to be able both to cover the rear entrance to the house and still get a good look at anybody approaching the front through the College.

The appearance of a traffic warden on the scene solved the problem. Ward strode up to her as an irate member of the law-abiding public, and explained how he'd seen two lorries forced to squeeze past an inconsiderate motorist in the neighbouring street. The warden promised to act swiftly, just as soon as she'd finished giving another offending vehicle a ticket.

Ward and Lucy ran round to the front of Queen's College and, nodding in a friendly way to the porter, made their way through the quadrangle towards Professor Coleman's house. They only had to wait a couple of minutes before the warden kept her promise and approached the parked Cortina. Immediately her bulky form blocked the view through the College passageway, they sprinted up to the front door and let themselves in.

"So far, so good," grinned Ward, as they both

flopped into armchairs in Coleman's sitting-room to wait for Colonel Green. "But we can't stay here too long in case Messenger and his crowd pay a return visit."

"But we must get the cipher. What exactly did Messenger say about it?"

"Not much, but he did assume that I'd read it and that I'd got a copy in clear."

"Surely he knows it was in cipher?"

"Definitely, but something has left him with the idea that I'd cracked it. The only way he could know that would have been for either Green or Coleman to have told him, or for his men to have found some evidence from his papers that he had in fact succeeded."

"Green certainly didn't tell him any such thing and presumably the papers weren't much help either."

"I agree, but we're ignoring one possibility which is now becoming more than probable: that Messenger, or one of his crew, actually spoke to Coleman before he died and that he admitted he'd cracked the code."

"Then why all the searching through the house?"

"If Coleman really had succeeded, he wouldn't be too keen to admit it to Messenger because, presumably, Messenger himself is on the List and Coleman would have ruddy well known it."

"So Coleman had a visitor the night he died," said Lucy grimly.

"I'd bet on it. The old boy decrypted the whole list and then realized its significance. Somebody on the List, or just somebody involved with MI5, then turns up and starts getting interested. It's all possible."

"So we haven't been looking in the right places for the List. We'd assumed that the key could be found in his papers, but he may have actually tried to hide the List or even disguise it, so Messenger couldn't get it."

"Which in turn might be why Green said he couldn't find anything to do with the List anywhere. What the security boys didn't take, Coleman might have hidden."

"Exactly. We must turn this house upside-down again, for the sake of Coleman, if for nothing else." And at that moment the telephone rang.

"I assume it's safe for me to return now," Green asked.

"No problem; come on home. Lucy'll make you some tea."

7

Colonel Green sipped his steaming mug of tea thoughtfully. "You were quite right, that chap followed me about like a faithful bloodhound. Didn't seem too pleased when I went into the call-box, though. Obvious piece of skulduggery."

"But necessary, I assure you," said Ward. "We're going to have to be on our way soon as we can't risk them kicking the door in, but I'm going to need some transport."

"Don't worry about that, young man," said Green. "You can borrow my Rover. It's in the garage and you won't have to go into the street to get it either. You can use the kitchen entrance to the garage. But where will you go?"

"As far away as possible," said Ward. "Messenger will be furious now, and it's far too dangerous to stay in the country. He'll probably add assault to all the rest of the charges he's ready to have me arrested on."

"And what about the List?"

"The List is somewhere in this house. Without it I haven't got a chance. I'd never be able to persuade them that I haven't read it. With it, at least I've got a weapon . . . I know who *not* to trust."

"But the whole house has been covered," protested Green. "I've searched and so have the professionals."

"But you haven't known what to look for," explained Lucy. "Suppose the Professor realized the danger?"

"But in that case he could have hidden it anywhere," said Green. "The possibilities are endless."

"The most obvious places are the safe, his desk, the leaves of the books in the library, the bedrooms and the cellar," said Ward.

"So what are we waiting for?" said Lucy gaily, and the three of them set to work. Ward went upstairs and checked all the bedrooms while Green searched the study and library. Lucy began to examine the books on the shelves, but after two hours they had made no progress and Ward was becoming increasingly restless about staying in Oxford any longer.

Finally Ward made up his mind and dialled a continental number while the other two continued the search in vain. He was quickly through to Evita in Vienna, and he explained his predicament.

"You're the only person who can help," he said, "I can't stay in England. Once the Security Service rope in the police, they're bound to get me. My face is not exactly the most beautiful in the country at the moment and there aren't many places I can go. If they tell everyone I'm demented and suicidal, people will ruddy well believe it . . . I've admitted as much in a signed statement already. I can't even rely on friends in that situation. At least you know the truth."

"Of course I'll help, but I need some time. When do you want to leave?"

"As soon as possible . . . like yesterday."

"Have you any papers?"

"Only Cooper's driving licence. I suppose I could use that again if I have to, but that'll mean getting to Heathrow tonight. I doubt they'll be much quicker in getting my actual description to the passport desks."

"I'll do my best," she promised. "I'll call you back as soon as I can. If you have to change location, give me a call again in, say, two hours. That'll give me enough time to plead on your behalf. By the way, how long will it take you to get to the airport if we decide to go that way?"

"Not more than ninety minutes. It's mostly motor-way now."

"Fine. I'll call you soon." Her businesslike efficiency dropped for a moment. "It'll be good to have you back. I'll meet you." And with that the line went dead.

Moments later, Lucy danced into the room looking triumphant and told Ward and the Colonel to sit down. "Now where would you expect a man like Coleman to hide the Blue List?" she asked.

"If we knew that," snapped Ward, "we wouldn't have been wasting the last few hours turning this house inside out."

Lucy seemed not to care. "If you think for a moment what the List is . . . a whole lot of names and addresses. If one was going to conceal it, the most unlikely place to look would be amongst other names and addresses."

"Of course," cried Green, "the man's ruddy address book. I know that's still around somewhere . . . I've seen it."

Lucy held out her hand and revealed a rather battered tartan-covered address book. "This is it, and in the back are a whole lot of new entries. The last five pages are covered with what must be the Blue List . . . from 'A' for Astor to 'W' for Westminster."

She handed the little book to her brother. "This has just got to be it," said Ward, with excitement. "This is the Blue List."

Together the three of them pored over the pages. "That old fox," murmured Green. "He really did manage to crack it after all."

"But at the same time he managed to keep it from its protectors," rejoined Ward. "We'd better make some copies of it before it vanishes."

"No wonder they were so keen to grab it," said Green, as he ran his eyes over the tightly printed names. "A lot of these I don't recognize, but some I certainly do. One or two of my old colleagues, in fact. Here's Messenger." He pointed out the MI5 chief's name and address. "Several of these chaps were quite close to Churchill. A couple of them worked for the Cabinet Office. God knows what senior positions they hold today."

"Just look at these names! If only a fraction of these people were Soviet agents, or have been blackmailed, there can hardly be a secret in the country the Russians don't know," said Ward.

"A lot of these fellows were quite open about their German sympathies," said Green. "For example, I recognize a few from such pro-Nazi organizations as 'The Link' and the Anglo-German Friendship Society. All fairly respectable. Open membership and so on."

"But would they have participated in a *coup*?" asked Lucy.

"That's the part that makes the whole thing so unbelievable," said Green. "Co-operating with a pro-German Whitehall junta is one thing, but I'm sure many of these people would have baulked at actually seizing power themselves. 'The Link' was formed in 1937 and its backers included the 12th Duke of Bedford, Admiral Sir Barry Domvile, Major General Fuller, Admirals Parry and Powell, Sir Lionel Hawarth and Brigadier Blakeney. They had over 4,000 members by 1939 in 35 active branches. 'The Link' published pro-Nazi propaganda like *News from Germany* and the *Anglo-German Review*.

"There were other organizations, including Mosley's British Union, the Imperial Fascist League, the Nordic League, the British People's Party and William Joyce's National Socialist League. These were the covers, and points of contact, for the people on the Blue List."

"But if it could be proved that they had been involved in a Soviet-inspired plot," said Ward, "then the List takes on a special significance. From the way people have behaved since the List turned up, I think it's fair to assume that it wasn't a cocktail party that all these characters were being invited to," said Ward.

"I grant you that," replied Green. "But is Six's

version of the plot really plausible? You don't think he exaggerated a little?"

"I don't think so," said Lucy. "I tried to find out about this Paddock business as soon as my idiot brother told me. It must still be quite a secret – I had quite a job getting anyone to admit to knowing anything about it. It did exist, though, and it's still there, which is why people are so cagey."

"How did you find out?" asked Green, obviously intrigued.

"I asked a friend in the BBC if he knew anything about it and he suggested I try the Public Records Office. I spent a whole afternoon there, but couldn't find much positive information. What I did see, though, was that the government was unprepared for giving essential departments deep-shelter accommodation. All the secret papers, released under the thirty-year rule, show that the best they could do was to try and reinforce a few existing basements. Even the famous War Rooms under the park weren't protection enough from the big bombs, so I changed tack and considered the government converting something already very deep. Don't forget Churchill's quotation of Paddock being 'far from the light of day'.

"Quite a lot of tube stations in London have disappeared off the London Transport maps from before the war, and I made them a starting-point. It wasn't too difficult to find out what had happened to them, but people were a bit tricky over two. One was in Down Street, just by Piccadilly. That was turned into a special centre to co-ordinate the railways and, located deep under Mayfair, it was fairly impregnable."

"And the other?" asked Green.

"It used to be known as the 'Bull and Bush' station, halfway between Golders Green and Hampstead stations. Nobody seemed to know much about it, so I went and chatted up one of the engineers at the Golders Green Depot. It's there all right. Paddock's main entrance is in the disused station and even has its own platform. It's heavily protected, even now apparently, with heavy steel doors, inside and out, and has an emergency exit shaft going directly up to the surface. It's also the deepest underground site in London."

"So what you're saying is that Six's claims about the place are true. If it's both unknown and well-fortified, it would have been the perfect place to isolate all the decision-makers."

"That's about the size of it. Six does make sense. Everyone scuttles down this hole in the ground as soon as the 'Cromwell' code is given, the warning that an invasion has started, and it would only have taken a handful of the men close to Churchhill to seize control and run the show."

"It's incredible," murmured Green.

"It's getting more credible every moment," said Ward, "and I don't want to be the one who's odd man out."

"I think the best thing for you is to get out of the country for a while, but the List must be brought to the attention of the authorities. At least we know who not to trust."

The three of them were still making plans an hour later when Evita telephoned from Vienna.

"We can get you out this evening," she said, "but you'll have to move quickly. We can get you on an El Al flight to Rome at 2045 your time. Check in at Terminal Two as soon as you can . . . there'll be a ticket in the name of Cooper waiting for you. The El Al staff are expecting you and they'll get on the aircraft with you. Trust them. You'll be in Vienna by midday tomorrow and I'll meet you."

"What about documentation?" asked Ward.

"Leave all that to our man at Heathrow. It'll all be organized."

"You're bloody marvellous. I'll see you to-morrow."

"There's just one thing." Evita said hesitantly. "I've had to get all this cleared through Tel Aviv, and they've put a price on the operation."

"The List?" ventured Ward.

"I'm afraid so. My bosses need it, but at least they're on your side."

"There just isn't time to bargain," answered Ward. "I'll bring you a copy of the List . . . deciphered."

"You managed . . . ?"

"At a cost. Have you a contact number in case something goes wrong?"

"Just call the airline desk, identify yourself and ask for Jeff."

"That's perfect. I'll leave now."

"Take care." The line went dead.

"You'd better borrow my car," offered the Colonel.

"That's very kind," said Ward, as he joined Lucy in copying out the Blue List. "You keep the address book. If they haven't thought of it up to now, they may overlook it, if they come back. Even if they do find it, we'll have a copy too."

"What do you intend to do?" Green asked.

"What do you recommend? I can only give it to the Israelis. It's my ticket out of this mess."

"Very well," he replied. "I'll do what I can to put these people out of action from this end. The List must reach the proper authorities."

"Provided your proper authority isn't on the List." He caught himself. "Perhaps I'm being rather too paranoid. Do your best. We'd better be off."

Lucy and her brother followed the Colonel through Coleman's kitchen and into the darkess of the garage. He flicked a switch, illuminating the early evening gloom and handed Ward the keys to his 3·5 Rover.

"There should be plenty of petrol in the tank. Wear my hat as you leave and they may just think it's me. Lucy can drop you off and then return the car to me. By then it'll be too late for them to do anything."

They said their goodbyes and then, with Lucy crouched down in the passenger seat under the dashboard, drove out into the lane behind Queen's and followed the twisting road down to the High. As they made their way past the Botanical Gardens and over Magdalen bridge, Ward could see the faithful Cortina following. At the roundabout Ward ignored St Clements and continued onto the Iffley Road. As soon as he made the turn and the tail was out of sight, he gunned the Rover at full power and sent the car surging forwards, taking the first opportunity to turn off to the left. They were in a quiet residential street of terraced houses. The Rover was moving quickly, the tyres squealing as Ward weaved through the backstreets. For a moment they emerged onto the Cowley Road, but they quickly crossed the busy street and headed north, uphill towards Headington. Both knew that it wouldn't take the driver of the Cortina long to realize what had happened, but by choosing this part of Oxford to lose him, they were given quite a choice of routes to take; there just wouldn't be time for them to get help over the radio to cover all the possible roads.

Ward hammered the Rover up towards the Polytechnic and then headed for the A40, the London road. The police were sure to be watching the roundabout, Ward reasoned, but they would be looking for two people in a Mini unless the Cortina was linked direct into the Thames Valley radio net, and this, he reckoned, was unlikely.

He slowly approached the A40 junction and there, beside a garage forecourt, was a police patrol car. Another was stationed on the other side of the ring-road in a lay-by. Ward manoeuvred the Rover sedately through the traffic and onto the A40. Within minutes they had left Oxford behind and were on their way to Heathrow.

They made the journey without incident, using the backroads as far as possible to avoid attention. They could imagine the scene as Messenger realized that his prisoner had well and truly escaped. Coleman's house would be searched again and the men in raincoats would finally put two and two together. And even given the worst possible co-operation between the Security Service and the Thames Valley force, it would be but a matter of half an hour before every traffic cop and Panda in Berkshire was on the lookout for a maroon Rover 3·5.

Once at Heathrow, Ward pulled up outside Terminal Two and instructed Lucy to wait a couple of minutes while he located the El Al desk and made sure that Evita's arrangements worked. At the airline check-in Ward asked for Mr Cooper's ticket and was quickly introduced to "Jeff", a small olive-skinned man in a neat powder-blue suit.

"I'm glad you could make it, Mr Cooper," he said, "if you'll just step into my office we'll take a couple of Polaroid pictures and complete your . . . ah . . . papers."

Ward agreed, but told him he'd first go and see Lucy off. As he walked back to the terminal entrance, he realized how foolish he was to expose himself to further risk. He got to the glass doors and then saw Lucy beside the Rover. There were two policemen in conversation with her. At length one moved to the rear of the car, checked the boot and then started talking into his radio. As a white Triumph police-car drew up, Ward knew that Lucy wouldn't be able to talk her way out. She had been caught, red-handed, with Green's Rover and that meant the terminal would be searched at any time. Reconciled by the knowledge that it would be useless to walk up and try to bluff the little group of officers around Lucy, Ward turned and went slowly back to "Jeff's" room.

"How long have we got until the plane takes off?" asked Ward as his photograph was taken.

"About two hours," replied the Israeli. "Have you got the list of names for Tel Aviv?" Ward handed the Blue List over, together with the original cipher.

"My sister has been arrested outside, though she hasn't done anything illegal. Would it be possible to find out what'll happen to her before I leave? I can't just dump her after all her help. I must know what charge she's being held on. Can you find out?"

The Israeli looked amazed but put the camera down. "There's nothing I can do. If she's committed no crime the police will have to release her. If necessary I can report back to the Embassy and they can stir a little tomorrow . . . maybe a Fleet Street journalist enquiring."

"That's not enough," reiterated Ward. "We must do something now. If the police surrender her to the Security Service, we can just forget about it all."

"Jeff" looked concerned. "I would help if I could, but if she's been arrested, there's little we can do right now. Give them twenty-four hours."

"Never again," replied Ward. "I won't go if they're going to use her as a hostage. We must find out what she's charged with. If they haven't got anything we might get her released."

"Very well. I'll call the police station and ask what the situation is." Moments later the Israeli was connected with the Heathrow Station Sergeant, with Ward listening in on the extension.

"Good evening, Sergeant," said the Mossad agent cheerfully. "Eric Viner here, from the *Express*. Any arrests today?"

"Nothing that would interest you," said the policeman. "Pickpockets and mini-cab drivers."

"Is that all?" persisted "Jeff".

"Why do you ask? Expecting trouble, were you?"

"Not really. Only a whisper that you'd picked up a bird outside Terminal Two not long ago."

"I couldn't really tell you much about that," said the Sergeant. "Out of our province." "Jeff" glanced at Ward. "When did you get your whisper?"

"Never mind, it's a non-starter," said "Jeff", putting the receiver down.

"You see," he said, "there's nothing in it."

"Not bloody much," said Ward. "When he said 'not my province', he meant that he, the uniform branch, wasn't involved. It's a CID job, and here that means Special Branch. Those bastards from Messenger have probably got her already."

"But there hasn't been time," protested "Jeff".

"It only took a phone call. You don't realize that

half the porters in this place are SAS men. As soon as she was spotted, the permanent Special Branch here would have contacted Messenger. It's how the system operates."

"So she could have been taken off Heathrow already?"

"Not necessarily. If a uniform arrested her, presumably for taking and driving away, it would take time for her to be released into Special Branch hands. There's probably still time."

"To do what?"

"To find her. Call your man back again."

"But he won't tell us – you said yourself he's uniform and therefore out of it."

"There are certain formalities that have to be gone through, whoever is involved," said Ward. "Even when a KGB agent was set up for defection last year, the police at Tottenham Court Road had to charge him with failing a breathalyzer."

"So what do we gain by calling again?"

"We find out who the arresting officer was, and then maybe what's happened to her."

"You know the drill, you do it," said "Jeff" dialling the number again.

When the call was announced Ward asked the switchboard operator for "Reserve". After a short delay he was put through. "Which relief is doing late turn?" asked Ward.

"B. Relief," replied the officer at the other end, instinctively aware that he was being addressed by a colleague.

"Who pinched the Ward girl?" asked Ward.

"Excuse me, but who's asking?"

"Commissioner's Office," replied Ward coldly. Few outside the Force knew that Scotland Yard was not in fact a police station, merely an administrative centre.

"P.C. House, sir."

"When's the prisoner being collected?" demanded Ward.

"Being collected by two Branch officers I believe, coming in by plane any time now."

"Thank you," said Ward courteously, ending the conversation. As soon as he put the receiver down, he was dialling again. He asked Directory Enquiries for the number of Kidlington Airport, Oxford. He was quickly given the code and number. "Jeff" watched as he was put through to the Control Tower.

"Have you had any aircraft cleared to Heathrow during the last hour?" asked Ward.

"Only one to Heathrow," replied the voice at the other end. "Golf Echo Delta Yankee. A Beechcraft Executive."

"Many thanks," said Ward. His next call was to Air Traffic Control, West Drayton.

"Have you got a flight plan for Golf Echo Delta Yankee outbound from Heathrow now?" he asked.

The ATC assistant punched some buttons on the console in front of him. "Inbound from Kidlington; outbound cleared to Glasgow and Fort William."

Ward thanked him and replaced the receiver on its cradle. He thought for several minutes before apparently making up his mind. He then dialled a long-distance number. "Colonel Green?"

"Speaking. Is everything all right?"

"Not entirely," admitted Ward. "Lucy's been arrested at Heathrow. So far I'm free."

"I've had another visit," said Green. "They were pretty tight-lipped but I guessed you'd got away. They're not too pleased at being conned over the car, though they haven't said much."

"There's a good chance that Lucy's going to be taken up to Scotland . . . Glasgow and then possibly Fort William. Does that make any sense to you?"

"Not much. Didn't they threaten to ship you off to Scotland?"

"Into the care of a Doctor Schofield. Did you know him?"

"It's possible. There were several psychiatrists at our place at Ham Common . . . Latchmere House. Schofield could have been one of them. It was a long time ago."

"Think carefully," instructed Ward. "Do you

connect Glasgow or Fort William with Messenger and his crew? Does Schofield or Latchmere House fit in?"

There was a pause. "Ham Common was known as Camp 020. There was another place like it – two in fact. One at Guildford and one in Scotland."

"What can you remember about the one in Scotland?" pressed Ward.

"Not a lot I'm afraid. I think it was run by Special Operations Executive, like a lot of establishments around there, right in a Prohibited Area."

"Do you know where exactly?"

" 'Fraid not. It was simply called Inverlair. Could be the name of a town or a region for all I know. I remember Professor Foot mentioned it briefly in the official history. Don't tell me Messenger is involved with that place?"

"A plane is coming to collect Lucy from Heathrow . . . the same plane I was supposed to travel up to Scotland in. By a strange coincidence Air Traffic Control tell me it's filed a flight plan up to Fort William. My guess is that the place has never been stood down."

"But that's impossible," protested Green. "Someone would have found out."

"Not necessarily," said Ward. "If this place was super-secret during the war . . . why not now? Maybe it's easier to keep on an old location rather than spend Treasury funds buying new premises. Whatever the answer, I'll bet Lucy is on her way up there."

"Are you suggesting that place in Scotland has been constantly used by Messenger's people . . . ever since the war?"

"Perhaps not, but don't forget that since Sillitoe in '46, every Director-General has been an organization man . . . White, Hollis, Furnival Jones and Hanley. The old tradition of outsiders has been discarded."

"A deliberate cover-up?"

"Hypothesis only," Ward admitted, "but something is going on that we have to put a stop to. I'll try and check out the Scottish place."

"Good luck," said Green, "but go carefully. Messenger is dangerous."

"I know."

The next morning found Ward not in Rome or Tienna but in a small two-bedroomed flat in Holland Park Avenue. He and "Jeff", whose real name turned out to be Tom Yariv, were talking. Yariv confided that his chief occupation was keeping the El Al flight guards in logistics. He supplied them with long-barrelled, semi-automatic Beretta .22s that had been specially selected and adapted by the weapons experts at Mossad. They had adjusted the trigger mechanism to make its action easier, so the gun could be fired more quickly, and increased the tension on the firing-chamber spring so the low-velocity ammunition would still operate the automatic-loading system of the Aleph. Every bullet had to be modified to carry light powder loadings and these had to be constantly replaced.

Yariv had not only been impressed by Ward's ability to gain official information from previously unco-operative sources, but had been surprised by the ease with which he'd "tapped" into the police.

"Not so difficult really," explained Ward. "We were all linked together in Northern Ireland – the RUC, the Army and the various intelligence groups."

"And who were you with?" asked Yariv.

"A separate bunch. The MRF – Military Reconnaissance Force. My regiment seconded me for a few months."

"Nothing to do with the intelligence organization?" asked Yariv.

"Different purpose. We only identified terrorist groups. We operated from the Palace Barracks, a couple of miles outside Belfast, and were separate from SIS and the Security Service. Once we'd nailed a suspect the others would move in."

"Hence your knowledge of police procedure."

"More or less. The Intelligence Corps run courses on how our counter-measures integrate. All quite effective, except it means that some of the 'hired assassins' become exactly that. They are highly trained in a particular job which is legally un- acceptable in civvy street. That's why so many SAS personnel become 'fringe soldiers' – mercenaries or employees of muscle shops like the independent security companies."

"And you?"

"I'm unemployable . . . a cripple if you like. But I won't let Messenger get away with this lot. By tonight I'll be up in Scotland and I'll deal with Messenger in my own time."

"You can count on our support, within certain parameters," promised Yariv. "We cannot be linked to your activities, although we support them. Will you leave the country as soon as you have confirma- tion that Lucy has come to no harm?"

"Probably, but I'll take a lot of convincing that Lucy is safe."

"What have you in mind?"

"A visit to Scotland for Mr Cooper."

8

For the time of the year the night was cool; a slight mist enshrouded the dark valley sides and dew covered the heather on either side of the road.

Ward parked his rented Ford Cortina beside the Spean Bridge signpost and walked the remaining two miles to the gates of Inverlair Lodge, the Security Service's psychiatric "cooler". It was almost a full moon and this remote part of the Highlands seemed as quiet as the grave. There'd been no traffic on the road from Roy Bridge and it was as though there was still a curfew in the area, so few people daring to venture out of doors, just as there had been some thirty years earlier. In the pub in Killiechanate a couple of the older regulars had told him of the war years and the difficulties of living in a Prohibited Zone. The Cameron Highlanders patrolled the whole

area, ostensibly "on exercise" and thought nothing
of scaling the mountainous peaks surrounding Loch
Laggan, perhaps bivouacking away from camp for
ten days at a time.

The legendary General Gubbins had selected the
western coast of Inverness-shire for his agents' training bases not just because he knew the region, its
wild beauty and its harsh surroundings, but because
the Admiralty had restricted the place to ensure complete security for their naval establishments. The
thinly populated, barren countryside was ideal cover
for both Commando courses and the less conventional training given to the SOE spies before going
into the field. Far from inquisitive eyes and lacking
in roads, the various fringe service organizations
could operate with a virtually free hand. Occasionally stories from some of the camps would leak out to
the sturdy locals, but that would have been as far as
the rumours ever got. The Highlanders valued their
privacy and were respectful of the privacy of others
. . . especially of the Scottish regiments that were
deliberately selected to guard the Spean district.

There was little that Ward could glean in the
rough, smoke-filled bar in the pub, apart from the
knowledge that Inverlair was still "a very special
place" and that he would be unwise to be up on
the moors after dark.

He did have more luck on his visit to the second

of the three local airfields where he was able to confirm that three passengers had been met from the plane that landed the previous night, though the man he'd spoken to could tell him little else. He only refuelled the aircraft when they needed it and the tower-controller who'd specially come on duty to switch on the lights was now at home. So far as he knew the Army at Inverlair didn't keep any equipment on the field: they just flew in the brass from time to time and never stayed for long.

Surrounded by broad Highland accents and quizzical glances as he tried casually to get any information, Ward knew that he was making himself conspicuous. In any small community, whether it be the hills of Armagh or the moors of Scotland, people had to be reassured about a visitor's reasons for asking questions. Rather feebly, he felt, he'd offered the explanation, when asked, that he was a television journalist on the lookout for suitable film locations. A poor cover, but he hoped he wouldn't be around for more than a day, two at the most. In between Glasgow airport and Queen Street Station, he'd grabbed the opportunity of buying a thick pullover and anorak so that his clothes resembled those of the thousands of other tourists visiting Western Scotland.

As Ward padded round the corner on the road to the tiny hamlet of Fersitin, wearing Yariv's tennis shoes, he caught sight of a light showing weakly through a window of a lodge. As he came closer, being careful to remain as silent as possible, he glimpsed a much larger building screened by trees. This must be Inverlair. Cautiously he worked his way up to the lodge and flattened himself against the wall, close to the window. Inside he could see two shirt-sleeved men playing cards in front of a coal-fire, steaming mugs of tea on the table beside them. On the backs of their chairs were slung the blue serge uniforms of the Ministry of Defence Police.

Ward moved slowly away and walked around the stone perimeter wall. It was only about nine feet tall, easy enough to scale, especially in the places where some of the parapet had crumbled through old age. A few yards off the road, the wall was replaced by a newer wire fence with a coil of barbed wire at the top. The links all looked in good condition and the prowler suspected that the wall close to the road was probably deceptive, perhaps backed up by some sophisticated electronic surveillance system. The fence continued through the trees up a slight incline and round to what must have been farm buildings at one time.

From where he was now standing, he had quite a clear view of the house, a grey stone-built place, with two storeys. All seemed quiet, with only a single light showing on a back door. In the dim light, Ward could make out bars covering most of the windows and the four small skylights in the roof. He recognized that assuming he was able to find out exactly where Lucy was being held, he would have little chance of breaking in and freeing her . . . He walked on slowly, occasionally testing the fence and always keeping an eye out for the give-away signs of an electronic detection system. He found none, but was able to choose a spot that appeared to be out of sight of the house and lodge and therefore a reasonably safe point of entry. Suddenly the noise of barking dogs broke the silence. A door had opened in one of the outbuildings and Ward could see a figure silhouetted against the doorway; in his hand was a dog-lead. If this was the start of a dog-patrol around the grounds, thought Ward, he would be better off back at the car. No point, he reasoned, in putting any of the opposition on the alert before he'd even had a chance to formulate an escape plan.

Ward made his way back to the road, skirting round the lodge. It was going to be quite a problem to get Lucy out. Perhaps an even bigger source of trouble would be in getting clear of the whole area; their choice was limited. By road, they could only go back up the lane towards the main road where he'd just left the car. If they got that far, they would only have two alternatives, to turn right towards Roughburn and Loch Laggan, which would eventually bring them to the main road to Inverness, or else to turn left, the way he'd come this evening, towards Loch Lochy and Fort William.

Either way, they would be at risk if Lucy's escape was discovered immediately. It wouldn't take long for the police to block the roads and anyway there were probably well-thought-out plans to cover the contingency of an escape attempt.

The only other route would be overland, and that would mean climbing a couple of thousand feet and trekking across some of the most desolate country-side in Scotland. He ruled this out as it would keep them too long in the immediate vicinity of Inverlair, exposing them both to unnecessary risk. He could also not be sure in what sort of condition he would find Lucy.

Still deep in thought, Ward climbed into his car and drove slowly back to his hotel in Fort William. He knew that he would have to take action soon, but he didn't relish the prospect of having to break into a Secret Service prison – and then break out again.

The following morning Ward woke early, unrefreshed from his few hours in bed. It seemed to him that what he had in mind was almost impossible and every few minutes he returned to the task confronting him – Inverlair with all its fences and bars and Alsatians. From the short time he had sat observing the house, he hadn't really been able to judge accurately the number of people in the place but the size of the building, he reckoned, suggested that an obvious assault, relying on diversions and confusion, would never work. The building might look old enough, but he was prepared to put a good deal of money on there being some pretty heavy investment in electronics, either in the way of television surveillance or seismic detectors, to track down unwanted visitors.

As he got in the hired car and headed south, Ward had found two things to give him some comfort. One was that so far he hadn't been caught; the other was in the nature of Lucy's prison. It was designed to keep the inmates from escaping rather than actually to prevent intruders. After all, he reasoned, the most famous escapes from high-security wings in England had all been directed from the outside. In fact, the man serving the longest sentence in British legal history, and therefore the country's most-guarded prisoner, George Blake, had achieved total success when he was sprung from Wormwood Scrubs, in October 1967. And all apparently with the help of just one Irishman and practically no finance. If, as Sean Bourke had later claimed, between them they used just a walkie-talkie and a flowerpot, then there must be hope for this operation.

By early afternoon he had reached Edinburgh and went straight to Broughton Street close to the Cathedral. Murtie's are the best theatrical costumiers in the North and have a vast stock to cater for every taste from Roman gladiators to spacemen. Ward already knew what he was after and was able to complete the hire of the items he'd selected quite quickly. His next stop was at a motorists' accessory store in Princes Street where he purchased a lightweight, hydraulic-action jack with a universal fitting for the top, and a detachable handle. Finally he called at a pet-shop in Queensferry Road, explaining to the owner that he was in the film business.

"We're taking some test-shots for a commercial tomorrow," said Ward, behaving as much as he could like a movie man. "Unfortunately the Alsatian we brought up with us has met with rather an unfortunate accident and we need a replacement urgently. Can you suggest somewhere we could borrow one for a few hours?"

The shopkeeper, a short, bearded Scot, seemed anxious to be associated with Ward's production and recommended a dog-breeder at Kirkliston, some way beyond the airport. A telephone conversation between the three of them ensued and the deal was made: Ward would collect the animal the following morning and return it the same evening.

"No," reassured Ward, "a handler won't be necessary. We have a very competent production team experienced with dogs."

Ward then completed one or two other purchases before the shops shut and then, feeling well-satisfied with the day's events, booked himself into the Metropole Hotel for the night. But after dinner he didn't go straight to sleep. Instead, tired though he was, he continued his preparations for his assault on Inverlair. Amongst his visits to the shops had been a call at Woolworths where he had bought several sets of chrome letters and some fabric adhesive. It was more than two hours later when his job had been completed.

In his mind he had begun to tackle the problem of getting into Inverlair, daunting as it was. The next hurdle was to find a way out and then a way to get clear of the area. He knew his plan could only succeed at night and this rather limited his escape routes. What was essential to the whole plan was that Lucy's escape should not be noticed for at least half-an-hour. If they were that lucky then he judged that they had a reasonably sporting chance. With that thought in mind, Ward happily succumbed to a deep sleep.

*

The next day, as Ward's car swung off the main A8 road to Kirkliston, he knew that the next twenty-four hours would be vital. He reckoned he had some slight advantage over Messenger in knowing where Lucy was. Breaking into Inverlair would certainly take Messenger by surprise, but Ward had no doubt that his reactions would be swift. He had not taken the trouble to contact Colonel Green for several reasons: by now Messenger would be certain of his complicity with Ward, and the arrest of Lucy in his car would only serve to confirm what he probably already suspected, especially bearing in mind the dash through the back streets of Oxford. The question that remained in Ward's mind was what action Messenger would take against Green. Did Messenger know that Coleman's death would be mentioned? Perhaps more importantly . . . did Green really believe that the professor had been put out of the way by Messenger's thugs? There were too many imponderables. Some alternatives just weren't worth contemplating . . . that Green himself might now have been "turned" by Messenger. Green had served in MI5's "B" Division. Where did his loyalties lie now? Would Messenger persuasively go to work on him? Ward could just imagine the tall suave former DDG explaining to the Colonel how Ward had been bought – by the Israelis perhaps – and was trying to get some blackmail material for use against government ministers. It was always a possibility. The previous evening he had read the Blue List from top to bottom. Most of the names meant little to him but Messenger was there and so were one or two other people whose names he recognized from newspapers. It was all very curious reading, these alleged collaborators with a British Nazi government and yet some, like a man who'd featured in a spy scandal in the early fifties, had since shown themselves to have sympathies with quite the opposite end of the political spectrum.

There was a lot of consolation to be found in the absence of Green's name from the list, for at least it showed that not the whole of the Security Service had been rotten. But if only a few key people in the Double Cross operation had been on the wrong side then the damage would have been incalculable. Those MI5 officers had been in daily wireless contact with the enemy.

Who actually checked the information that they were sending over to the Germans? When he examined the idea more closely, he could see how dangerous the whole game had been; a proportion of the intelligence radioed to the Abwehr must have been authentic because otherwise the Germans would soon realize they were being duped. But who made sure the balance was right . . . that they had slightly more phoney material than the real stuff? If

MI5 was full of right-wingers ready to help topple Churchill, then it was only a small step to provide the other side with war-winning intelligence.

Ward smiled at how thoroughly efficient such a spy-ring might have been . . . acting with the knowledge and help of the only organization in the British Isles authorized to mount counter-espionage operations. The idea, or so he hoped, was too good to be true. He imagined the top planners from SHAEF sitting round a huge table littered with maps, pointing out to the MI5 Double Cross planners what future operations they were mounting against the Third Reich. What better way to find out Allied intentions? The idea was appalling, but it was, from what little Green had told him, eminently practical. One would be heavily reliant on the individual "turned" spy and his case officer as soon as they were given their instructions. Each would see clearly, from what they had been told, how to give the opposition the true intelligence. Certainly a heavy responsibility to live with.

The whole organization lent itself to corruption unless it was carefully monitored. Few people in Britain, even within the Services, then knew, or for that matter knew today, much about the officers, the structure or the workings of the Security Service. The "need to know" principle must, Ward reckoned, have left even those closely involved with its operations and methods fairly ignorant of what other departments were up to. If there had been even a couple of bad apples in the basket, the whole system might not have just blown, but might have been made actively to work for the other side. Ward smiled. What a catastrophe for all those smug men who were in the know!

But would the politicians who must have been consulted for authorization of the project have given their approval if there weren't checks on the system? After all, just one defection or one leak would send the thing wrong. Would they have risked that? Surely, Ward asked himself, they must have known that it was inevitable that there would have been the odd traitor? There were quite a few treason trials after the war to deal with those who actually went over to Germany. Amery and Joyce were hanged. The Legion of St George men had been imprisoned. How could the politicians be sure there wouldn't be others changing sides? No doubt whoever had initiated the dangerous game was persuasive enough to get their way, but there would always have been the risk.

He thought for a moment of the role that Coleman had played in the affair. He, presumably, was the ultimate check on the intelligence reaching Berlin. Once the Abwehr outposts in Lisbon, Madrid and the rest received their spies' messages they still had to get them to Hitler's headquarters and that obviously meant using the Enigma code-machine. The final verification on the quality of information believed by the Nazis was their own signals traffic.

Ward felt a little more comfortable. Too many people at Bletchley would also have to be traitors for the Double Cross system to be turned round on its operators. Since the codebreakers came under the auspices of the Secret Intelligence Service, who had little love for their St James's Street rivals, he knew that they would have had no hesitation in revealing a leak in MI5.

But if Messenger's name was on the List, then clearly the SD believed him to have been at least sympathetic to their cause. Green had recognized some of the names as having been his colleagues in "Five"; and Messenger's own brother had been shot down in a German aircraft.

Ward racked his brains to imagine the extent of their collaboration. After the *débâcle* of Paddock and the cancellation of Sea Lion, were the people on the Blue List approached to do more work for the Germans? Did they use the List to blackmail more co-operation? The only person who could answer that was Messenger himself and from Ward's point of view the question had already been answered by the attempt on his life.

Could it be that Messenger still retained a special

section, loyal only to him, within the Security Service, perhaps with its ultimate masters the Soviet Union? More to the point, would it be possible for him to maintain a sort of private army within the Service and get away with it for years? Ward knew from his own experience in Northern Ireland that when elite groups were set up, like the Military Reconaissance Force which he had served, it was difficult to maintain effective day-to-day control of their operations. Once the politicians had authorized the general principle they were discouraged from taking too close an interest in the running of the system. And all too frequently, provided there wasn't any adverse publicity and results were achieved, the politicians didn't really want to know about the nuts and bolts of the thing. Was it possible for Messenger to be operating an illegal, parallel team under the umbrella of MI5? He knew there was every chance, especially as Lucy was now languishing in some kind of a Security Service cage, having been flown there by plane. The illegal section was well-financed and well-covered. Ward's only chance was to spring Lucy so that she couldn't be used as a lever to obtain the List. He also realized that if the attempt failed and Messenger discovered he'd passed a copy to the Israelis, neither of their lives would be worth much. If Messenger didn't repeat his trick with an exhaust pipe, he'd use Ward's signed statement to discredit

him. Either way there wasn't much in it for either
of them.

Ward drove through the little cluster of houses
that made up the centre of Kirkliston and turned
into the road beside a large hoarding advertising
Alsatian puppies for sale. As he approached the
bungalow at the end of an ill-kept path, the barking from the kennels beside the house reached a
furious pitch. Mrs Campbell, the owner of the
establishment, came out to greet him and wished
him good morning. For a few minutes they stood
outside the front door and discussed the commercial
that Ward was in the middle of making . . . Mrs
Campbell, a large, red-faced lady in thick tweeds
and tightly pulled-back hair, listened attentively,
apparently satisfied that her animal was going to be
well looked after.

"He should be fed this evening, at about five,"
she explained. "Try and give him a good walk this
afternoon and he'll be as good as gold. Quite the
easiest one of his litter. You'll have no problems."

Ward listened to her instructions and followed
her round the wire enclosure that contained the
dogs – at least a dozen as far as he could judge,
and not all Alsatians. From one of the kennels she
selected Ben, who, Ward was pleased to note, was
doing a little less barking than the rest. A lead was

quickly attached to his collar and the three of them set out for a short walk together to acclimatize Ben to Ward. They strode briskly down the garden at the back of the bungalow, Mrs Campbell telling the movie-director how many prizes her pedigrees had won the previous year. Ben was now apparently too old to show, but he was still a fine, strong brute, eager to be let loose in the fields beyond the hedge.

"Try and keep him on the lead as much as you can," said Mrs Campbell. "Ben has always been a one for the sheep and there'll be trouble for you if a farmer or shepherd catches him. Will you be going far?"

"Only to Dunbar," lied Ward. "We've completed most of the work there already. Ben will be in good hands, and he'll be back with you late tonight."

At the end of the walk, Mrs Campbell was given £75 cash, from the funds lent to Ward by the ever-helpful Yariv, and Ben climbed into the back of the Cortina and curled up on the back seat. Ward made his farewells and started back in the opposite direction to Dunbar, heading towards Stirling and the road to Fort William.

On the journey he thought further about getting out of Scotland once the balloon had gone up. If Messenger was acting with full Cabinet authority he wouldn't hesitate to start a wide-scale police search which would obviously involve roadblocks – which excluded using the car. Even if he was working "illegally" he could quite easily fabricate some story about an escaped dangerous patient which would achieve the same result. Ward knew that if there were any awkward questions for them to answer afterwards, he could always wave the statement about. A boat from Fort William would take too long to charter and would attract attention; a private helicopter would be the answer, but he doubted if Yariv's co-operation would stretch that far. Add to that the time of morning that he intended to carry out the operation and the idea was ruled out. A telephone call the previous evening had established that there were only two trains down the west coast, an early morning stopping-train down to Glasgow with a connection to London, and the evening sleeper which left at about six from Fort William. Neither was too promising but he would keep them both up his sleeve in case nothing else worked.

Ward reckoned that if he could manage to get as far as Glasgow without detection, he would be able to make it the rest of the way. He doubted whether Lucy would have been photographed yet and if Ward's service photos were dug out of the Army's files, they wouldn't really be recognizable.

His face had been badly scarred since they had been taken and he felt safe enough with Cooper's identification. There was a long way to go, but he'd done the groundwork. It now remained for him to get into Inverlair.

9

Fourteen minutes to four the next morning found Ward sitting quietly in the heather above Inverlair. Through the damp mist he could see the vague outlines of the house silhouetted against two of the security arc lights that were burning over the southern rear wing of the building. The moon was on the wane and the night was unbearably quiet. Occasionally he heard one of the guard-dogs bark and, during the past hour, he'd seen a patrol pass through the grounds. Ben, squatting on his haunches, never stirred, but his head darted round in anticipation each time Ward changed position.

He was dressed in the dark-blue serge uniform of a Ministry of Defence police sergeant, the original division letters on the tunic epaulettes having been replaced with the chrome letters, "MD". In one hand he had a tight grip on Ben's lead. The other held a policeman's peaked cap with a black-and-white checked band, and a small satchel containing his other purchases from Edinburgh.

Slowly Ward got to his feet and quietly whispered a few words to his fellow-conspirator, Ben. Crouching low they made their way down to the perimeter fence and Ward paused for a few moments before extracting a pair of heavy-duty wire-cutters. He made five snips through the links and exposed a gash some two feet off the ground. Before going through, he replaced the cutters and pulled out a can of AntiMate dog-repellent. Ben growled softly as Ward sprayed the area around the hole before pulling him through. He repeated the performance on the inside so as to ensure that the breach wouldn't be immediately discovered and started boldly up the grass to the house itself, making straight for the ground-floor window that he had selected earlier. It was almost directly under one of the arc lights and was in clear view of both sides of the building, but he had little alternative. The west side was in spitting distance of the guard-hut and there was no unexposed window to work on. Anyway, he didn't intend to be there for more than a minute and a half at the outside. He could only pray that no one looked out of the two curtained, gabled windows that were closest to him, and that the tea-drinking guards didn't decide to put in an impromptu check. He tied the dog lead to one of the four bars over the window and pulled out the jack from the satchel. Deftly he placed the jack's head between the two centre bars. In the hotel the previous evening he had shortened the universal fitting on the top with a hacksaw so that it would fit. There was an inch-and-a-half to spare. He quickly fitted the pumping handle into its socket and gave the jack three or four pulls to get it rigid against both bars. Then with two hands he put his weight to the handle and felt the hydraulic lift inside the jack increase in pressure. He kept on pumping until he could see that the centre of the bars moved outwards. Ward smiled in satisfaction; when the guards did find the bars bent aside, they would be mystified by the strength needed to achieve the gap he had forced. As soon as he reckoned the bars were bent enough, he released the hydraulic lift and took the jack down. He stopped for a second just to check that he wasn't going to be disturbed for the most difficult part of the exercise.

With his heart thumping in his chest he replaced the jack in the satchel and stuck a handful of plasticine against the pane of glass closest to the latch fitting on the inside of the window. Once the sticky material was firmly in place, Ward ran a diamond-headed glass cutter round the outside of the frame, as close as he could make it to the putty.

Then with a couple of taps on the grooves he'd made, the glass came away cleanly in his hand. With a twist of his wrist the pane was brought back through the hole and laid silently on the ground. Moments later, the window was open and he, Ben and the satchel were through the bars and through the window.

They were in a small dispensary, the walls covered with medicine-filled cupboards and filing cabinets. A small desk was close against one end, the top cleared of all papers. There was a slight smell of disinfectant in the air and the atmosphere of a hospital institution was reinforced by two trolleys parked against the opposite wall beneath a swivel-lamp. Both were piled high with kidney dishes and syringes. Ward dropped the satchel to the floor and closed the window behind him. There was no going back now, he thought. The feeling difficult to suppress at this second, he thought, was that unfortunately there wasn't a single person he could rely on to get him out if he was caught. He sensed the same gut-feeling that he'd experienced when he'd been at school and was close to being discovered in the act of some unforgivable misdemeanour. On this occasion, as he knew only too well, there would be no back-up, no overwhelming force to bail him out when things got tricky; no platoon of Green Jackets within calling distance when the operation became too much to handle. He was on his own, and he wished to God he wasn't. Even the presence of Ben did little to reassure him. If ever a dog looked confused, Ben was earning an Oscar. For an animal usually employed to guard premises from break-ins, Ben showed all the reluctant characteristics of a less-than-happy accomplice. Ward tugged at the lead in order to get him over to the door and pressed his ear against the woodwork; there was not a sound to be heard. With military precision, he placed the police cap on his head and made his way out of the passage. The corridor was well-lit and seemed to run almost the length of the building, a green baize door blocking further view at either end. Ward closed the door of the dispensary silently behind him and followed the corridor round to the right and towards where he judged the main staircase would be. As quietly as his rubber-soled boots would allow him, Ward led the now inquisitive dog through the door and into a large entrance lobby. His first priority, Ward reminded himself, was to locate Lucy. Somewhere in the distance he could hear a faint buzzing sound as though a generator was operating; the whole place gave the impression of a slightly seedy health farm or a geriatric clinic . . . the walls were covered with that two-tone sickly-green colour one normally associated with the services or a hospital, neglected for too many years by an under-financed Health Authority. So far, though, the security aspect of the premises seemed to leave a great deal to be desired.

At that moment Ward noticed that directly above him was a small circular mirror. In its distorted glass he could make out the reflection of a man seated behind a desk on the first-floor landing. He cursed himself for not having spotted such an obvious device for keeping the whole of the ground-floor corridor under surveillance. He told himself that it was fatal to turn back now and that he had to continue up the stairs if he wanted to get away with the plan. As soon as the white-coated guard at the top came into view he saw that the man was gently dozing, a paperback in his hands. Each step seemed to take an age. Ward prayed that Ben would remain quiet. The dog quickly padded past and attracted no attention at all. As he turned the corner into the narrower first-floor passage, Ward felt the sweat pour off him. He paused for a moment and considered the situation; if the guards were to start a patrol of the grounds, there was a fair chance that one of them might notice the bars across the window downstairs had been forced open. He was confident that it wouldn't be a dog that would sniff him out as he had left a generous dose of repellent around the ground outside. There was only one way to trace Lucy and that was to cover the whole building until he found her. He accepted that a challenge might come at any moment, but he regarded his progress so far as being something of a triumph.

On either side of the corridor were doors with numbers painted on them. After a few yards, when he judged that he was safe from interference from the uniformed slumberer on the landing, he tried the nearest. It was securely locked – as was the next, and the one following. The fourth yielded, though, and appeared to be a small, poorly-furnished sitting-room with chairs placed round a central table. Ward pulled his reluctant companion into the room and glanced at a couple of magazines on the table . . . an out-of-date *Punch* and the *Illustrated London News*. It reminded Ward of his dentist's waiting-room, and he gave an involuntary shudder. The following two rooms were also empty, the walls covered with bookshelves. The green baize door at the end was marked "No Entry for Category A". Through the small glass pane in the centre of the door, he could see there was an improvement in the living conditions. Instead of just bare boards, there was a slightly worn carpet covering the floor. The dim green lightbulbs had been provided with shades. This area didn't seem to be any more promising, thought Ward; he was beginning to give up hope of finding the right room. Further progress was frustrated by his inability to get through the baize door. Nothing short of an attack on the sleeping guard was going to give him access to that wing of Inverlair, he concluded.

Just as he turned and was about to head back to the central landing, he heard a door close right at the other end, and, in the dim, greenish light, could see another white-jacketed man striding purposefully towards him. Ward was filled with an almost irrepressible desire to make a run for the stairs but he knew that the other man would get there first. He tightened his grip on Ben's lead and murmured "steady boy", keeping his head down so that his features would be hidden under the visor of his cap. Just at the second that Ward felt he was going to be challenged, the guard executed a swift left-wheel and clumped noisily past the man sitting at the desk. Without stirring, the dozing guard opened his eyes and acknowledged his colleague, who was by this time several steps down the stairs. His head turned vaguely towards Ward but by the time his eyes focused, Ward had passed from view and was leading Ben quickly down the corridor. The same series of doors led off from the passage and at the end was another green baize firedoor . . . only this time it wasn't locked. He opened it and walked slowly through. Immediately on the other side was a passage at right angles, lit by the same green bulbs, giving the place an eerie look. A newspaper was left on the top of a small table stationed halfway down the corridor, no doubt where the white-coated man had been sitting. Each of the five rooms here had small Judas-holes cut at eye-level through the wood. Ward briskly moved along the doorways, quietly pushed the covers away from the holes and peered into the rooms' interiors. Beside each doorway was a typed card with just a series of coded numbers on it, and a lightswitch. He briefly pressed the switch and for a few moments the first room was illuminated; inside the fittings were sparse . . . a bed, two chairs and a cupboard. Over the back of the bed was draped a dressing-gown and a pair of trousers.

Ward replaced the eyepiece and moved on to the one next door, but the room was unoccupied. The third room was Lucy's. Surprisingly, the door wasn't locked but as soon as he noticed the other side, he realized why: there was no handle at all. He kept the lights off and as gently as he could woke her up.

"Who the bloody hell is it?" she demanded.

"Not anybody who's going to make unreasonable demands on you, bad luck for you," said Ward.

Lucy sprang up in her bed. "Mike . . . " she exclaimed, lost for words. "How on earth?"

"Don't worry about a thing," he replied casually. "Me and my trusty companion have come to take you away from all this. Are you OK?"

"Never better," she laughed quietly. "Actually, the food's quite good."

"You can give me the details later. Right now you've got to become a policeman, Ministry of Defence variety." He thrust the black plastic parcel into her hands. "Get dressed quickly. I'll just check the door." The self-closer on the door had been frustrated by Ward jamming a waste-paper basket into the gap. Carefully he removed it and poked his head round the corner. The man in the white coat hadn't returned.

"What's with the police bit?" whispered Lucy. "We'll never get away with it." She was struggling with her uniform trousers.

"There are a whole load of police forces in this country, you know . . . some of them rather like private armies, but all with the same basic uniform. The Ministry of Defence have their own and they guard quite a lot of the more sensitive places like the nuclear stores and Security Service buildings. They've just recruited you."

"I'll never fool anyone," Lucy complained. "You may not have noticed, but I'm the wrong shape for this gear."

"You're tall enough and that's the important thing. Pull the cap down over your eyes and with any luck we won't be challenged. Ben will give us a little authentic colour."

"Where on earth did you get him?" she asked, amazed.

"I've borrowed him, like the uniform. Are you ready yet? Our friend might come back at any time."

"How do I look?" she grinned.

Ward adjusted her clip-on tie. "Bloody marvellous," he commented as he examined her in the thin pencil of light shining through the gap in the door. "Now let's get out of here."

"As simple as that," she murmured, as Ward pushed the waste-paper basket away and let the door close behind them. Together they walked back towards the stairs but as they rounded the corner the man who had been dozing behind his desk stood up and eyed them both. Lucy inclined her head slightly so that the brim of her peaked cap hid much of her face from view, and Ward stepped smartly between the man in white and the staircase to block his vision.

"What are you doing up here?" asked the guard. Lucy continued on down the stairs and left Ward to answer the questions.

"We had to make a security check," said Ward somewhat weakly.

"But you know you're not allowed up here," insisted the man. "I'll have to report it in the log."

"You do that," suggested Ward. "I'm only following instructions," and with that carried on down the stairs to join Lucy who was waiting at the bottom.

He quickly led the way back to the dispensary, Ben padding along at their heels. With a sigh of relief they closed the door behind them and replaced the latch on the inside.

"I thought he'd got us then," said Lucy who was still quivering. "Whatever gave you the daft idea you could just come in here and collect me?"

"I didn't think you'd be coming out any other way. The next step is to get through the window and then walk slowly across the lawn down to the bushes at the far end. I've left a gap in the fence there. When do you think they'll miss you?"

"Perhaps not till morning. I don't think they do spot checks. How did you know where I was?"

"Genius," murmured Ward as he opened the window. "I'll go first. Try and be as quiet as you can." At that moment he heard the crunch of gravel and both instinctively dropped to their knees. Some fifty yards away a uniformed dog-handler strolled along the path that bisected the lawn, but he was paying little attention to the house. A minute later, the man had disappeared from view.

"We'd better give it a rest for a while. There's a hell of a lot of activity in the garden, isn't there?" said Lucy.

"We can't wait here," said Ward. "Someone might come in at any time, and the guy at the top of the stairs might decide to check on us at the front door or the guard-lodge. We have to go now."

He handed Ben's lead to Lucy and noiselessly climbed through the window and squeezed past the two bent steel bars. Apart from the occasional rustle of the trees and a bark from the direction of the kennels at the other side of the house, the night was quiet. "OK," he whispered and Lucy, peaked cap in her hand, scrambled through after him. After a couple of encouragements, Ben sprang up onto the ledge and jumped down onto the ground. As he landed, he must have smelt the AntiMate because he started to bark. Desperately Ward commanded him to keep quiet, but to no avail; he exchanged worried glances with his sister and started across the grass leaving the window open and the satchel just inside. Feeling extremely conspicuous in the artificial daylight of the arc lamps, they dragged Ben towards the bushes at the end of the garden. The other dogs in the kennels were now barking furiously and at any moment they both expected a voice to challenge them. As soon as they were in the cover of the shrubs, they broke into a run and reached the fence, but with their eyes unaccustomed to the darkness, it was difficult to know which way the hole was, and now they no longer had the wire-cutters.

"Where's this famous gap then?" whispered Lucy urgently.

"Bit further on, I think," replied Ward as he pushed his way through the undergrowth with the noise, as he thought, of a herd of charging elephants. At last Ward recognized where they were. "Here it is, thank God," and with that he pushed Lucy and Ben through the wire before following.

Once on the other side, they trotted up the steep incline of the hillside and then followed the contours round, giving the perimeter wall a wide berth. It was heavy going in the police boots they were both wearing, but Ward wanted to avoid the road in case the alarm had already been given. They continued on, out of breath and stumbling in the darkness, until eventually Ward pointed to the railway bridge over the road.

"I've left some clothes for us up there," he said to Lucy as he climbed up the side of the banking.

"What have you got in mind now?" Lucy gasped as she clambered up the steep sides after her brother.

"We have two alternatives. One is to get to the car which is about a mile further on. It's off the road and fairly well-hidden behind some trees. The other is a trek along the railway tracks. I wasn't sure what condition I'd find you in, so I had the car as a standby, but frankly I don't think we'll get very far. There are only two roads to take and it's pretty obvious that they'll be well covered as soon as you're missed. If we go west, we'd have to go through Tulloch, Roybridge and Spean Bridge before getting to the main road and even if we got that far we wouldn't be safe."

"What about the other direction?"

"If we head east, we would eventually have to go through either Newtonmore or Dalwhinnie, a good thirty miles away. They could find those bars at any time and the road-blocks would go up pretty quickly. There just aren't that many roads up in this part of the world."

"Where do we get to if we follow the railway?"

"This is the main line from Fort William to Glasgow, and there are two trains a day –"

"Don't tell me," interrupted Lucy, "you were going to stop one of the trains and get on."

"More or less," Ward admitted. "It's not as daft a scheme as you think. The only other way is to trek over the mountains but I'm not very keen on that idea."

Lucy was pulling off the heavy serge uniform and changing into the sweater and jeans Ward had provided. "We don't stand a chance on the road and I don't much fancy a whole day walking, so I suppose it's got to be the railway. It'll be a bit awkward if we can't jump on one, though."

"I hope it won't involve anything quite as strenuous as that. As you can see, this is a single-track line, but it does have passing-places at intervals. The idea is that we hide beside the points at one of the passing-places and doctor the signal: the train stops and we jump on."

Lucy pulled on her anorak and gave Ward a big hug. "For an ex-Army officer, you're absolutely brilliant. Those bastards can search the roads as much as they like and they'll never find us."

"Well, that's the theory anyway. I expect they'll check the stations too, in case we tried to get on the Glasgow train this morning. After that, they'll probably start a full-scale search with choppers over the mountains." He picked up the uniforms and dropped them into a freshly dug hole that he'd prepared earlier the previous evening, then covered them with turf. "I've left a couple of misleading clues in the car just in case we didn't need it. When they do find the car they'll probably start a search of the Caledonian Canal. That should give us a little margin as well."

And with that, Lucy, Ward and Ben started along the railway track, heading south.

It was in bright sunshine, eight miles later, that Ward and Lucy came to the first passing-place on the track. Below them, still partly shrouded in mist, was Loch Treig and all around them the Highlands towered up to three thousand feet. In the far distance they could just make out a plume of smoke rising from a shooting-lodge on the far shore. The wind-patterns on the surface of the Loch were only faint, and the view was truly magnificent.

"We're about ready for the train here," said Ward. "What do you think? We could carry on to the next passing-place but it might be a bit risky."

He glanced at his watch. It had taken them nearly three hours to cover the distance from the bridge at Fersit and they were both tired and hungry. The tension of getting in and out of Inverlair was now taking its toll. "The first train from Fort William leaves at about nine and, according to the timetable, gets into Tulloch thirty-five minutes later. I guess that we have at least an hour and a half before it arrives. With any luck though, a goods train may get here sooner, in which case we can hitch a ride on that."

"What about Ben?" asked Lucy.

"We'll take him with us. I'll bet it was him that got us through Inverlair. Who'd argue with a brute that size? He may be able to help us again." He put down the lightweight hiker's backpack and started to take a reel of thin electric wire from it. "This is what is going to stop the train," he announced.

Ward walked over to the post carrying three signal lamps further up the track and removed the back-plate from the bottom red box. He connected the end of the wire to a small six-volt bulb and suspended it close to the glass in the front of the case, then closed it up again, leaving the wire trailing to the ground. Deftly he unscrewed the covers of the other lamp and took out the bulbs. He picked up the reel and began to walk slowly back past Lucy, paying out the wire as he went. "This is more or less what the Great Train Robbers did," he explained. "As the driver approaches the passing-place, he's warned that he might be stopped by a yellow, flashing light. That means slow down and proceed with caution. The second lamp will either show red or green and will tell him to stop or continue. By disconnecting the red and the green from this first signal we can get the train to slow right down. I've substituted my own flashing bulb which will show yellow through the lens. All we have to do is climb aboard. It shouldn't be too difficult. The next lamp up the track won't have been interfered with and will probably be green, in which case the driver will put on speed again, knowing that the track ahead is clear. He might report at the depot that one of the signals was flashing caution without any apparent reason, but that'll be all."

He brought the reel into the gorse bushes and clipped the wire with a pair of wire-cutters, connecting the leads to a six-volt battery. As soon as he pressed the wires onto the metal contacts on the battery, completing the circuit, the yellow signal started flashing.

"Bravo!" clapped Lucy. "This beats queuing on a platform any day."

"Now all we have to do is wait for a train," said Ward.

Just ten minutes later, sitting in the bushes, Lucy watched a small dot in the sky grow slowly bigger. She gave her brother a nudge and pointed out the approaching helicopter. Gradually they could distinguish the noise of the engine and for a good twenty minutes they watched it move over the moorland, sometimes sweeping down low. Twice it came quite close overhead, causing Ben to growl fiercely, but their camouflage was excellent and the chopper soared north towards Glen Spean.

"I bet they're in a right panic now," observed Lucy. "Messenger will go berserk when he finds out I've gone."

"Did he come up with you in the plane?" asked Ward.

"I've still not met him," said Lucy. "There were frantic telephone calls from the police station at Heathrow when I was arrested, and then Messenger's heavies carted me off up to here. They wouldn't tell me where we were going and I didn't even know the name of the place. I was put in my room and more or less left there. They searched me pretty thoroughly and asked if I had disposed of any documents, but I rather had the feeling that the chap asking me the questions didn't really know what he was after."

"Did he ask anything about me?"

"They asked me if I knew where you were going and which flight you'd taken, but they didn't pursue it. I got the impression that they were waiting for Messenger to come up and take charge."

"That's what I reckon," agreed Ward. "I think they would have used you to get me to give myself up, though they had no idea that I'd got a pretty good clue to where you were going to be taken."

"I'm glad you did. They only let on that they hadn't got you when they started the questions about what flight you'd taken. And even then, I assumed you wouldn't find out about my arrest until you decided it was safe enough to get in touch with Colonel Green again."

"What a bloody mess," said Ward forcefully. "We're right back at square one: Messenger is after our blood, as no doubt is most of the Scottish police force; and we're no nearer getting the Blue List to the people that matter, whoever they are. If I ever managed to persuade, say, the Prime Minister that I wasn't a raving lunatic and that the Security Service was being run by people with highly dubious records, I'd still have to explain giving the List to the

Israelis. That act of desperation won't have won me any friends – except for a few in Tel Aviv, and who needs *them* on a moor in the middle of the Scottish Highlands?"

"I don't think things are as bad as that. Your Israeli contact can complete his part of the bargain and get us out of the country for a while. You've delivered your part of the deal, but he hasn't done much yet."

"I don't think he'll be over-enthusiastic about either of us and anyway he only agreed to smuggle one of us out. Still . . . we'll think of something."

At that moment, Ben's head lifted off the ground and he got to his feet. "Can you hear anything?" asked Ward, peeping over the top of the gorse.

"Not a thing. I'll just check the rails." She got up and walked over to the railway lines and put her ear to the track. "There's a train coming," she shouted, her voice filled with excitement.

"Can you tell from which direction?"

" 'Fraid not. Let's hope it's going our way."

Some minutes later, they both heard the unmistakable sound of a diesel cruising round the side of the Loch from the direction of Tulloch.

"Ours, I think," muttered Ward, as he connected the leads to the battery and started the warning signal flashing. Lucy pulled Ben down into the gorse and gripped his lead tightly. The train came impressively into sight and they both stared at each other . . . it was a goods train headed south. It slowed to walking pace as it clunked over the points down the line.

"Let's go," said Ward, pulling Lucy to her feet. The cab and half-a-dozen tankers and flat-cars passed them by. They started trotting beside the trucks and Ward selected a box-car with open sides. He now realized the difficulty of climbing aboard. Although the train had slowed right down, the level he had to reach was easily five feet; the problem was not so much for himself but for Lucy and the dog. In a few moments, the driver in the cab would see the green signal at the end of the cutting and he'd accelerate away. Quickly he hoisted himself up onto the platform, suffering some splinters from the rough, wooden surface on the way, and turned round to help Lucy.

"Grab my hand," he shouted urgently, but instead she passed him Ben's lead. The dog was loping along the uneven surface of the track. With one swift movement Lucy hauled herself up onto the wooden floor. "How the hell are we going to get Ben up here?" shouted Ward. The train was now picking up speed and out of the corner of his eye, Ward glimpsed another signal go past and heard the noisy clank of the train moving over points. Neither of them would be able to jump back to the ground to retrieve Ben and he certainly wouldn't be able to jump the distance and get a good footing.

"Come here!" screamed Ward. "Get in!" The animal loped steadily forwards and seemed to sense the dilemma. Both of them were now shouting encouragement to Ben and suddenly he leapt forward but never even came within reaching-distance.

"Good boy . . . try again . . . up!" they encouraged.

Seconds later the Alsatian hurled himself towards them and they both grabbed him. His back legs were scrabbling madly for a foothold and both Ward and Lucy hung onto him as they rolled over backwards. He was safely on board. The train was surging forward, the rolling stock banging together noisily on the downgrade. When they had recovered their breath they were able to see Loch Treig vanishing behind them; they were on their way south.

They rattled on beside the river that flowed down from Leum Uilleim and sped through the simple wooden platforms that made up Corrour Station. Normally the morning train to Glasgow would have stopped here and a dozen other places along the line, but the goods train just kept on going, past some of the most breathtaking landscapes in the Highlands. They thundered over countless bridges, followed the glens into Tayside, and continued without stopping over Rannoch Moor and the Grampians.

At one stage the train slowed to a halt and there was a five-minute wait. Cautiously they both looked round the side of the car to see the cause of the delay. Suddenly an express thundered past . . . the overnight sleeper to Ford William, on schedule and due to arrive at ten-seventeen. They were soon on their way again.

The open-sided box-car was not uncomfortable, but the slipstream whistled round them both and Ward knew that if their destination was the Glasgow freight-sidings, their trip would take at least four hours. The rest of the journey was undisturbed except for the few occasions that they gave way to the up-train.

Ward tried, mid-morning, to imagine Messenger's rage when he learned of Lucy's escape. He wondered if anyone would have the courage to mention the two extra Ministry of Defence policemen that had patrolled the first floor, or whether that would be conveniently forgotten. Inverlair was supposed to be a secret establishment and by the same token, "spring"-proof . . . Sooner or later someone would have to own up to what had happened, if only because there was no way out of a self-shutting and self-locking room with undisturbed bars over the window. Perhaps in his paranoia, considered Ward, Messenger would think that it had been an inside job! Until they found the satchel . . .

Obviously he had supervised the cordon around the area and it would have been equally obvious that Messenger would have been confident of an early recapture. The country was among the most inhospitable in the islands and once news had been spread of the two dangerous Sassenachs on the run, there wouldn't have been a door north of the border they could knock on.

If the system was efficient, as he rather supposed it was, the roads would all have been sealed off and all civil aircraft grounded within a matter of an hour or so. The railway stations would be swarming with Transport Police, and maybe the Fort William train to Glasgow might have been searched. Once those few avenues of escape had been covered, it was simply a matter of sitting back and waiting for the fugitives to show themselves or give themselves up. Barring the intervention of an Israeli commando troop, or a flight of helicopters, the result would be inevitable.

In spite of all that, however, he had to hand it to Messenger, or whoever was in charge of the operation, for alerting the search-aircraft so quickly. He had hoped that by leaving a copy of an Ordnance Survey map, suitably marked around Fort Augustus and the Caledonian Canal, on the floor of the Cortina, he would throw the pursuers off the scent, but it clearly hadn't worked. He considered for a moment that perhaps the car hadn't been found yet, and then dismissed the idea. The roads to Spean Bridge and Newtonmore would have been thoroughly scoured. The Ford hire-car was less than three miles from Inverlair and carried easily checkable plates. In less than four minutes, the patrol car would have an answer from the regional computer revealing it to be owned by Godfrey Davis . . . One call to the Fort William office and a further check with the police computer would show the hiring to be fraudulent . . . and all within the space of just a few minutes. Their conclusion, though, would be wrong. They'd assume that their quarry were trying to make it slowly across the moors, while in fact they were speeding south at an average speed of thirty-seven miles per hour.

"This is the difficult bit," announced Ward. "We've just passed Bishopbriggs and I reckon that we'll be coming into Glasgow at any moment."

Lucy roused herself from a fitful sleep. "Will we go straight into a goods yard?"

"I'm not really sure," answered Ward. "It rather looks as though we're going straight into Queen Street, in which case, I suppose we'll be shunted out to a freight depot or round to Motherwell, which is the main collecting centre for Glasgow . . . Either way, it's going to be a bit tricky."

"What have you got in mind?" asked Lucy.

"You've done all right so far." She gave his arm a gentle squeeze of encouragement.

"To be honest, I never really thought we'd get this far, but just in case, I checked up on the ways out of the city." He fished out a notebook from the rucksack. "There's a regular two-hourly shuttle flight down to Heathrow. You only have to book in ten minutes before take-off and, so they tell me, you're guaranteed a seat. Otherwise there's a train that leaves from the other station at ten-past-two and ten-past-four. What do you think?"

"I have a feeling that MI5 will have thought of London flights already," commented Lucy.

"The train was an earlier invention," pointed out Ward, "and so was the internal combustion engine. We could always hitch a lift on the motorway."

"What about renting a car?" Lucy asked brightly.

"Not so good, I'm afraid. The driving licence I've got at the moment is in the name of Cooper, thanks to you, and I'm willing to bet that the name Cooper won't win any prizes in Scotland today. By now they must have found the Cortina and traced the hiring. If we just showed our faces at a car-hire firm we would be courting disaster. I think it's down to hitching and the train."

"I don't reckon hitching. The police always seem to be 'anti' and we can't afford an identity check."

"Which rather leaves good old solid British Rail," muttered Ward.

The train had now slowed down and was negotiating a complex system of points and interchanges. A signal box beside the track announced Glasgow. "I suggest we skip off here rather than wait to go into the station; Messenger may have more sense than we credit him with, and there might be a reception committee."

"Anything you say," said Lucy unconvincingly. They both jumped off the box-car together, pulling a reluctant Ben behind them. The train continued on, unaware that its passengers had got off. They picked their way across several sets of railway lines and started to walk towards a group of sheds some two hundred yards away, close to a lorry-park.

"This must be some kind of freight depot," said Ward. "If we can get out of here without being spotted, we can grab a cab for the other station." Warily they continued on, sticking to the protection of a line of stationary rolling-stock. They were just crossing the gap between two coal-tippers when a voice rang out behind them.

"Oi, you two! What do you think you're up to?" A uniformed man was running towards them, a dog straining at a lead. Ben growled menacingly. Desperately Ward surveyed the scene but there was nowhere to run to. He gave Lucy's hand a little squeeze and decided to bluff their way out of the situation.

"Do you think you could help us?" said Ward. "We're a little bit lost. Our dog ran away and we came in here after him. Can't find our way back now." The man in the uniform approached them. "This is all British Railways Board property," he insisted. "No one's allowed here unless they're on official business." He glanced down at Ben, who was baring his teeth.

"We couldn't just leave him in here," said Lucy weakly. "He might have caused an accident. We've got him safely on his lead now."

"D'yer know where it was you came in?" asked the guard, rubbing his moustache. But Lucy had won him over.

"We were just walking the dog," said Ward. "He just ran off somewhere over there . . . " he gave a vague wave behind them, "and so we tried to get him back. You know how it is."

The guard seemed uncertain what to do. Lucy must have sensed this because she kneeled down beside Ben and admonished him. This made up the mind of the suspicious Scot.

"You'd better come with me," he said finally. "I'll escort you to the gate before you get in any more trouble." And with that, the three of them trotted off past the sidings and the sheds, the two dogs following beside them. They went straight past the security-post at the main entrance and were shown into the road.

"For goodness' sake, keep him on a lead round here in the future," the guard warned as they parted company, and as Ward and Lucy walked towards Glasgow, they congratulated themselves on their good fortune . . . not only to be caught by a dog-lover, but to be waved past the security precautions on the way out of the depot.

They soon caught a cruising taxi in Springburn Road and completed their journey to Central Station where the Inter-City expresses connect to London. Although Ward didn't know the centre of the city at all, he realized as they sped under the M8 motorway that they were approaching what had once been one of the most important commercial nuclei of the Empire.

"Could you drop us in the street that runs quite close to the station?" asked Ward.

"Do you mean Union Street?" responded the driver.

"That's right . . . Union Street. Drop us there."

The taxi turned left from Castle Street into George Street, and took a short cut through the back streets until they got close to the station. "Here we are," announced the cabbie as they drew into the kerb. Ward paid him off, and made a deal with him. For an extra £20 he would take the Alsatian to the RSPCA and report it as a stray. They could then ensure his safe return to Mrs Campbell.

The procedure they'd adopt had already been decided. Once they got to the main Glasgow Central booking-lobby, Ward developed a very pronounced limp; Lucy struggled to support him and called a porter to assist her.

"We're trying to catch the fourteen-ten to Euston," she explained. "Would you be kind enough to buy two single tickets?"

She passed him £45 exactly. "Meet us at the platform." Ward continued hobbling painfully as the British Rail man raced off. There was not a lot of time to spare and this simple precaution would evade any of Messenger's eager bloodhounds. They wouldn't be able to cover every platform, but it was a fair bet they'd at least cover the ticket-office. Ward dragged his leg past the departures board and onto the platform. The porter caught up with them as they reached the gate and received a generous tip. Minutes later they'd taken their seats in the second-class carriage and the train pulled out . . . they were on their way to London, on their way to freedom. For the first time in days both felt entirely at ease. They were travelling like any other passengers to the nation's capital. Nothing picked out either of them as being anybody special. Indeed nobody would in the normal course of events give them a second glance. They had achieved the impossible – escape from the Security Service prison – and were heading for the safety of the big crowds of London.

10

It was shortly after the Carlisle stop, when Lucy and her brother were safely dozing in their seats, that ex-Detective-Inspector Digby, late of Special Branch, spotted his two quarries in a closed compartment of the London train. Since the alert, some four hours earlier, he'd started taking the down-line connections to Penrith. Just those twenty miles were enough for him to walk up and down the swaying carriages and make a visual check on every passenger. His instructions, delivered by teleprinter earlier in the morning, had been to identify and maintain surveillance on the two "rats". Occasionally he'd been instructed to do the same thing, but the brass had never taken a personal interest before. Usually the form had been some punter on his way down from Holy Loch or one of the nuclear establishments, who was a potential target for a drop or an exchange. The difference was that on this occasion he'd been told to report making contact and then pass on the case to the next officer. This was unusual, because the normal procedure was that any officer involved would tag on in the background, either to give assistance in the event of an arrest proving necessary, or to complete his report in the presence of a senior officer. This time he was to leave well alone once he'd found them. He'd call the Freefone number but that would be as far as he'd go. In many ways he felt slightly disappointed. It was rare that in this part of the world the Security Service had anything of interest apart from the routine of spot-checks on sensitive government employees. Maybe London would order a phone tap for no obvious reason, but that was about all. This sort of work, at such short notice, was indicative that something was brewing. Digby didn't even know their current names but their descriptions had been given in detail. In all probability, he'd been told, they'd be travelling together, without any luggage. He had wondered about that. Not many people travel without even a briefcase.

He went back along the corridor, feeling rather like hangman Pierrepoint catching the briefest glimpse of his victim. He experienced no feeling of doubt about his identification. He paused for a moment to consider what crimes against national security they were guilty of . . . indiscretion, naivety or espionage?

To the ex-DI's horror, the girl suddenly opened her eyes and looked him straight in the face. With accustomed ease, he glanced at his crumpled newspaper and continued up towards the first-class section. You couldn't help wondering, he said to himself, what sort of case you were getting into. If ninety per cent of them were a waste of time, you could be forgiven a small flicker of interest when you met the real thing. Quite soon, of course, the whole matter would be taken out of his hands, but in the meantime he was the officer on the case. He was the man who'd picked them out in the early afternoon from several hundred other passengers . . . no easy task . . . perhaps worthy of some commendation. He popped into the toilet at the end of the carriage and spent a couple of seconds jamming the "engaged" sign. He then returned to the corridor and leant against the end-compartment as though he was waiting for a stomach-troubled passenger to purge himself.

After a while he felt the train slow. No one had come out of his suspects' section and Digby felt pleased and confident when he got off the train at Penrith and made his way towards the public telephone next to the exit. It was only after he'd dialled the number and asked for his chief that he felt the unmistakable pain in his kidneys. The barrel of a gun was rammed into his back. Reluctantly he replaced the receiver and laid both his hands on the pay-phone as the soft-spoken voice requested. This was no time for heroics, Digby told himself. The man behind him sounded calm enough but the menace was real. Arguments could come later.

Without looking round, he walked slowly back to the train and got in. The muzzle in the small of his back never wavered; perhaps he was getting too old? Nobody would be suicidal in a situation like this. Just follow instructions and try to remember all the details for the report . . . if there was a report. He realized that he was sweating. His shirt felt damp and his confidence had left him.

"Turn right," said the voice behind him. "Get into the toilet."

"This won't do you any good," Digby said. "It'll count against you. I might be able to help."

"You might at that," said Ward, thrusting the discarded cigar tube in his pocket harder. "Put your hands against the window and lean on your fingertips."

The ex-Detective-Inspector obeyed and felt a hand frisk him. He could tell that whoever was carrying out the search was experienced: this man knew exactly what he was doing.

"I'll try and help you if I can," continued Digby. "Nothing is ever that serious. Give me the benefit."

He still hadn't had a chance to examine the face of his assailant, though, from a brief glimpse in the British Rail mirror, he was fairly sure that this was the man who had been quietly dozing next to his girlfriend minutes beforehand.

"Are you a police officer?" the voice asked.

"Not exactly," Digby replied. "I'm . . . retired."

"Are you from the Security Service?"

Digby paused for a moment. "Even if I was, I wouldn't be able to tell you," he said with rather a nervous laugh. He began to think that his colleagues had let him down. No one had warned him that the bastard was dangerous. Christ, he reflected, he wasn't even carrying a shooter. This could turn out very nasty. Ex-Detective-Inspector Digby was worried.

"I'm going to ask you three questions," said Ward. "If you answer them correctly, I'll know that you're MI5. If you mess about, you'll be telling me something I suspect already. Do you understand?"

"I think so," replied Digby. This was beyond bluff and his hands were beginning to ache.

"What's the room number of the conference room at Leconfield House?" Ward knew that practically any Security Service employee would have to come into contact with the conference room sooner or later. He himself had once spent an afternoon there being briefed on outside agitators before being posted to the MRF.

"I can't remember the number," said Digby with irritation – the "muzzle" bit deeper into his back by way of encouragement, "but it was on the fourth floor . . . the eastern end of the building."

Ward made no comment. "Where's the canteen?" This was the only other piece of information about the Security Service's HQ in Curzon Street that he could remember from his brief visit. After his film show, he'd been offered a little Civil Service hospitality.

"On the top floor, the seventh floor. It's rather a nasty shade of red," added Digby.

Ward was satisfied. The nervous figure in front of him was definitely an employee of Sir David's, but what was left unclear was exactly how close he was to the former DDG. Was he an "official" or one of Messenger's private thugs?

"How long have you been working for the Security Service?" he demanded.

There was a gap of a few moments before Digby resolved himself. "I'm not prepared to answer any more questions," he replied. "You have put yourself in a very dangerous situation, Captain Ward, or Mr Cooper, whichever name you prefer. Assault with a deadly weapon is a serious charge."

"From this end of a gun, the right end, that sounds

fairly academic," remarked Ward drily. "Are you trying to say that you are arresting me?"

"Since you appear to be so familiar with Leconfield House, I'm surprised that you don't know the Security Service have no power of arrest. Incidentally, how did you spot me? Do I know you?"

"My sister spotted your flat feet. If I hadn't stopped you telephoning, what would you have done – tailed us until we got off?"

"I'm not saying anything else."

"How did you know that we'd be on this train?" He was answered by silence, and he knew that he would learn little more from the ex-policeman. The shock of being discovered had obviously upset him and Ward had taken full advantage of his opportunity, but the last few minutes had given him a chance to recover himself and his mouth would be tight shut from now onwards.

"Would it make any difference if I were to tell you that I suspect Sir David Messenger of being a Soviet agent and that because of the incriminating evidence I've uncovered, he tried to have me killed?" There was no response. Ward knew the effort was in vain.

"Can I stop leaning up against the wall yet?" requested Digby.

"Not unless you want the lower part of your abdomen shot away," replied Ward, keeping the cigar tube in position, and wondering how long he could keep up the pretence. The man before him could have been an excellent source of information but he accepted that nothing he could say would persuade the ex-copper to be disloyal.

"When do you plan on releasing me?" demanded Digby.

"Soon," said Ward. He realized only too well the enormity of the task before him . . . to convince someone in authority that one of the most trusted public servants in the country had at least at one time conspired to topple the wartime government and to prove that this information was probably known to the KGB who wouldn't hesitate to use it for blackmail. So who should he turn to? The obvious answer was to clear out of the country and leave the problem in the hands of the Israelis but they couldn't necessarily be relied upon to act on the Blue List. Outside of the elected members of the Cabinet, the people he considered approaching were either the Permanent Under-Secretaries, those faceless mandarins responsible for wielding so much of the Cabinet's power, or the members of the Joint Intelligence Committee or, even more unapproachable, the Chief of the Secret Intelligence Service.

Ward's mind was spinning with the inevitability of defeat. He knew, from a recent newspaper article, that Ian Fleming's "M" published his home address and even his private telephone number in *Who's Who*. But there again, he thought, even if he could get together enough documentary evidence – the evidence of the Blue List and the incident in the back of the Ford Transit – he still wouldn't be believed. His humble offerings would be weighed against a signed statement that admitted a state of mental insecurity. Now, in the face of one of Messenger's men, one who in other circumstances he would have considered relatively incorruptible and trustworthy, he felt utterly resigned to the hopelessness of his task. No one would believe him, no one would give him a second hearing. By his own admission he was a candidate for the 1969 Mental Health Act.

Digby seemed to realize the desperation in his captor's mind because he offered no argument when he was ordered to leave the toilet and walk down the corridor past the section where he had first spotted the two fugitives. As instructed, he walked on past the buffet car and came to a halt at the rear of the train by the guard's van.

"So what's this all in aid of?" asked the ex-Detective-Inspector nervously. "You won't gain anything by this."

But Ward was resolute. There were few people he could rely on now. Under more usual circumstances, the cowering man before him would have been co-operative. He was only one of several thousands who worked for the Security Services. But the difference was that Ward felt that they were on opposing sides, whether by design or accident. There was so much at stake that it was too late to enter into meaningless semantics. As Lucy pulled open the partition door into the parcels van, Ward ordered his prisoner to shift the wooden, exterior sliding-door. Suddenly, the slipstream came rushing into the limited space in the car. Ward glanced at his watch, keeping the cigar tube in his pocket firmly in contact with Digby's back. It was nearly four o'clock. In less than twenty minutes they would be arriving at Oxenholme. Ward had already weighed up the possibilities and he felt he had little choice. Remorselessly, he grabbed Digby by the arms from the rear and suddenly propelled him through the open door into mid-air. Lucy gasped out loud at this barbaric action, and her brother turned to her.

"So what should we have done?" Lucy couldn't answer. In spite of all she had experienced in the past two days, she hadn't been conditioned for this.

"In cowboy terms, it was either him or me," said Ward. Quickly he corrected himself "– him or us." This made no visible impact on Lucy. "I couldn't shoot the bugger because I haven't got a flaming gun. Yariv refused to supply me with one. But be absolutely sure, if I had let him get away, he'd have turned us in. My try at explaining . . ." she turned her head sceptically, "yes, my rather feeble, unbelieved attempt to convince him was utterly without hope. Right now, he's picking himself off the grass and trying to work out where the nearest telephone is. And I can assure you," she looked unconvinced, "if he does find a telephone before we get off this train, we are both destined for a country lane and a dose of carbon monoxide."

Lucy seemed riveted to the spot but after a while the colour came back into her cheeks and she moved forward to close the doors. The tension of the two disappeared as quickly as the cold air stopped rushing round the interior of the car, but the atmosphere seemed strangely pregnant. Lucy was acutely aware that if she hadn't called her brother's attention to the rather tall, lean man who had examined them both twice from the corridor, he might still be alive. She tended to ignore that, without this natural flash of female intuition, neither of them might be enjoying the relative freedom they both, albeit temporarily, enjoyed now.

"Assuming that Digby survives that little experience, he'll be on the telephone within half an hour." The train was speeding through the Cumbrian countryside towards Kendal; occasionally they rumbled over a road-bridge or through a short tunnel. "It'll take them a little time to get organized but if we hang on here, we'll be caught by the rest of Messenger's mob for sure. If they're quick, they might board the train at Preston, or even Lancaster, which is not too far away now." He glanced at his watch. "I'll bet that copper was the only one to cover this line. If he was, then our chances are considerably improved, but we'll still have to get out at the next stop."

"Where's that?"

"Oxenholme," he quickly flipped through the pages of his notebook. "According to the timetable, we'll be arriving at sixteen-eighteen. It's either that or out the door like that poor bastard. If we do that and they stop the train at Lancaster for a thorough search, they'll just work their way back up the line."

"They'll do that anyway," observed Lucy coldly. They were both close to capture and they knew it.

"Yes," agreed Ward, "but we'll have just that margin of time on our side if we wait for the station. It's that much further on and you've never done any parachute falls."

"Where the hell did a parachute come into all of this?" asked Lucy with surprise.

"They teach you on a parachute course to land properly. If anyone's going to survive a jump from here, at least he'd have to know how to fall without hurting himself. And that's no guarantee."

The train had slowed slightly and they moved out of the guard's van and back into the corridor. They were passing through Kendal and the bright sunshine of the morning had given way to darkened clouds and the threat of rain. Gradually the train lost speed as it approached Oxenholme.

"We're bound to be remembered getting off here," said Ward, "but it's too late to worry about that. If we are traced as far as here, they'll still be behind us."

The train pulled into the station, its platforms thronged with holiday-makers. From the vantage point of the carriage window Ward tried to see if there was a reception committee waiting for them, but there were too many people milling around. The wheels jolted to a halt and they jumped off feeling conspicuous because they were practically the only people there without luggage. Lucy led the way, forcing a passage towards the barrier. The small queue delayed them for a while, but then they were quickly through, and into the station-hall. Suddenly there was a sharp call and the ticket-inspector strode after them, leaving a bewildered group waiting to have their tickets collected.

"What's the problem?" asked Ward as Lucy walked ahead and out into the carpark.

"These are valid for Euston," pointed out the inspector. "You don't want to waste them. If you wait a few minutes, I'll give them to the booking-office and get them endorsed."

"That's very kind," replied Ward casually. "I'll be just outside. We had to get off the train in rather a hurry." The railwayman returned to his duties and Ward joined his sister, who had found a taxi.

"I was beginning to think I'd seen the last of you," she laughed. "What happened?"

"The man on the gate noticed our tickets and wants to save us some money, but we can't wait around. He's going to remember us, but it just can't be helped."

"I told the driver we'd like a hire-car for a few days, and that our luggage is already at our hotel." She winked mischievously. "He thinks he can find a car for us and he's gone to telephone. It's the height of the tourist season and it's quite difficult to get a self-drive."

"With any luck he'll be contacting a local firm so he gets commission and that means Messenger will find it rather tricky to trace us. He should have no problems covering the national organizations, but a hole-in-the-wall garage would be just the job."

A short young man with greasy hair walked through the station entrance and climbed into the driver's seat. "A friend of mine's got a car he can let you have," he announced in a broad Lancashire accent. "It's only a Mini, but it's his last one. How long will you be wanting to keep it for?"

"Just a couple of days," said Ward. "How far is it to Morecambe?"

"About twenty-five miles," said the driver, starting the engine. "It won't take long, though if you came off the Glasgow train you'd have done better to have stayed on until Lancaster."

As they set off to the holiday town the rain started to pour down. It was a depressing scene, but the taxi's two passengers were elated. If their friend from the train had managed to survive the fall, and had got as far as contacting his masters, the delay had given them the chance to escape. Nothing short of road-blocks throughout the country would catch them now. For the benefit of the taximan, who, they were confident, would be questioned about his two fares, they asked plenty of questions about the area and sought one or two recommendations. Quiet country hotels were what they were after, Lucy explained. By the time they got into Morecambe, they reckoned that they'd laid enough false trails to keep Messenger busy for a week.

The taxi pulled up in the forecourt of a large garage in a sidestreet, just off the sea-front, and the driver got out to find the manager. Ward gave Lucy the driving licence made out in the name of Cooper and told her to start filling out the hire-form while he telephoned Yariv.

Half-an hour later, Mr and Mrs Cooper were on their way to London on the M6 in a slightly clapped-out blue Mini. Ward had spoken to Yariv and had been offered a room. They were expected in Holland Park Avenue later in the evening. Yariv's only news was that Colonel Green had twice telephoned him in an effort to contact Ward. Ward promised to return the call as soon as they reached the safety of the capital.

"Hello, Colonel, I gather you wanted to talk to me," said Ward jovially. "What can I do for you?"

"Are you all right?" demanded Green with concern. "Your last message to me was rather cryptic."

"We're both fine. Lucy's with me, no thanks to Messenger's heavies."

"That's what I wanted to call you about . . . they've been in touch again. Firing on all cylinders, so to speak."

"Would it be better if I called you back in a few minutes in a coin-box? These characters are pretty active."

"Very well," replied Green. "Tell me where you are now and I'll ring you right back. That should do the trick."

Ten minutes later, Ward and Lucy squeezed back

into the telephone kiosk in response to the call from Oxford.

"We're secure for the time being," assured Green. "Tell me your news. How come Lucy is back in the land of the living?"

"That's all too long a story to go into now," said Ward, "and anyway I don't suppose that you'd approve. We're both in rather a lot of trouble. We should be back on our way within a couple of days. It's not the ideal solution, but beggars can't be choosers."

"Don't be too hasty," said the Colonel. "I've been making a little progress and I've got someone I want you to meet."

"Not Messenger again," said Ward wearily.

"Definitely not. His superior, if you like."

"Can you trust him? Is *he* on the Blue List?"

"Please believe me, he's trustworthy. He answers directly to the Prime Minister. I think it's important that you come and see him."

"Not likely," said Ward evenly. "If he's anything to do with MI5 it's out of the question. Those bastards are up to their necks in this and I still don't know what the hell's going on."

"It's making more sense now," reassured Green, "but it seems to be rather more serious than either of us imagined."

Lucy frowned. "So what's serious, Colonel? The

professor has been murdered; they had a good go at me; Lucy's been locked up in an Army nuthouse? Tell me what's not serious?"

"This chap is in a position to answer all your questions," said Green. "He's the Intelligence Co-ordinator to the Cabinet and has never served in Five."

"How did you find him?"

"He was the only person outside Five that I could turn to. After our last conversation I got very worried. Peter was in SHAEF and that's how I first met him. He and I used to discuss our Double Cross deception with the Five case officers and the LCS. Peter went into the Civil Service after the war and ended up in the Foreign Office. He succeeded Dick White as Co-ordinator of Security and Intelligence. I can promise you he's above suspicion. You must see him quickly."

"You rather lost me on the first part. Tell me more," instructed Ward, determined to extract every piece of information on the man. He was only too aware that sooner or later he'd have to trust someone and that, at his present rate, he would end up with some faceless man in Tel Aviv. Perhaps Green could supply the right person.

"During Double Cross, as you know, I led a team of VIs – Voluntary Interceptors – especially trained radio-hams to fool the Germans. As well as a VI, each turned agent had a case officer who was generally a Five man. Tar Robertson, who ran Bl(a), assigned a CO to supervise the day-to-day requirements of the agent. We had a regular meeting with LCS, London Controlling Section, represented by Dennis Wheatley, where the overall strategy was discussed and the feedback from Six's Ultra material was examined. Peter came along from Norfolk House to tell us what we could give to the Germans. He was a soldier, right outside of MI5."

"Why didn't you approach someone in Five?" asked Ward.

"That was all quite a while ago, and anyway, I don't have that much confidence after this Blue List business. My two friends were Tommy Harris and Guy Liddell and both are dead. Peter knew them all and I reckoned was in a good position to advise."

"You don't think he'll just hand me over to Messenger?"

"I promise you he won't. Obviously I can't queer his pitch, but I can tell you that the PM is in on this one."

"Are you saying that the Prime Minister approved of those two thugs and their mobile execution chamber?"

"I wouldn't put it quite like that," replied Green defensively. "All I'm saying is that you ought to see Peter. He does have all the answers and he has the power to free you from all this nightmare."

"How can he be above Messenger?" persisted Ward. "I thought the head of the Security Service only had to answer to the Cabinet?"

"That was true while Dick White was running MI5, but in the mid-fifties he did a switch and was appointed to SIS. He's the only man ever to have done both jobs; probably something to do with Philby . . . I'm not sure. When the time came for him to retire, apparently he wasn't allowed to, and a new post was invented specially to keep him in the saddle . . . Co-ordinator."

"Rather a case of being too valuable to lose."

"That's right. I would have seen White first but after all he was a Five career officer and I didn't want to risk it. Even if I had wanted to, I wouldn't have succeeded . . . he's abroad for a while, according to his house in Sussex. I knew you wouldn't have anything to do with someone connected with Five."

"Damn right," answered Ward. "I have an apparently unreasonable ambition to stay a little longer on this earth. MI5 aren't helping my prospects much."

"If you see Peter, I think he'll be able to sort it all out and put a stop to Messenger. Thank God you managed to get Lucy back."

"Don't worry, I'll see your man, but it will have

to be on my terms. We've risked too much already.
I have a feeling that most of my nine lives have been
used up."

"Very well. Tell me what you want to do. Alternatively you could contact him direct. He has a room
in the Cabinet Office."

"If he wants to see me, he'll have to do as I say.
I'll tell him how to make contact if he comes to this
telephone kiosk tomorrow afternoon."

"Where are you?"

"In South Kensington Tube Station, the box at
the eastern end. He can check the number to make
sure he's got the right place. I'll call him here at
four o'clock exactly and give my instructions."

"Agreed," said Green. "Take all the precautions
you need. I know it'll work out. Tell me what
happens." With that he rang off, leaving Ward and
Lucy curious.

"So what was all that about?" asked Lucy. "Are
you determined to commit suicide?"

Ward shut the door of the telephone kiosk behind
them. "I'm no keener than you are on a return visit
to the Transit van special, but we can't ignore
what Green says. He reckons the Prime Minister
is involved."

"All that means," Lucy insisted, "is that instead
of being a martyr for democracy in the fight against
socialism, you'll end up the unsung hero of the

British Civil Service's determination to keep its skeletons intact."

"Not if I can help it. As I see it, we have two alternatives: either we accept that the Security Service is infiltrated and therefore dominated by ex-Nazis, or at least people susceptible to Soviet blackmail, or else we come to terms with the fact that Messenger is playing some kind of dangerous game – one that leaves the likes of you and me completely expendable. If he's on the level, then there must be some overridingly good reason to force Messenger and his crew to adopt terror tactics."

"I won't state the obvious," said Lucy, "but at this rate it's getting increasingly difficult to see who's wearing the white hats and who's got the black ones."

"If the Co-ordinator is all that the Colonel says he is, we'll know tomorrow."

11

In a light drizzle, the Co-ordinator of Intelligence and Security in the Cabinet Office emerged from an Austin Princess and walked briskly for the cover of the South Kensington arcade. The time was almost four minutes to four. He stationed himself outside the telephone box at the eastern end of the concourse and stepped inside moments later when the telephone rang.

"Wilkins," he answered.

"Can you tell me your exact date of birth?" asked Ward immediately.

Without hesitation the older man answered, "Fifteenth of April, nineteen fourteen. I see you've done your homework."

"If you want to meet me, look in the S–Z directory in the box you're in now. There's an envelope there;

inside are your instructions. Don't talk to anyone. You'll be under observation from the moment you leave the box. That's all."

The Co-ordinator smiled inwardly as he replaced the handset onto its rest and lifted up the S–Z London telephone directory. Instinctively glancing around him to see if he could spot anyone watching, he opened the plain, unaddressed envelope he found and read the instructions quickly:

"Go straight down to the District Line platform and take the first train to Wimbledon. Do not attempt to communicate these instructions to any third person. Get off at the fourth stop and make your way to the entrance of the station. Turn left and keep walking until you see another telephone-box on the opposite side of the road. Wait there for further directions. If for some reason you are unable to keep the rendezvous, I will call this kiosk again at the same time tomorrow."

Sir Peter Wilkins hadn't travelled by tube for some time, and certainly had not indulged in basic tradecraft for a decade. He felt a surge of youthful enthusiasm, qualified by a reluctant respect for Captain Ward, late of the Royal Green Jackets, as he consulted a London Underground wall-map to see where his destination was to be. He found the Wimbledon line and traced his finger towards South Kensington; the fourth station from South

Kensington was Fulham Broadway. Even if he had taken the precaution of having all calls to the box monitored, which would have been possible in spite of the short notice, he would have been obliged to carry a walkie-talkie to let anyone else know where he was headed. The good captain, he thought to himself, had been thorough. It's surprising, he concluded, what deceitful skills a soldier could pick up in Northern Ireland.

Sir Peter made his way down to the platform and let the first train, a Circle Line, go past. After a seven-minute wait, a train rumbled into the station bearing the Wimbledon plate. As he stepped into the second carriage he took a good look at his companions; only three others had joined the train and any one of them could be one of Messenger's operatives. Naturally he hadn't bothered to inform the DGSS of the meeting, but he was aware that Colonel Green might have passed on details to Messenger . . . part of the uncertain world we inhabit, he considered. Certainly his own staff had been instructed to keep away from the area, but there again, with so many interests involved, it was difficult to predict who might want to barge in.

Wilkins stepped off the train at Fulham Broadway, making sure that he did so just as the doors were beginning to close. Only one other person had got off, a coloured woman with a big Tesco bag.

Not likely, he thought, but possible. He paused for a moment to let her get clear of the platform and then he walked slowly towards the escalator. She didn't hesitate for a minute. At the gate at the top he surrendered his ticket to the collector and strolled, umbrella in hand, to the entrance of the arcade. He emerged into the Fulham Road at almost exactly twenty-one minutes past four, and turned left, walking towards Chelsea. Suddenly he began to feel rather like a target. If he had been followed by anyone, now was the time it would show. There hadn't been enough time for a car to make the journey from South Kensington without attracting attention; that left the possibility of a team directed from some central position. Ward had definitely done his homework, it being well-known that portable radios are notoriously unreliable in tunnels.

In spite of this reassurance he still felt vulnerable. The last time he'd felt anything like this had been some ten years ago in Saigon, and even there he'd always had protection outside the Embassy compound. His old instincts made him size up the newspaper-vendor outside Lloyds Bank and the driver of the black cab cruising past, his meter showing he was engaged although there was no one in the back. A sense of exhilaration gave way to a numbing feeling in the small of his back, as though several pairs of eyes were piercing into him.

He ambled along the road towards the football ground, becoming increasingly aware of the other pedestrians. He stopped for a second outside a newsagents to watch the reflections in the plate-glass window. There didn't seem to be anyone taking an interest in his progress; none of the tell-tale signs, no pedestrian pausing to light a cigarette, no scruffy van pulling into the kerb. He walked on, keeping an eye open for a red telephone box, but on the other side of the road there were only a few once-pleasant buildings now being redeveloped. He walked on past the football ground and crossed Stamford Bridge. He had rather assumed that the kiosks would be closer to the station, but he'd seen none. The traffic flowing west was gradually building up but he tried to memorize the cars as they went past in case the same one passed twice. He continued down the Chelsea side of the bridge and spotted a pair of post-office red boxes set back from the road beside a boarded-up church. A girl was hunched over the telephone in one of the boxes . . . the other one was free. Almost as he got to the door he heard it ring. Pulling open the heavy-framed door, he answered the call and heard the pips of a pay-phone on the other end. A girl's voice told him to walk on along the Fulham Road and take the first turning on the right into Hortensia Road. He should then turn right again into the King's Road and head for the next telephone box. The line went dead.

Sir Peter followed the instructions, with just a hint of impatience, and walked down Hortensia Road, past Chelsea School. As he reached the corner of the King's Road, a yellow Ford Cortina drew up and Ward poked his head out of the passenger's window.

"Good evening, Sir Peter," he said, "I gather you want to see me?"

Wilkins walked around the front of the car and climbed in. As he did so, the girl who had been in the coin-box next door to him approached the car and got silently into the back.

"I don't think you know my sister, Sir Peter," he said. He smiled rather nervously at the grey-haired man.

"How do you do, my dear," he responded. Ward leaned over and casually frisked the Co-ordinator. "I hope you'll forgive this little formality but I've become a little paranoid recently, as I'm sure you can appreciate."

"What do you propose now?" asked Sir Peter. "You've dragged me half-way across London for this. Are we permitted to speak now?"

"Please don't think me completely uncivilized," replied Ward as he let out the clutch and turned east into the King's Road, "I thought we might go and have a quiet drink. There's a place down the road where we won't be disturbed." They travelled in silence until they got to Gilston Road, where the two men got out.

"There's a wine-bar just here which should suit us," said Ward as he led the way through the late-afternoon throng and into the sudden peace of the Nose Bag. They selected a rough wooden table away from the window and ordered two coffees from the hovering student waitress.

"When I spoke to Colonel Green yesterday, he said that you might be able to help me," started Ward. "I'm sorry about all that cloak-and-dagger performance, but I'm not high on the government's popularity list at the moment."

"Do you trust me?" asked Wilkins, taking a sip from his cup.

"Sir Peter, I know very little about you, if you want me to answer truthfully. There's not a lot in *Who's Who* and I don't know much about the role of the Co-ordinator."

"Well, that's a good start," commented Wilkins. "You're not supposed to know much about me."

"And as for trusting you," continued Ward, "the last time I met a man in MI5, I nearly wound up choking to death with carbon-monoxide poisoning."

"Not much in the way of encouragement," admitted Wilkins.

"If I was guilty of espionage, I would understand that Messenger's men were justified in nailing me into a coffin but the fact is that their behaviour is proof enough that much, if not all, of the Security Service has been infiltrated."

"Is your evidence the Blue List?" asked the Co-ordinator.

"A part of it, yes. From the moment that fighter was brought up in Cowes there's been an all-out campaign to bury me and the List. The diver who organized the recovery has apparently 'gone on an extended holiday' and can't be contacted. The Naval officer in Portsmouth who claimed the wreck for the Admiralty has been posted elsewhere and is also 'beyond reach'. Add to that the probable murder of an eminent historian, an abduction and an attempted murder, and you can begin to see how one might take these things personally."

"What do you believe is the significance of the Blue List?" asked Sir Peter.

"At first, I had no idea that the List *was* a list. It was just a few scraps of film covered with a German cipher. It was Dr Six in Germany who told me that it was a list. From that moment I assumed that a few of the people on the List were still alive and quite anxious to have their past indiscretion, their flirtation with Nazism, remain a secret. Obviously, they had an interest in putting the List right back in the sea. If, as Six claimed, the people on the List were influential enough to reach into the top levels of Churchill's government, then it's not difficult to imagine what influential positions they hold today. When I approached Coleman to break the cipher, I warned him to be discreet. Obviously the sudden involvement of the Security Service can only point to their complicity. The names on the List included those of men right at the seat of power in the intelligence world.

"They were extreme right-wingers in the late thirties and forty years later they're still hiring thugs to cover up the plot. If the professor was murdered, then they had a hand in it . . . "

Sir Peter listened quietly to Ward and occasionally raised his eyebrows or rubbed at his stubbly moustache with a nicotine-stained forefinger. When Ward had finished, the Co-ordinator was silent for a few moments and then said: "In any kind of a democracy there comes a time when you can no longer rely on conventional tactics and certain compromises have to be made."

"Am I one of those compromises?" asked Ward. "Or is Lucy?"

"Neither of you is, but you came close to being one," he replied. "You are talking about the lives of two individuals being at stake. You know as well as I do that those sort of terms are meaningless to the Russians."

"This has little to do with the Russians," countered Ward. "This is apparently our own counter-espionage service, not the KGB, although I admit it's a little difficult to tell the difference these days."

"The Security Service cannot remain a mere defensive organization," explained Sir Peter. "It is a practical impossibility for them to be mending holes and patching up cracks in security all over the country. Certainly there is an investigation branch for just that purpose but if we were to wait for breaches and then act, we would be playing entirely into the Russians' hands. Ever since the days of the First World War, the Service has always taken the initiative, maintained the offensive. It's a variation on the old principle that the best form of defence is attack. You probably know quite a lot about the 'Double Cross' operations during the last war; your Blue List is a relic of those days. In normal circumstances the Security Service wouldn't be much interested by your digging, unless perhaps you were going to endanger the life of one of our retired agents. Unfortunately the Blue List has a direct bearing on a current operation and that is the basic explanation for what has happened."

"So when Sir David warned me off originally,

he wasn't just protecting himself and his dead brother?"

"It would be difficult to exaggerate the importance of our operation. It is so secret that, apart from myself and the Prime Minister, only the Head of the Secret Intelligence Service and the last two Secretaries to the Cabinet are in the know.

"Please let me assure you, before you sound off about Whitehall cabals and mandarins plotting, that the secrecy is essential not only to keep alive the operation, but to ensure that for the next decade we retain the upper hand in the intelligence field. So far we have been successful. Your activity, combined with Sir David rather underestimating your capability for survival, has jeopardized all of that. I'm unwilling to elaborate further; too much has been said already. In case you're not entirely satisfied, I've been authorized to give you this letter from the Prime Minister. You may read it here but you can't take it away. If you require further confirmation, you can telephone Downing Street."

"I'm grateful for what you've done," said Ward, "but I'm afraid it's all a little late. I appreciate that you're not bundling me into the back of a van," Ward ignored Sir Peter's grimace, "but you don't seem to realize that I've read the Blue List. When Professor Coleman cracked the German cipher, he made a clean copy of the List and hid it from the

Security boy-scouts. We managed to find it, and handing it over to the Israelis was the price of my survival. They have a clean version too."

Wilkins looked thoughtful and replaced the Prime Minister's letter in his overcoat pocket. "That's not necessarily the end of the world," he said casually, "but I must have all the copies of the List. Are there any others circulating?"

"Only the one with Mossad. But I've still read the List."

"So you reckon you know what the current operation is?"

"I think I've a pretty fair idea. You've hinted that it started during the war, or even earlier, and it's still absolutely vital. One name on that List links up with that and the need for this extreme secrecy."

"I won't deny it. The man at the centre of the operation is at risk every day of the year. He has made a truly historic sacrifice for the West, one that won't be known for at least a generation. He must be protected at all costs and so must the work he has achieved. Your death would be a small and insignificant event compared to what's at stake. If the Russians, who incidentally are always alive to the possibility of the operation, should become aware of what has happened, the whole effort has been largely in vain. So much has been gained that it would be madness to throw it all away."

"How can you prove to me that Kim Philby is still an active operation?"

Sir Peter Wilkins paused for a few moments. "Since you insist on knowing, I appear to have little alternative but to explain. Please remember that this knowledge may well put you in more danger than the Blue List ever did."

"I accept that," replied Ward, "but if I am to believe that the country I served in Ulster has not got a completely rotten core, I'll have to know, however reluctant you are to tell me. I reckon I can piece together quite a lot. Mossad should be able to fill me in on the rest. Only I may not believe it unless I hear it from the horse's mouth, so to speak."

"Very well, but on your own head be it. What I'm going to tell you now will remain secret for the rest of your lifetime. I consider you responsible and enterprising enough for you to realize its full import. Tell others at your peril."

"I accept your terms," said Ward grimly.

"Most of the names on the List were recruited either in this country or on visits to Berlin during the early thirties. They were people from various walks of life, but all with a common interest in the Nazi system. Naturally MI5 penetrated the front organizations quite early on, which resulted in the expulsion of several of the key German undercover men. One was Doctor Thost, a personal friend of Goebbels and the London correspondent of several Nazi newspapers. He and his colleagues spent their time building up useful contacts with sympathizers within the British circles of power. In spite of our penetration, Thost was fairly successful; he and Doctor Rosel, the Partei District Leader for Central London, managed to accumulate an impressive group of disaffected patriots or traitors.

"Mosley's British Union of Fascists and William Joyce's National Socialist League provided ample volunteers, as did the mushrooming right-wing, anti-Semitic clubs and the groups of Irish, Scottish and Welsh Nationalist extremists.

"By the time war broke out, MI5 had achieved a spectacular success. Their round-up of Category A, B and C suspects and aliens before special tribunals left the German military intelligence service without much assistance in the British Isles. Canaris struggled on, as has been well-documented. What was less well-known was that the SD assault on England was thought in Berlin, at least, to be thoroughly established. Their list of potential collaborators included a certain H. A. R. Philby, a war correspondent in Spain for *The Times*, one of a number of people connected with pro-Nazi organizations in London.

"At the time, no one knew about the SD list but the Abwehr soon began laying down the basic intelligence groundwork for the invasion of Britain. Most of the four hundred-odd spies on the Abwehr books in 1939 were picked up through the 18B Detention regulations, as were a lot of the SD contacts. A few, though, survived and they were supplemented in the days running up to Operation Sea Lion by agents parachuted into the country. These hapless men and women formed the backbone of the Double Cross game. But even Admiral Canaris' eager young officers weren't to be fooled by the radio reports from England. On several occasions they sought, and got, confirmation that their agents were in place and operating normally.

"In the first year of the war, the SD took on the dual role of planning the government of Britain after a successful German invasion, and of acting as watchdog on the military intelligence service. It was not long before MI5's Double Cross became active, turning the variety of under-trained enthusiasts and plain crooks who were sent over to spy, into reasonably plausible agents. The process of capturing and persuading the agents wasn't too impossible, but what did prove difficult was keeping the SD at bay. Fortunately their interest in Britain waned after the cancellation of Sea Lion, but up until that point they retained an unhealthy interest in everything that was going on, both in the Abwehr and MI5.

"MI5's Double Cross had been initiated some considerable time before the war and the officers involved were always acutely aware that if just one of their turned spies was betrayed, the whole system would be in danger. Furthermore, because the object of the exercise was deception, the Germans might learn a good deal of the Allies' true intentions if they were able to determine what we were willing, literally, to give away. Of course, it was all fraught with danger, but at the time it seemed to work. In order to keep the profit and loss account balanced, several juicy pieces of good intelligence were included from time to time, but there was a continuing possibility that the SD would learn what was going on. To guard against this, a second Double Cross was built up, in some cases without the active co-operation of the subjects, to fool the SD. The difference between the two was that whereas the Abwehr was dealing with people of a generally low intelligence and high ego, the SD already had in place a group of committed and influential people, politicians who couldn't be browbeaten into espionage by the bright boys of MI5.

"By 1941, the scenario was complete. The Double Cross operation was well under way and the Nazi top brass believed that there was a traitorous groundswell within the United Kingdom that could be activated at almost any time. MI5, of course, had a fair idea of the composition of the Blue List, but could only rely on their own investigations. As it turned out, only a few of those the SD had selected to support a German *coup* in London were actually prepared to betray their country. Mosley instructed his followers to remain loyal and only a single aide, a man named Tester, disobeyed him. Plenty of others were put out of the way of temptation on the Isle of Man for the duration, but as a rule the Blackshirts denied Germany active help.

"Several of those named on the Blue List were approached through the Spanish Embassy in London to carry out apparently harmless chores for the SD, usually in the way of providing political reviews and social gossip for the eventual consumption of an interested, but unaligned, audience. One such person was Kim Philby, then still a *Times* correspondent, but on the brink of joining Special Operations Executive for war work.

"The contact was immediately reported via Baker Street to the Secret Intelligence Service and in particular, MI5's Tommy Harris. In order to encourage the connection, Philby joined Felix Cowgill's counter-espionage section with special responsibility for the Iberian Peninsula.

"By 1944, Philby had proved himself to be an exceptionally gifted controller of agents and also skilled in manoeuvre through the minefields of inter-office rivalries. With his work directed against the Germans, Kim maintained a close relationship with senior officers of MI5 and when he was asked to head a special anti-Soviet section, he was assigned a female officer of unusual qualities.

"Jane Archer had been a career intelligence officer and what made her so important to Philby was that she was the person who had been selected to 'debrief' General Krivitsky, the chief of Soviet operations in Western Europe, who had defected to America in 1937. In her interrogations, she had learned of an informal contact between the young English journalist and the NKVD. When challenged by Guy Liddell, Philby made no attempt to deny his liaison but maintained that it was all fairly innocent. As the emphasis switched in SIS from the Nazis towards the Soviets, so Menzies authorized a build-up in the Philby-Russian link. The Double Cross operation had been so successful when used against the Germans it was thought that a similar scheme might be launched against Moscow.

"Of course, there were several hiccups to start off with. One incident which threatened to smash the plan straight away was the defection of an NKVD officer stationed in Istanbul. In return for protection and asylum, he was offering the names of three Soviet spies in England . . . one of them the head of a counter-espionage section in London. Volkov would have been quite a catch, but Philby's penetration of the KGB was judged to be more important in the long term. In the end it was arranged that an indiscreet warning should be given to the Russians over a tapped telephone line. This, combined with Kim's messages to his contact, was enough to have poor Volkov picked up and shipped back to Mother Russia.

"The danger of defectors 'blowing' Philby to the West was always present and it was good fortune that the NKVD tightened up their security later on, so that when a cipher clerk, Igor Gouzenko, defected to Ottawa the same year, he had no knowledge of the traitor in SIS. He did, however, manage to put the finger on Nunn May and remove some of the pressure that was being applied to our decrypting operations. We had been decoding Russian signals for some time, and with Kim's help managed to nail Klaus Fuchs and the atom ring in America. Bletchley had been breaking the Russians' traffic from the Consulate General to Moscow since early 1944 and this gave invaluable clues to spies already exposed by Philby. Naturally we had to keep the Philby source a secret, so on a couple of occasions we had to tolerate known Soviet agents, wherever possible feeding them with misinformation."

"Were Burgess and Maclean also doubles?" asked Ward.

"Not that they ever knew. Maclean had never been a close friend of Kim's, rather more an acquaintance from their university days. Maclean had been identified as a Russian source shortly after the war and code-named 'Homer'. Immediately it was known the Head of Chancery in the Washington Embassy was a Russian agent, steps were taken to isolate him from atomic secrets. He was Secretary to the Anglo-American Combined Policy Committee on Atomic Development, which entitled him to a fairly free hand, but his permanent pass to the Atomic Energy Commission HQ was withdrawn. In 1948 he was transferred to a less sensitive post in the Cairo Embassy.

"The danger for us was that in May 1950, Maclean suspected that the net was closing in on him as he had less and less access to secret information. He suffered a traumatic breakdown and was brought back to London for several months' treatment. In the end it was clear that he was 'blown' to almost everyone, including the Russias. Our problem was that he was in a good position to betray our own man, Philby to us, so it became necessary to have the Russians remove him before he could jeopardize the operation. Burgess was instructed to contact Maclean and give him his route back to Moscow because the Russians were aware of the high level of surveillance covering the FO man passed as fit by the SIS psychiatrist. The plan didn't go completely smoothly, as Burgess, on the spur of the moment, also decided to flee.

"Although this removed the danger of two minor sources who might at any time confess to the British that they were part of a ring that included the SIS link-man with the CIA, it had also made the game more difficult. Philby had had very close ties with Burgess, including sharing a house with him in Washington, and he quickly came under American suspicion, which eventually led to his resignation from the Foreign Office.

"Unfortunately, contact also had to be broken off with the Russians who became desperate to find out whether their star had come through the MI5 interrogations, but they were unwilling to compromise him by organizing a meeting. Our handling of the situation was a success and the Soviets were certainly ready to take their source on board again when yet another defector, this time from the Soviet Embassy in Canberra, announced that Burgess and Maclean were not mere homosexuals caught by the FO with their trousers down, as had been suggested in the newspapers, but that both of them had been long-term spies recruited at university. Furthermore it was hinted that a third man had tipped off the two diplomats that they were under suspicion, which aided their escape.

"Of course the truth of the matter was that our Double Cross operation was once again at risk. We couldn't tell everyone to keep quiet, thus warning off the Russians, so we were obliged to come into the open. An MP was leaked Kim's name as the third man and reluctantly the Prime Minister, Harold Macmillan, defended him in the House of Commons.

"That the KGB would still be interested in him after all that was practically beyond belief, but they were. In order to establish exactly what his standing was, they kidnapped and interrogated the chief of West German intelligence, Otto John, putting particular emphasis on his knowledge of intelligence operations involving Philby. John protested that he believed Philby to be loyal to SIS, and the Russians were convinced that their spy had maintained his cover successfully.

"The next stage, after having Kim publicly cleared, was to infiltrate him back into Soviet confidence and the opportunity arose when Kim was appointed 'stringer' by the *Observer* and the *Economist* in Beirut in August 1956.

"His SIS assignment was deliberately to avoid contact with the Russians . . . to play hard to get. He was to limit himself to Arab affairs and his reintroduction into the field was a closely guarded secret. In communicating with London he had to go through the Beirut Head of Station, the only SIS officer in the know in the Middle East. For the next six years, Philby operated more or less on his own, feeding his Soviet masters with a mixture of fact and fiction and effectively checkmating each of their moves in the super-sensitive playground of the great powers, the Middle East. The game could have continued on much longer, especially since the Russians were so desperate for SIS intelligence after the arrest of George Blake in 1961.

"In spite of their apparently insatiable appetite for SIS intelligence, the Russians remained very wary of Philby in this his last period in the field. The delicate double-agent balance of profit and loss had to be handled with great care. We were reluctant, due to the nature of the operation, to sacrifice too much for the benefit of the opposition, and they themselves were acutely aware that they were dealing with a man exonerated by the then Prime Minister.

"The operation then moved towards its final and most crucial stage. The Russians knew that Blake had made a full confession of his activities, but they couldn't be sure if he had been aware of Philby's deception. The two double agents had met several times in Beirut shortly before Blake's final recall to London and the Moscow centre suspected that their star from Berlin might have compromised Philby. Worse, though, was to follow. Anatoli Golitsin, a senior KGB officer, defected to the Americans early in 1962 and there could be no doubt for the Russians that Kim had been well and truly blown. Golitsin was secretly flown to England where he filled in details of several Soviet operations. The interrogation resulted in the arrest of Vassall, a homosexual Admiralty clerk, and pressure from the centre for Philby to flee to Moscow before the British came and arrested him. Philby was now in an awkward position: if he went to Moscow, he knew that he would be cut off entirely from our protection and there would be little chance of ever returning to the West. If we revealed the Double Cross, it would have made much of the previous twenty years' deception meaningless. One thing was certain: Kim could not remain in Beirut. The CIA, who hadn't been party to the operation, were livid, and determined to finish him off once and for all. They had been aware that Philby was an identified risk from the moment they'd photographed him paying a visit to Colonel Abel, the Russian masterspy, in New York some fourteen years earlier. At that time they agreed to leave the problem to the SIS, provided Philby was never given access to American secrets. The other condition was that he be kept out of the United States . . . terms that the Double Cross operators accepted.

"Now, though, the cat was out of the bag and

everyone was after him. The breaking-point was reached when the Lebanese chief of security offered to have him bumped off or arrested for transport back to England.

"The position was impossible and with the greatest reluctance Philby agreed to make use of the escape route provided for him by his KGB contact, though not before there had been a lot of heartsearching. It was a tense situation, and Kim was under enormous strain. The Beirut Head of Station, an old friend of Kim's who had acted as his controller since 1960, returned briefly to London over Christmas of 1962, to confer on what action should be taken and then explained to Kim what his mission would be. Only days later, on 23 January, Kim slipped aboard a Polish cargo ship, the *Dalmatova*, bound for Odessa.

"The ultimate and most dangerous part of Philby's deception began. For six months he underwent the most punishing debriefing far from Moscow, but he succeeded in gaining the confidence of the KGB and after a brief period with the News Agency, *Novosti* (officially his Moscow cover), he was appointed to the Dzherzhinsky Square headquarters of the KGB with responsibility to advise on espionage matters in Western Europe."

"The final goal?" Ward asked.

"If you like, yes, but he will always remain at risk until he retires or is brought back."

"And what was the danger of the Blue List?"

"It became fashionable for the MI5 heroes of Double Cross to publish somewhat exaggerated accounts of their wartime activities, which posed an awkward problem for us. We were keen for the Secret Services to get just a little credit for some of its successes, especially when there was so much ridicule being aimed at the Services. Unfortunately the two outstanding successes, the breaking of the Enigma cipher machine and the build-up of our code-breaking operations simply had to remain secret for as long as possible. Eventually, Winterbotham was – reluctantly – given permission to publish an account of Bletchley, and that rather opened the floodgates. At about the same time, there were several journalists probing what had happened to all the German spies sent to England during the last war and a picture of the Double Cross deception operation began to emerge. Sir John Masterman wrote his version of the Double Cross system, and that raised more fears for our man in Moscow. In order to counter all the publicity, we frequently encouraged journalists, some of them ex-SIS themselves, to write about Philby, laying particular emphasis on the length of service he gave to the Russians and the devastation that he managed to create.

"The difficulty about the Blue List was that a

number of those on the List were approached by the Soviet Secret Service after the war and were threatened with exposure unless they co-operated. Of course we cannot know for certain how many people experienced this as we never had a copy of the List, but a number of contacts were discreetly reported to MI5. Each time the instructions were the same: appear to be ready to help . . . we'll operate you as a 'double'. In the years following the war, a substantial part of the Russian espionage effort was entirely misdirected. If they even suspected that this was the case, Kim would be at serious risk and thirty years of work would be up the spout. It remains an absolute priority that officially the Blue List should never fall into the hands of the authorities in England. How the Russians got hold of it we don't know; its power would be lost overnight if Moscow knew we also had a copy."

"The List came from Gestapo Muller," said Ward. "My friend in Mossad said they had suspected he'd been kidnapped from some hideout in South America and shipped behind the Iron Curtain. He at least had had the foresight to keep a copy of the Blue List. There were only three others. Two were burnt in an air-raid on Berlin, and one was submerged under the Solent."

"Obviously the Russians never found out about Captain Messenger's version."

"That would make sense," observed Ward, "but it's just about all that does. If all the fine, upstanding citizens did eventually come to MI5 and co-operate with another Double Cross, only on a bigger scale, how did they explain away their take-over plot in 1940?"

Sir Peter looked puzzled. "What plot?" he asked.

"Their plan to seize Paddock at the first sign of invasion."

"I'm afraid I'm not with you," replied the Co-ordinator. "You'd better explain."

Ward briefly recounted how he'd "brought a little pressure to bear" on Dr Six, forcing him to reveal a Soviet plan over thirty years old to stage a coup from within Churchill's secret War Room.

"Have you any evidence that this place, Paddock, even existed?" asked Wilkins. "I can assure you that I've never heard of it. I think perhaps your Dr Six felt obliged to give you your money's worth."

"Supposing I told you that my sister had actually been to Paddock, a matter of days ago, and that it does exist?"

"Then I suppose I would have to believe her," replied Wilkins thoughtfully.

"Correct me if I'm wrong, but if Paddock is there, and there was a Soviet plot . . . then some of your Double Cross performers have, in the

immortal words of *Private Eye*, been 'slightly less than frank'?"

"That is a possible conclusion, I admit," said Sir Peter gravely.

"That is a problem that I leave to you," said Ward easily. "It seems to me that the double-agent game is rather too dangerous. The margins between truth and deception have a habit of getting blurred at the edges. Tell me this . . . Philby worked throughout your operation in that grey area. Can you really be sure which side he was on . . . or is still on for that matter?"

"This Paddock business puts a new complexion on it all," muttered Wilkins thoughtfully. For the first time he seemed deflated, unsure of himself. "If there was a joint Soviet–Nazi scheme to take over the government in 1940, I have never heard of it. Come to that, I've never heard of Paddock. Are you absolutely certain of your information?"

"There's no doubt in my mind," replied Ward. "The way I see it, Messenger and his lot were acting for the NKVD right from the word go. All the subsequent Double Cross palaver was nothing more than a blind enabling the Soviets to conduct their espionage with a free hand. The events you have described, using double agents to mislead Moscow, can be interpreted in an entirely different way. Far from being a patriot willing to make the ultimate sacrifice, your precious Philby has conned the system rotten. He must have a good chuckle every time he communicates with London, if he still does."

"He does," groaned Wilkins. "If – and I'm not saying you're right – there was an undiscovered Soviet plan for a *putsch* in 1940, it would mean that most of MI5's postwar activities might have been completely and deliberately counter-productive. It's too ghastly to contemplate."

"All the more reason to put an end to it straight-away. If you won't, I will. It's time Messenger and his ilk were dealt with, once and for all."

Wilkins hesitated, and then got to his feet deci-sively, reaching into his pocket for some coins which he placed beside the empty coffee cups. In the same movement he picked Ward's Xerox of the Blue List from the table. "Let me handle this. I shall have to make some rather urgent enquiries, but come and see me tomorrow. Don't come to my office. Meet me at White's Club just after midday. I'll have to consider what you have told me. In the meantime, please don't do anything precipitate. Too much is at stake. Do I have your word?"

Ward reluctantly gave his consent. "A few hours won't make much difference to me. I'll be there tomorrow."

While Ward and Wilkins had been deliberating,

Lucy had been parked on yellow lines fifty yards up the road, with the engine running just as a precaution. She saw the older man leave the Nose Bag, and then edged her Mini closer to the wine bar's entrance. Moments later her brother emerged and climbed in. From force of habit she started to drive towards Thurloe Street and on the way Ward explained the position.

"Wilkins seemed okay, genuinely shocked by the implications of the Paddock plot, which was all news to him. He had come well prepared though, a really detailed cover story tailor-made by Messenger. He even had me believing some of it at one stage. But the gaping flaw in the whole affair is the Soviet involvement in the *coup* attempt. That really had an impact."

Lucy looked quizzical. "How did he account for Inverlair and what had happened to me?"

"He didn't even try. He had been briefed with an elaborate tale, which no doubt came from Messenger originally, which involved MI5 running agents against the Soviets via the Blue List. A rather complicated Double Cross operation that is somewhat undermined by what we know was to have happened at Paddock. He seemed a little sceptical at first but I think he was convinced by the end. It looks as though everyone has been taken in by Messenger's version of events. Even the Prime Minister."

"So will he have Messenger arrested?"

"I doubt it. I'm to meet Wilkins tomorrow, and I've promised not to approach Messenger again until then, but," he added darkly, "there's nothing to prevent us from making a few contingency plans, anticipating the worst. Messenger won't rest until he has recovered the Blue List, and that's a weakness we can exploit. Care for a drink? Up at the Bull and Bush?"

Lucy grinned mischievously, and without bothering to answer, turned the Mini north, towards Hampstead Heath.

12

Just after noon the following day Ward sauntered along Piccadilly, past the Ritz Hotel, smartly dressed in a pinstripe suit, wearing his regimental tie. He crossed over the top of St James's Street and then turned down towards Pall Mall. After just a few yards he climbed the steps up to the unmarked entrance to London's most exclusive club, and pushed his way through the two mahogany and glass double doors, into the hall. As he entered, the uniformed porter leaned through the hatch from his narrow cubicle.

"May I help you, sir?" he asked, recognizing that Ward was not one of his members.

"I've an appointment with Sir Peter Wilkins. My name is Ward."

The porter consulted an unseen notepad and then

asked Ward to follow him. They walked across the hall, past a chattering news-service printer and through a doorway into a larger lobby, dominated by a magnificent red-carpeted staircase. They continued past the stairs, and turned left into a narrow, passage-like alcove filled with half a dozen dark-suited members. So this was the famous White's bar, thought Ward. He saw Wilkins at the end of the bar, cashing a cheque. At the porter's approach he turned to acknowledge Ward, and offered him a drink.

"Two Bloody Marys please, Morris," ordered Wilkins. As the barman turned to mix the cocktails, Wilkins whispered conspiratorially to Ward, "Morris knows more secrets than most statesmen. He hears all the gossip, and he goes back to when Sir Stewart Menzies used to run MI6 from this very spot."

Ward was unimpressed, but decided against any remarks on the lines that that fact explained a lot about MI6's record. When the drinks arrived Wilkins took them both and gestured for Ward to follow him. They moved away from the bar and into a long billiards room. At one end was a group of leather armchairs and sofas gathered around an ornate fireplace. None were occupied, and Wilkins selected a small table between two of the battered but comfortable chairs and placed the glasses carefully on the top.

"We shan't be disturbed in here," he explained. "It only fills up after lunch, when the racing starts on the television." Ward glanced across at the large TV set which looked somewhat incongruous in such a grand, colonnaded room.

"And now to business," Wilkins said abruptly. "I saw the Prime Minister this morning, and I have a suggestion to put to you." Ward listened attentively.

"I am inclined to believe everything you told me yesterday," he continued, "and I for one do not subscribe to the notion that you are deranged. Nor do I think you are an irrational conspiracy theorist. The key, of course, is the Paddock plot, call it what you will. I have done some preliminary checking, and there was indeed a second, secret War Room that conforms to your account. Churchill hardly used it, but that is immaterial. If there truly was a Soviet scheme to mount a *coup* in 1940, we are all agreed that it would radically alter our perception of MI5's supposedly effective Double Cross operations against the Russians. However," he paused, "there is no proof of any plot, and no proof of Sir David's involvement."

"But if there was proof –" interjected Ward.

"Proof comes in two varieties. The legal kind, for the lawyers, and the intelligence sort, as relied upon by counter-intelligence agencies. We need either if we are to act, and in terms of Messenger's involvement, we're talking of something more tangible than the presence of his name on the Blue List. But if there were proof, then I have been authorized to take certain action."

"For reasons of self-preservation I have a plan to smoke Messenger out," confided Ward, "but I would have to know what you have in mind for him. My reservoir of trust and goodwill towards the authorities has been exhausted, I'm afraid."

Wilkins looked uncomfortable, but understanding. "Very well. I accept your terms. If I disclose the government's thinking on this, I will need your assurance that it will go no further." Ward nodded in consent. "I will also need your undertaking that nothing you will do in consequence will embarrass me, or compromise our contact. I only agreed to see you because Colonel Green is an old and trusted colleague, whose judgement I value. You mustn't let me down."

Ward stirred uneasily. "I will not abuse your confidence, but I can't be expected to give guarantees about my behaviour. Have you forgotten, Messenger tried to have me knocked off? He very nearly succeeded, and he has certainly wrecked whatever reputation I may have had by forcing me to sign a statement admitting I was unbalanced. If any of this comes out, the government will be embarrassed."

"Well, you still can't be sure that Messenger was definitely responsible for all your, er . . . misfortunes. There may have been an element of over-zealousness on the part of subordinates."

"But nothing to incriminate Messenger," suggested Ward.

"I wasn't going to say that," said Wilkins defensively. Clearly there was part of his proposal that he anticipated would not be received well by the man beside him. "Messenger may indeed be guilty of misconduct, even heinous crimes, but our options are limited. That is why you could be so vital. We hope you will agree to convey an offer of immunity from prosecution, in return for his full co-operation." He went on quickly before Ward could object. "I've talked this over with the Attorney-General, and he feels there is no real chance of obtaining an admissible confession. It could be withdrawn at any time, and obviously he would need a pretty powerful incentive to reveal the truth. There is also the public interest to consider. A trial might have very damaging consequences. No, the only solution is to gain his help and recover some of the lost ground. If he were really committed, we might even be able to turn this sorry episode to our advantage. The Prime Minister agrees."

"So another traitor gets off scot-free?"

"Immunity is a useful weapon," countered Wilkins. "The Soviets would be the first to acknowledge how effective it is. It is the one inducement we have that can be used to break into their clandestine organizations without tipping them off. It's an opportunity to turn the Double Cross back against Moscow. You yourself acknowledged how vulnerable the whole arrangement is. If you could trap Messenger, get him to accept immunity, it would be in everyone's best interests, including yours."

"And this is not an offer you want to make to him directly?"

"We can't. Messenger would be bound to deny the allegations and we have no evidence to place before him. As for your testimony, I'm afraid it would be worth very little as evidence. He has made a thorough job of discrediting you in advance. Besides, he may yet be completely innocent. We only have your word for all of this, and I don't suppose the good Doctor Six will be prepared to repeat his story in a public forum, or submit to cross-examination. No, you are our best bet. If you succeed, it will be a major breakthrough and at least we will know the scale of the damage. We might be able to do a few running repairs. But if you fail, we are powerless to act."

Ward thought over Wilkins' proposal. "And how, exactly, am I supposed to tackle Messenger

. . . How do I get close enough to suggest the immunity?"

"That," said Wilkins, "shouldn't present much of an obstacle to someone as young and resourceful as yourself. If your tale is true, that will be the least of your problems."

At that moment the uniformed hall porter reappeared before them and told Wilkins that his lunch guest had arrived. Ward took his cue and, thanking his host for the drink, made his way back to St James's Street, and the real world.

Later the same afternoon, after a second reconnaissance mission to Hampstead equipped with a bolt-cutter and two padlocks, Ward put the finishing touches to a plan he and Lucy had formulated the previous evening. At first, Lucy had been utterly opposed to the scheme suggested by Wilkins.

"All the public-interest stuff is codswallop," she said forcefully. "Messenger deserves rather more than the reassurance that he will never be put in the dock. He's guilty of old-fashioned treachery and back in 1940 he would have been hanged. Why should he be let off now? We have hardly an inkling of what damage he has inflicted on this country in more recent years. He makes Philby look like a novice."

"Wilkins is a realist," stated Ward. "He knows

that a trial means legal evidence, and there is none. Furthermore, Messenger has had years to weave a very plausible cover. Look at the number of people who have been taken in by this double-agent and triple-agent nonsense. Even Wilkins believed it up until yesterday. You should have seen how earnest he was, dropping terms like 'national security' and 'lives at risk'. It all sounds very impressive. The trouble is, we are about the only ones to really know it is all a sham. The authorities can't take a risk with Messenger and give him the third degree. They are powerless to act unless there is something concrete."

"So you're to do their dirty work?" insisted Lucy. "You are being used – we both are."

"Maybe," admitted Ward, "but it's true we do have the one thing that Messenger wants – the Blue List – and he'll be keen to get his hands on it. Trouble is, we won't be safe from him and his cronies until he does. Our only hope of peace is to force Messenger into incriminating himself in such a way that he feels completely threatened. Then we hit him with the immunity. It has to be presented as an attractive, soft option. Once he's hooked, he will have no reason to go after us again. Anyway, Wilkins will be supervising him."

Once Lucy had been persuaded, Ward went over the final details of their plan, and then placed a call to Messenger's country home. The retired Deputy Director-General answered the telephone himself.

"Sir David, this is Michael Ward. Listen carefully, and don't interrupt. I'm willing to make a deal. The Blue List, and all my copies, are yours. They will be in a safe place ready for collection at exactly ten o'clock tomorrow morning."

"Where?" demanded Messenger, apparently quite shocked by Ward's message.

Ward said just one word before he replaced the telephone receiver: "Paddock."

13

Soon after eight the following morning Lucy and Ward sat in her Mini in Wildwood Grove, barely two hundred yards from the Bull and Bush public house on North End Way. On the opposite side of the quiet residential cul-de-sac where they were parked, almost obscured by foliage, was a small squat brick building, barely fifteen feet high. It was windowless, but surrounded by a series of narrow metal slats mounted horizontally. The ugly but functional structure, enclosed by a chain-link fence, had the appearance of an electricity sub-station, of the kind that are so common in London's streets. But this example was nothing to do with any utility. In fact it was all that remained on the surface of a tube station unused since before the war. The original building had been demolished long ago, leaving only the bare minimum above ground to cap the main vertical shaft and to provide ventilation. Directly underneath, a couple of hundred feet down, was the original Bull and Bush Northern Line station. Ward and his sister had paid a visit the previous afternoon.

They had established the exact position of the station deep under Hampstead Heath by travelling back and forth between Golders Green and Hampstead on the tube. Equipped with flashlights, they had fleetingly illuminated the abandoned site by shining their torch beams out of the carriage windows, along the side of the tunnel. Roughly two-thirds of the distance to Golders Green station the monotony of the black tunnel, lined with cables, had given way to grimy tiles, and a short platform. Apart from the distinct change in the sound of the train as it rushed through what remained of the old station, there was nothing to indicate its presence.

Armed with the knowledge that the site was rather closer to the north-western edge of the Heath, Ward and Lucy had toured the few streets in the vicinity to find whatever remained on the surface. The electricity sub-station was the only likely candidate, so bolt-cutters had been bought to deal with the padlocks securing the chain fence and the door into the housing itself. Inside they had found a dark, unlit chamber containing heavy ventilation equipment. Enclosed in a cage, positioned at head height over a deep shaft, was a free-moving extractor fan, idling slowly round on air pressure from below. They negotiated a second steel bulkhead door, and then began a long walk down a steep spiral staircase.

It had taken them a full ten minutes to reach the first of the station's two levels. The lower they went, the louder the sound of the air rushing through the confined space. When a train had thundered through the station on the second level, the noise had been deafening. But apart from the eerie atmosphere, heightened by their belief that the site had not been visited since the war, their explorations were trouble-free.

The station itself conformed to the standard pattern of single mid-line stations of that vintage, with twin northbound and southbound tracks, and a single platform in between serving both. One side gave access to the up line, but the other had been bricked up, leaving a long gallery stretching the length of what had been the down line platform. It had been partitioned off into a series of small rooms where, Ward presumed, the War Cabinet staff were to have been accommodated. The additional construction work consisted mainly of cement blocks, without the benefit of any plasterwork. Evidently wartime austerity had prevented more than a makeshift finish.

The two trespassers had made a thorough inspection of Paddock. None of the doors were locked, although a few were hanging off their hinges. The place had not been vandalized, but its occupants had stripped it of anything that might indicate its secret purpose. Some of the wiring had been ripped off the walls, and in places there were untidy piles of rubbish and obsolete equipment, including a few ancient telephone handsets. In one room, clearly a telephone exchange, what remained of the switching gear was propped in a corner. The floors were all perfectly dry, but covered in a thick layer of filthy dust. It was a scene of desolation and dilapidation, occasionally lit by the tube trains as they shrieked past. Ward had thought it odd that although he could see clearly the passengers crammed into the carriages, and so many of them seemed to be gazing out of the windows, none could see him. Indeed, few could know that only a matter of a few feet from where they were standing, Churchill had once taken refuge from the Luftwaffe. It had been an odd sensation.

It was while they wearily retraced their path up to the surface, taking the stairs slowly, that they had discussed the possibility of luring Messenger back to the scene of the ill-fated Paddock plot.

"Provided he came alone, it's the perfect place to deal with Messenger. There would be no fear of interruption, and whatever gadgets he brought to communicate with his minders, none would work so deep underground," observed Ward. "It's also so completely secure. You couldn't walk along the tracks when the trains were running, and this shaft is easily sealed off. I wouldn't mind locking Messenger in one of the rooms and just leaving him there. No one would ever find him, and it would be rather appropriate retribution."

Now, some thirty-six hours later, Ward and Lucy were back in Wildwood Grove. They were still discussing Paddock's merits as a suitable rendezvous for Messenger.

"It must have been utterly impregnable," remarked Lucy, rather glad that their agreed plan did not call for her to go back underground. "When it was in use it was the deepest tube station in London. It's got the protection of Hampstead Heath on top, and anyway the Northern Line was dug right under all the other tunnels so in one way it's got twice the advantage of the other stations that were used as bomb shelters."

Ward nodded in agreement. "One can see its attractions. But look at the paradox. Its isolation is what made it vulnerable. If the tunnel in and out were blocked, perhaps by sabotaging a train on each line, there was only one emergency exit upwards. Taking control of that would have been child's play unless it had been heavily fortified, and if it had, then its secrecy would have been compromised. I don't suppose much thought was given to local subversion or a *coup d'état*."

"I don't think Churchill would have been able to handle all those stairs. I expect he would have been quite content to wait for the trains to start again," laughed Lucy. "Which route will Messenger use?"

"He'll have to use the tube. He'd have been terribly reluctant to go through all the official channels to get this shaft specially opened up, and I don't really see him scaling the fence and then breaking into the housing. My guess is that he will try and bluff a train driver into stopping a train *en route*. It's risky for him either way but the last thing he wants to do is leave a paper trail linking him to Paddock, today of all days. Anyway, even if he does arrive up here with a key, or accompanied by a man from London Transport, he still won't be able to get in now that we have replaced the locks. If I were in his position, utterly determined to get into Paddock at the appointed time to retrieve the Blue List, I wouldn't want anyone to come in my place. From his point of view, there's too much at stake. If there had been more time I'm sure he would have made elaborate plans and taken lots of counter-measures. But just this once, Messenger has got to work alone."

"I can't believe he would really walk into such an

obvious trap," replied Lucy. "If I were him I'd send a minion."

"But think of the psychology," protested Ward. "I didn't instruct him to come to a certain place at a certain time. I simply said that the Blue List would be there, ready for collection. Now in those circumstances, given that he can't really confide in any of his regular thugs who think they're protecting an elaborate intelligence operation, wouldn't he be more inclined to make the collection himself? He won't want anyone after the event to talk about a visit to a disused Underground station to collect a set of documents. Even with MI5's arcane activities, I bet such a venture would be judged to be a little out of the ordinary, especially if there is a chance that the whole Paddock affair might be revealed at a later stage. Messenger will want no one else involved, and my bet is that he'll come alone. If I'm wrong, we'll have to try another tack, that's all. It won't be the end of the world."

"Will being caught inside Paddock really be enough to make him accept immunity from prosecution?" asked Lucy.

"How will he explain it?" Ward replied. "Officially he knows nothing at all about Paddock, and certainly not its actual location. How did he come by the knowledge? And if he is entirely above-board, why didn't he simply report my strange offer to the authorities? Those are the kind of questions he would have to answer instantly. There would be no time to manufacture cover stories or get outside help. If he turns up he'll be as jumpy as a rabbit and quite isolated. If I can't push him into accepting the immunity when he is at his most vulnerable, in sight of the Blue List, then he never will take it. His very presence will serve to confirm Six's story of the Soviet conspiracy, but he probably doesn't realize how much we know. When I suggested Paddock to him, it must have been quite a bombshell."

"You'll soon see how much of a bombshell," said Lucy, glancing at her watch. "It's time to move."

Ward double-checked his arrangements with Lucy for the last time, making sure she had the number Wilkins had left him in case he did not emerge from Paddock. "Don't come after me," he repeated. "If I'm not back by eleven, call Wilkins. Then he can deal with Messenger." A moment later he had crossed the road and disappeared into Paddock's shaft housing.

With the aid of a powerful torch Ward made his way down the long spiral stairwell to Paddock's lower level. There, among the debris, he found a battered cardboard packing-case on which to place the plain white envelope. It contained a photocopy of the Blue List, sufficient bait, Ward hoped, to lure Messenger into vulnerability. He placed a small flashlight on the box to illuminate the envelope, and then moved across the platform concourse to a conveniently sited cubicle that gave an unobstructed view of the main staircase and the box. Whichever route Messenger chose, Ward would be able to see him approach. He then settled down in the darkness to wait. He calculated it would take a couple of hours, but his reconnaissance work in Ulster had prepared him for his silent vigil.

After the first half-dozen trains had hurtled through Paddock's tunnels, Ward stopped count-ing them. There was nothing to distinguish them, just the perceptible change in pitch of the constant hum of air, then the sudden roar as each set of dull metal carriages thundered along the rails, and the wind of the air being displaced. For the few seconds they passed by the abandoned platform, an eerie flickering light was cast onto the tiled walls. The trains passed in both directions irregularly, until at last one made a slow approach. Ward glanced at the luminous dial of his Rolex. It showed half past ten.

The contrast with the rapid passing traffic made the rumble of the cautiously approaching carriages sound rather sinister, especially as Ward was unable to see the front carriage emerge from the tunnel. All he could see from his hiding-place was the single-beam headlamp lighting up the wall of the station.

until the front of the train drew level. A single door opened, and a tall man stepped out from the driver's compartment carrying a torch. A brief conversation ensued but even though he strained to listen, the revving of the train's electric motors all but drowned the voices. Then the driver's door slammed shut and the train moved off slowly towards Hampstead, leaving the platform in complete darkness. Moments later, as the red rear lamps of the last carriage vanished into the tunnel, the station was returned to the background noise made by the movement of air.

The man on the platform seemed to wait an age, just standing alone in the darkness. Perhaps waiting for his eyes to adjust, pondered Ward. Then he heard footsteps, and saw the torchbeam swing in an arc around the walls. The figure walked the complete length of the platform, as if carrying out an inspection, and then returned towards the staircase where Ward was crouched. The beam probed every corner of the station, and then drew slowly towards the stairs. As it did so, the illuminated envelope became visible, and the torch suddenly focused upon it. Ward knew that this was his cue to reveal himself. Silently he got to his feet and stepped out of the cubicle. As he did so, another train, this time heading towards Golders Green, roared out of the tunnel and shot through the station. Even if Ward had wanted to announce his appearance, the man holding the torch would never have heard him. A moment later Ward's face was bathed in light.

"I rather thought you might be here," said the anonymous figure, still unseen in the darkness behind the torch. "Is this some elaborate game or are you really surrendering the Blue List?"

Ward admired the calm of his adversary. He had not anticipated that Messenger would be so unperturbed. "Let's be clear," he replied, "that's the List all right. But it is the fact that you're here that's really important." He put added emphasis on the "here".

Messenger appeared to nod. "It's certainly appropriate. But you know," he confided, "this is my first visit."

"Maybe," replied Ward, "but you knew where it was. You were part of the plan to mount a *coup* right here in 1940 . . . to isolate Churchill and the War Cabinet. You were involved in a *coup* plot. A Soviet *coup*." Even in the gloom Ward could see Messenger flinch.

"This is a pipe-dream, your talk of plots and *coups*. This place is well-known. I'm surprised it isn't open to the public, like the one under Great George Street."

Ward knew he was bluffing. "The fact that Paddock existed is known to very few. Its actual location is a long-forgotten secret. Yet you never asked. You came straight here. That tells me all I want to know. It shows what you and your brother really were."

Messenger hesitated. "A Soviet plot?" He gestured to the envelope. "We're surely talking of people the Nazis believed might have become collaborators. That's the point of the Blue List. That's why I'm here . . . to recover it and make sure it is put to good use."

Ward switched on his torch to see Messenger more clearly. He looked shaken and uncertain, in spite of his bravado. "I know the full story," said Ward. "The List is just the key. None of your Double-Cross explanations will work now. You and Benjamin were Soviet agents in 1940 and you probably still are. There's no point in denying it, and there are others who know the truth. I am merely here to convey an offer. There's an immunity from prosecution for you in return for your co-operation . . . authorized by the Prime Minister."

"The Prime Minister," gasped Messenger. "Are you mad?"

"Not as much as you think. A deal has been agreed. All you have to do is switch sides again. You shouldn't find that too difficult. Look at the alternatives. It's your best hope."

Messenger seemed to be considering his predicament, pondering the validity of Ward's offer, when there was a scraping noise on the upper level. Suddenly there was silence again, but both men looked at each other quizzically. Both realized instantly that they were not alone. Someone else was in Paddock, and only a few yards away. Each wondered simultaneously whether the other had somehow hedged his bets. But Messenger was the first to move: he murmured a low oath and ran back towards the station. Ward hesitated, and moved towards the concourse, where he found Lucy negotiating the last of the steps in the vertical shaft.

"What the hell are you doing?" he demanded angrily. "You're supposed to be upstairs."

"Do you mind not shining that in my face?" Lucy replied casually. "I couldn't just sit in the car. You've been gone too long, and I didn't want to call the cavalry unless there was real trouble. So I popped down to check. Everything all right? I thought I heard voices?"

"Messenger's down below. I think he was more frightened than you when we heard you." His relief was evident in his voice. "I thought he might have turned the tables on us . . . just when I was broaching the subject of immunity. I must get back. Stay here."

"No way," she objected. "This place gives me the creeps. I'm coming with you. Don't worry, I'll keep out of the way."

With a shrug of resignation Ward turned and headed back towards Paddock's platform. He had wanted to tell Lucy to go back to the surface but there was no time to argue. It was imperative to find Messenger and get his consent to the immunity. When they reached the lower level the envelope was still perched on the packing case, apparently untouched. There was no sign of Messenger.

"Where's he gone?" whispered Lucy. "He can't have got past us, surely?"

"He's done a runner, thanks to you," replied Ward as he lowered himself down onto the track. "I'll go after him. For God's sake stay where you are. This middle rail is live." He swung his torchbeam onto the shiny central conductor as a warning. "There's only one other way out of here, and that's down the tunnel to the next station."

Ward set off, crunching along the gravel surface, into the impenetrable void of the tunnel, but after just a few paces, there was a sudden movement ahead. It was impossible to judge the distance in the dark, but the flash of light from Messenger's torch was unmistakable. Evidently he had taken refuge in the tunnel, and was now determined to make good his escape. Ward cupped his hands to his mouth to call out a reassurance, but at that moment the rails on either side of him began to hum with vibration. For a fraction of a second Ward wondered what had happened, and then the sound grew more familiar. A tube train was in the tunnel, and approaching them at full speed. Transfixed to the spot, Ward concentrated his vision on the occasional movement of Messenger far ahead, and watched in horror as two headlights came hurtling around the slight curve and suddenly picked out Messenger's frame directly in front of them. For a second or two he was silhouetted perfectly against the oncoming train, spread-eagled with one arm raised in a futile attempt to stop the onrush of the carriages. If he had uttered a sound, Ward did not hear it. There was a fearsome screeching of brakes, but Ward had already turned on his heels. There was nowhere to escape the train in the tunnel, no room on either side to avoid it, and none of the convenient refuges seen in the movies. Ward sprinted the few last yards to the mouth of the tunnel, the train racing after him in a crescendo of noise, and threw himself up onto the platform at Lucy's feet just as the train came rushing past, braking hard. He had been so perilously close to the driver's cab that he felt as though the slipstream had helped propel him through the air.

"That was a little close," Ward gasped. "Let's get out of here before that driver comes looking for me."

"What about Messenger?" asked Lucy, already sensing the answer.

"No need to worry about him again. He never had a chance."

Lucy helped her brother to his feet, and guided him up towards the concourse. They were both in a state of shock from the narrowness of Ward's escape. Slowly they climbed back up the vertical shaft. When they finally reached the surface, and the welcome daylight, they paused, grim-faced, as if looking for something to say.

All Ward's experience warned him that Lucy was in danger of going into shock when she realized fully what had just happened. He couldn't treat his sister as he would one of his squaddies – a stiff drink and a bit of time to relax seemed to be what Lucy needed – but the first course of action was just as the Army had taught him: find the subject something immediate to do.

"Would you mind driving?" he asked – this habit of lying was getting all too easy – "I banged my ankle coming over the edge of that platform, and I'd hate to ruin the gearbox on this valuable antique."

Over the second gin in Thurloe Street, Lucy was fully back in control, able to put the horror of the morning at the right distance. "So now what do we do?" she wondered. "Presumably I won't be whisked off to the Outer Hebrides, and you won't be heaved into the back of another rented van. But

Wilkins is going to have a bit of explaining to do, isn't he?"

"Not necessarily," said Ward, who had been furiously worrying about the same problem. "If Messenger hadn't completely forgotten all his field-craft – labels and so on – it won't be all that easy to identify him, and they may be able to keep it out of the papers. All the same, it might be tactful if we took ourselves out of range until the commotion – if there is any – dies down. Any ideas?"

"I was tempted," said Lucy, brightening perceptibly as she strode across to rummage among discarded invitations on the mantelpiece, "to take a look at this seminar in Florence. They're pretty hot on restoration – mind you, they need to be. And come to think of it" – she was by now quite back on form – "Graham's got this conference in Rome. If you'd only give the poor man his licence back, we could make a tour of it on the way home. What about you?"

"Well," said Ward, "I had wondered about taking a proper look at Vienna . . ."